MIDNIGHT SWEETS

Midnight Sweets

BETTE PESETSKY

Thorndike Press • Thorndike, Maine

Library of Congress Cataloging in Publication Data:

Pesetsky, Bette, 1932–
    Midnight sweets / Bette Pesetsky.
    p.   cm.
    ISBN 0-89621-900-3 (alk. paper : lg. print)
    1. Large type books. I. Title.
[PS3566.E738M54   1989]   89-31817
813'.54--dc20   CIP

This is a work of fiction. Names, characters, places, and
incidents are either the product of the author's imagination
or are used fictitiously. Any resemblance to actual events or
persons, living or dead, is entirely coincidental.

Large Print edition available in North America by
arrangement with Atheneum Publishers.

Cover design by James B. Murray.

For Louis

Contents

The Interview 9

Movie Star Cookies: 1986 16

Icebox Cookies: 1956 105

Bonitas: 1978 140

Mortimers: 1971 177

The Perfect Cookie: 1964 209

Movie Star Cookies: 1987 327

The Interview

I have always used my maiden name. Before it became the fashion. It just happened. Anyway, I work under my maiden name. I started baking under the name Theodora Waite. My mother always said that I was named after Theodore Roosevelt. Teddy. No, we weren't distant cousins.

God, but it's dark in here. Charlotte is forever snapping the blinds shut. She has this great fear of fading. Personally, I'll take light over fading. Charlotte works for me. You were asking about highlights in my life. Significant moments. I don't know if there are highlights. Divisions yes, highlights no. These divisions of mine are not chronological. Life goes back and forth, life selects. For instance, my Aunt Arlette — a woman whom I knew for a short time but long enough — if you listen to her, you realize that jewelry separates her life. Forget greed, this is not about greed. Take her conversations, the way they begin — When I bought the bracelet or Before my necklace clasp broke in the lobby of that theater or

When the rings were stolen. But if you asked her to define life's highlights, she wouldn't want to disappoint you. Look, she would say, pointing to that framed photograph on top of the piano when she posed in a sausage casing of white satin in the Chase Hotel one summer evening. What next? Why the usual catechismal or Shakespearean listing of life's poignant encounters. Who was born, who died, the child's first day in school. That is what Aunt Arlette thinks is expected. Life's great moments, so to speak.

My friend Dierdre — here's another example — now she believes that her life breaks evenly into when she was with Ben or after she left Ben or when she was with Ralph or after she left Ralph. But Dierdre actually calculates differently. We lived on Eleventh Street, she says. So that does it for her — not the lovemaking, the screwing. Life separates by her moves, those true coastal displacements, those travels down the East Side and up the West.

I think significance must be what we see when we close our eyes. The hand clasping the gold links. The shadows in three rooms. As for me, I say quite firmly that although my life has the same personal anniversaries as anyone else's, I divide my life by cookies. Yes, cookies. Which cookies? Picking the cookie in advance is as unpredictable as deciding which gold ring bears the burden of memory or which street address holds the tragedy. Some cookies just carry a certain weight. Significant cookies, I call them. I cannot set out to create a significant cookie. It is *afterwards* – in subtle ways – suddenly that cookie has meaning. Becomes important. Bas relief – so to speak.

Listen, would you like some cookies? I put a small assortment on this plate. Sugar, oatmeal, double fudge, chocolate chip. If there is a different one that you would prefer. Ask.

What are we working on now at *The Cookie Lady?* It's true that we have something in the oven. I can't say – a trade secret. Still, I'll go so far as to hint that it is not fully developed as yet. The birth of a cookie – unlike that of a human – has no defined parameters. Or perhaps I should equate its creation with love. It either happens or it doesn't.

Ideas for cookies come in different ways. A cookie evolves – I have no faith in "Eureka." The idea grows, synapses connect, events coincide. Then one day – it often seems falsely like one day – you have it. The new cookie.

And this is exactly what is happening with my *newest* cookies. A slow putting together of impressions – taste, texture, color.

I began baking cookies when I was a very

little child. Four or perhaps five. At my mother's side. Of course. In matching red-and-white aprons. *Icebox Cookies.* Yes, there's a significant cookie for you. An icebox cookie. A significant cookie in my life does not have to originate with me – might – but doesn't have to. Icebox cookies are not new. A nostalgic type of cookie, don't you think? *Bonitas* on the other hand were mine – named after my oldest daughter. Certainly a cookie of significance. My other children all have their own cookies, but not named for them. It became impractical – and some names did not yield themselves to being cookies. John – for example.

Those are pictures of my children on the piano – all five of them away at school. So we have *Bonitas.* Then there are *Mortimers* – no longer in the line – however, they *were* significant. Mortimer was my first husband.

I have a significant cookie that doesn't exist – so you can see that significance for me has a broad definition. The nonexisting cookie – I call – *The Perfect Cookie.*

I sought perfection. A recognizable adolescent dream. That's not to say that I have ever given up the thought that I could create a perfect cookie. But on the other hand, I now know the problems. When you are young – all goals seem to be at the tip of an arrow. Later that aim for perfection becomes confused, mixed up with the need to be known or to make money or to end up in the history books. As for me – I wanted to create the perfect cookie. I was fifteen, it was 1964. I had my notebooks, my recipes – and behind me – even then – ten years of baking. I never thought the perfect cookie would lead to either money or notoriety. I just wanted to bake it.

Of course, I didn't. I never created that perfect cookie – either I was never satisfied or I wasn't good enough – or it cannot be done. Which is what I believe today.

Our new cookies? Back to them? Rumors working overtime. I'm working on them. Yes, working on them. Everyone wants to know a secret. All right, Public Relations will kill me – but why not. By the time this appears, those cookies will either be created or abandoned. I call them *Movie Star Cookies*. That much, I'll say.

What touched them off? I'm uncertain. One day I saw three girls walking behind a man. Tab Hunter, one of them whispered to me, we've been following him since the Bronx. I saw the television news report of Clint Eastwood's election as mayor of Carmel. I don't think I personally ever saw him in a movie. But nevertheless movie stars do bombard the sensibilities.

Do I think these new cookies will be significant in my life? I don't know. Significant cookies are odd – they appear at uneven intervals. Once a decade or one following another quickly – I can't say. So other cookies might suddenly acquire meaning – and *Movie Star Cookies* will then just exist for me – the way chocolate chip cookies exist.

What has happened since I started work on *Movie Star Cookies?* You mean what falls under the rubric? We moved to this new apartment. It's large, but you have to consider that I have five children. My husband doesn't live here. Rudolf and I separated soon after I began working on *Movie Star Cookies*. I really prefer to say no more about that.

The Cookie Lady stands for a pure and wholesome product. Did you receive those sheets from my people on the history of *The Cookie Lady?* They tell the story. I have a fine, a wonderful team. I could never have done it alone. The history of a baker is the product – I do believe that. I am *The Cookie Lady*.

My personal life is my cookies. What did you expect? – The Confessions of *The Cookie Lady*. I got married, I got divorced, I got married, I got separated. Happens to a lot of women. I had five children. Maybe I like children. That's what's meant by human interest – isn't it? You're not talking about the cookies. Well, the cookies are what it's all about.

Are you saying that you can't describe some-one's life as *Icebox Cookies, Bonitas, Mortimers, The Perfect Cookie,* and *Movie Star Cookies?*

Yes you can.

Movie Star Cookies: 1986

How have movie stars touched my life? Ava Gardner. Now I knew very little about movie stars. I was never a fan. But I had this crush on Ava Gardner. An attraction based less on her movies than on a poster for a revival of *The Barefoot Contessa* on display in the lobby of the Western Star. I was a young girl, perhaps sixteen, and it was typical of my relation to movies even then that I admired the poster but did not go to see the movie. Nevertheless, I thought this movie star was exceptionally beautiful. I could see why people wanted to stare at her.

Had that been the end of it, why, the woman's image might have lingered with me and could have been used later. At any rate, I thought that Ava Gardner and I had parted company.

I moved on, grew older, and at nineteen became a rather silent and solitary girl. I was enrolled for my second year at the university. I spent the winter vacation period with my step-mother and her new husband. When your stepmother remarried, was that man your stepfather? Call me Dad, George said. He was a decent man but he was alien to me. The newly created family had moved from the town of Dover Beach, they now lived near Albany. Visiting them was as if I had taken a room in a bed-and-breakfast house where unfortunately I was forced to talk to the owners. The only joy was in the realization that I needn't go back. On the other hand, there was no other place to go.

I had pledged a sorority, having fallen in love with their stove. It was a marvelous stainless-steel Model 816. Within two months the cook came before the sorority's governing council. Either I went, he said, or he did. I found a room, it was late in the year and the choices limited. Lethargy kept me in the same quarters for my second year. Kitchen privileges but hardly worth the effort. All this altered my behavior, created mood swings, made me unhappy. I devoted myself to my studies. I was majoring in history. I wrote a freshman paper on "The Practices of Cooking in Sixteenth-Century France."

No question that my mood that year was depressive, and a perceptive nurse at the Student Health Services suggested that I talk to someone. What she meant did not coincide with what I did. I began to hang out at the Student Union spending my days drinking cups of coffee while every ten minutes someone played the same Ray Anthony record. My expression was hardly sociable, hardly inviting. But you can't discourage some people. Thus, I met Robert Lee. He winked at me. Hi toots, he said and sat down.

I arrived at the Union every morning at ten, Robert Lee came at noon — and we sat together until six in the evening, sometimes playing cards, sometimes staring into our fate. He had a dormitory food card and went to eat at six. Following the behavior pattern of people in my mood, I went home to bed despite the daylight and the hour. In February, Robert Lee informed me that he had passed none of his courses. They were going to throw him out, he said. At the mercy of his parents' money, he said. They had him by the balls. They called the tune.

Who paid my fees? I was at the university because I had won a baking contest. Robert Lee thought that was funny. He wanted to know if I had belonged to a 4-H Club, if I could milk a cow, if farmers really went in for bestiality.

We became companions, having nothing in common, and took part in the kind of dream-wish conversations that are dangerous when believed. Our talk centered around fame, around finding a huge, untraceable sum of money, around a secret relationship to a royal hemophiliac.

Physically, Robert Lee and I were an odd combination, we called attention to ourselves. It was all right to be strange, in the late sixties we were already into a period where looking odd was desirable. Yet, Robert Lee and I did not complement each other. Short men are attracted to tall women and tall men are attracted to short women. I didn't believe that at all. I wore flat moccasins in cold weather and hot. I would have done better to have cut off my legs at the knees, I used to say, after I met Robert Lee. He liked to hear that. Cut your legs off at the knees, he would repeat, and then maybe a little beheading.

But I was only a tall, ordinary girl — not exceedingly tall — or in any way someone who should be stared at. Robert Lee was short — a thin blond man. Standing side by side — I became taller and heavier and he smaller and frailer. He loved it. We look like a perversion, he said happily. We should have separated, but we didn't.

Leaving school was fashionable. I can't say that was true for either of us. We were not part of cultural trends. Robert Lee picked up only what constantly bombarded his senses. I never thought that what happened in the world mattered to me – or that I could affect it. Who made the decision to leave? And why together? This man and I shared little and we were lovers only to the extent that twice we had made love in my room. Robert Lee had undressed me, slowly and carefully. He was better at this than I had expected – either because he had heard how it should be done or had been patiently taught.

Robert Lee's parents sent him a letter. No more dough. I had two thousand dollars left from my Bake-Off prize money. Let's go, Robert Lee pleaded. Let's blow.

It was 1968, and we could go in style into the mainstream of society. Robert Lee swore that he knew thirty-three people who had dropped out of school. Why not us? Leaving, he told me, was where it was at.

Robert Lee wanted to go to the West Coast. But I thought New York City, we were in Buffalo at the time, and it was winter. I had no trouble persuading him – anyplace was as good as anyplace. We took the train to New York City. It immediately felt warmer.

We spent that first night in the Hilton. Robert Lee loved it. He said that he loved hotels, he loved the soap, the fresh towels each day. He would have stayed longer, but I said no. I didn't care much about money, but I understood it. We were not young people yearning for the romanticism of poverty. We simply had very little money. I can't say that Robert Lee wasn't escaping or getting back at his parents. But as for me, I had no particular place to go. No demands. My stepmother had remarried. She was no longer my immediate responsibility.

We rented what the landlord called a one-room apartment in a structure of time-softened wood above a barber shop on Avenue C. Robert Lee was good-natured about our quarters – perhaps our circumstances had the air of an adventure. We went to a Goodwill store, and bit by bit, carried back furniture. The alcove kitchen, separated from the rest of the room by a black-and-grey checked cretonne curtain on a string, held a chipped enamel stove labeled *Excalibur* and a half-size refrigerator. The curtain had to be pushed aside, and it threatened fire at all times. The kitchen, the entire arrangement, was all right for me, because I was in a fallow period. I had baked nothing for nine months.

There was no way that Robert Lee and I could have succeeded. Now that the drama of our leaving was over, we became irritable with each other. I had the money. We didn't have jobs. We didn't really want them. One evening we had an argument – he was sick of pizza, he said. Sick of pizza, sick of me. Robert Lee went out. Alone and uneasy, I went shopping. I started with one cookie sheet and just a few ingredients. I made classic chocolate cookies with a walnut half-embedded in each one. In the room and the outside hallway the scent of purity hung in the air.

When I woke up in the darkness of the room, Robert Lee was sitting at the table eating cookies. "Shit," he said. "These are good."

I thought I might make enough money from cookies to live on. Besides the Bake-Off contest, I had never thought of cookies as money – easy money. I located the store. The neighborhood hadn't been gentrified yet. Businesses were divided into the permanent and the floaters. The store I considered was the size of a walk-in closet with a window. Madame Marta – *Teller of Good Fortunes* – had moved out. One day she wrapped herself up in her paisley tablecloth, took her decks of cards, her magic water, and vanished. Owing, the landlord said with a sour breath. Owing. I had spoken to Madame Marta a few times, she was younger than she looked, a full-breasted woman who used pancake makeup for an authentic olive-colored complexion. She had dreamt of finding the right old lady whose life savings would be transferred to Madame Marta's keeping. Not on this street, I told her, but she couldn't afford the rent elsewhere.

The store was vacant and cheap. For such a hole, you needn't sign a lease. I paid for two months. It was Robert Lee's reaction that I couldn't understand. "Honey," he said, "we'll turn this shit-box into a little palace."

Robert Lee energized was almost frightening. He began to find things — two gallons of paint. Never mind that one was red and one orange. They were free. The paint was old and thick. Robert Lee thinned it, shook it, got brushes. The tiny store became red and orange. Late one night he appeared with a small wooden counter — two boys were carrying it for him. In front of that two-bit store a striped awning suddenly flapped in the wind. We were both pleased with that, we giggled, we punched each other. That night we made great love.

Robert Lee wanted to call the store *Robert Lee & Theodora*. But I thought that name too limiting. Early one morning I got out of bed and, walking in my bare feet not to wake Robert Lee, I went down the stairs before I put my shoes on. At the store, with gold paint and stencils, I made a sign — *The Cookie Lady*.

We worked shifts. The store didn't open until eleven. I baked most of the night. Robert Lee would carry the trays of cookies down to the store — a block from our room. I tried to make enough. Sometimes we would run short — then

Robert Lee would have to stay in the store while I went back and baked. I suspected that he took money but I wasn't certain. Anyway, the music was his idea. He found the phonograph, the three records, the table. "Honey," he said, "you got to seduce the customers."

We had a bad fight over ingredients. "Cut the sugar," Robert Lee said. "Half butter and half margarine — the jerks won't know the difference. And for God's sake, imitation flavorings."

"Never," I said.

The shop made expenses. That was what I had thought — volume too low for real profit. But it was doing what I had intended — we could pay our rent, buy our food. We had money for living. Also I knew that my depression had begun to lift. I felt better. I have never been by nature the sort of person who easily makes friends. By preference I would stay home alone and read or work on my baking notebooks. I thought that if it hadn't been for the listlessness that had accompanied my period of depression at the university I would never have known Robert Lee.

The more I baked, the more contented I became. I bought myself a good reading lamp. Odd that should be the point when Robert Lee stopped going out evenings. Where he went, I felt, was none of my business. But now he sat across from me talking endlessly about expansion. The store sold only five kinds of cookies. The size of my stove and storage space made this necessary. I couldn't be rude, I would have to close my book and listen as Robert Lee, making plans, grew excited, animated, and pulled at his blond curly hair.

"What's this?" Robert Lee said when he lifted the book of North American birds, and the picture fell out. The book was on top of a pile of magazines, he was trying to reach the magazines. We had board-and-brick bookcases.

I blamed a lot on the weather. We ran fans, but the wiring couldn't take more. Then too, the oven was on. Robert Lee didn't take too well to heat. His back had a red prickly rash. Robert Lee waved the picture. "What is this? Isn't that Ava Gardner? Isn't that her?"

"Yes," I said. "It's her."

"I can damn well see it's Ava Gardner," Robert Lee said. "But what are those lines on the picture – crisscrossing the picture." He looked more closely. "Like she was a box score. Who did that?"

"I did that," I said, "when I was a kid."

"Why?" Robert Lee said. He took a beer from the refrigerator, popped the can open, and was rubbing the cold sweat from the metal across his forehead.

"I believe I must have been measuring her face."

"Measuring her face?"

"Yes," I said. "Measuring her face and comparing it to mine. You know — how long her nose was, how wide the forehead. I had a picture of me — same size."

"Jesus," Robert Lee howled and let himself drop down hard on the bed. "You were comparing yourself to *her!*" he said. "My God, didn't you have a mirror?"

Robert Lee began during moments of intimacy to call me Ava. It was a joke with him. I knew how I looked. I was in every aspect a woman neither beautiful nor ugly. Yet when he called me Ava — it was an intensification of the peculiar appearance that we made when we appeared side by side. I never responded to this name, and a more sensitive man would have perceived that its continuous use was dangerous. Still, Robert Lee never lacked self-assurance. "Ava," he said over and over.

One night as we shared our bed, Robert Lee raised himself on one elbow and whispered, "Fuck me, Ava." It was a reflex action, I turned, my arm shot out, and I hit him solidly across the mouth. I split his lip in the corner and blood slowly found a path down his chin. At that moment I was horrified. I had never hit anyone in that way. The violence of my hand started a ripple of shock in me. At that moment he could have gotten any concession from me. If Robert Lee had handled the moment right, I would have begged his forgiveness. He would have had me. But Robert Lee pulled his knees up against his chest just beneath his bloodied chin, he pushed his back to the wall, his eyes widened with true fear. Now, I was only six inches taller than he and at best twenty pounds heavier. Yet his gestures, his movement backwards made me a bully.

Robert Lee said his feet itched to leave. West, he said. That's where it's at. A favor, though. Do me one favor, Theodora, have dinner with my parents? I was surprised, I thought they lived in North Carolina. Robert Lee said no, they lived on Staten Island, he had gone to prep school in North Carolina. What could I do? I went. My friend, Theodora, he said and introduced me. I was hardly a favored guest. Robert Lee's mother served cold cuts and potato salad on a plastic tablecloth.

"I can't stand her," his mother said in the kitchen.

"Whisper," his father said, "Listen, he was heading for nothing. She has turned him around."

"You can say what you will about Bobby

Lee," his mother said, "but he is not ugly. Bobby Lee is not ugly."

I was sorry to lose Ava Gardner. She would have definitely been one of the *Movie Star Cookies*, but I had no objectivity where she was concerned. Not because she lacked star quality – she would have been perfect – but I thought that my ability to perceive her accurately was biased. I might not do her justice. But Ava Gardner remained the first movie star I had ever thought about.

Going to movies has always been a prime activity for dating. I shouldn't make it sound as if I either never went out on a date or was never taken to the movies. I went to movies. The truth however was that at the movies I mostly dozed or thought about other things. But I was a good sport about it. I suppose that moviegoing might be related to family conditioning when you were a child. You either were a family who went to movies or you weren't. We weren't.

Rudolf enjoyed going to the movies. Maybe he thought it was necessary – a prelude – we went to a movie, we stopped for coffee and a discussion of the movie, we went to bed. At any rate, we went to the movies. Eventually I became serious about Rudolf, and then after the movie we would pass up the discussion about it and talk about ourselves.

Bit by bit, my confessions became deeper, Rudolf began to spend entire weekends with me, and he became acquainted with my children. I believe that he once told me who his favorite movie stars were – I listened – probably told him that I agreed with his choices. A deception of courtship, but surely not a vital one.

At any rate I decided that I would tell Rudolf everything before we married. It was at a revival series of comedy films, I fell asleep during *Hollywood or Bust,* but I woke up at the end, and then we went for coffee.

We exchanged tales revealing our pasts, I told Rudolf about many events. He thought my life was more complex than his, I thought it was simpler. He had lived with five, six women. He had spent a year in Finland. I had lived with only two men – Robert Lee and my first husband, Mortimer.

It was after *Hollywood or Bust* that I thought I ought to tell Rudolf about my fifteenth year – the year I was a thief. When I told him that I had reformed, he laughed and leaned over and kissed me. You're a darling, he said, you truly are. Imagine saying that.

It was not that I thought he didn't listen – or perhaps in my telling I deliberately deemphasized what happened – the length of time, the nature of my crimes. Perhaps he could not grasp the beginning and end of the events. And he was the *only* one I told. "The peccadillos of youth," he said. "Hey kid, I must tell you some time how on a dare I stole a basketball from Herman's Sporting Goods. Can you imagine walking out with a basketball?"

My evening's confession concluded, Rudolf dropped me off at my apartment, he had an early class to teach. The next morning Norma who looked after my children asked me what movie I had seen. I took out my appointment book and read her the name. I loved Martin and Lewis, she said. Broke my heart when they split.

What will happen? One day at a dinner table a friend will say that the source of *Movie Star Cookies* was adultery. Absolutely, the friend will say. And it won't matter that I will have denied that. Life was a straight line to some people. And if the friend were Dierdre – she would add archly that perhaps I should give Rudolf half the profits from *Movie Star Cookies*. If, of course, they were ever made. Some cookies were started and then dropped – I dropped them just like that.

It could be true that events concerning Rudolf led to the *Movie Star Cookies* – on the other hand, those cookies would probably have been conceived anyway – considering all that time I spent watching television after Rudolf left. I could visualize myself sitting and watching an old movie – maybe even the very *one* that triggered the idea.

Rudolf left – eleven years after those days of courting – after *Hollywood or Bust.* Of course he and I went to movies during the years of our marriage, but not as a regular activity. I can no longer remember any of the movies we saw. I always wrote the titles down so I could refer to them when necessary, but that notebook was lost. Name an actor or actress from one of those movies? I am afraid they were just faces to me.

At any rate, one day Rudolf and I were giving a party. All of this led up to *Movie Star Cookies.*

I called out to Charlotte, "Going out."

I was lucky. If you were lucky, you rode in an air-conditioned subway car in August. It was all chance, you couldn't plan it. The woman next to me nudged my shoulder, nodded in the direction of a fat black man in a red sweater. "Wool," she whispered. *"Meshugge."* I nodded my agreement, we were allied against wool. I left the pool of icy subway air reluctantly, climbed the stairs coated with sheets of flapping newspaper, an entire week at my feet. Two pigeons riddled a knockwurst with holes as it rolled off the curb, I moved out of the way. City birds weren't afraid of anyone. "Taxi," I yelled, but there was none. This not being the part of Brooklyn where taxis were the happiest. Still, I had that stored-up coolness, my jeans, my cotton top, my arms. I thought the chill would last a while. I was dressed for walking, sometimes I carried account books, a briefcase. But today I had some money in my pocket and a ring of keys. I could walk.

Was it dangerous in that part of the city? A bunch of streets from which the buildings have been torn away, leaving behind newly formed wilderness, instant forests of weeds irrigated by the last drops in soda cans. How can you walk there? my friends said. It is absolute madness, they insisted. Nothing, I replied. It's nothing. Most of the meadows have signs, sun-faded into permanent history, acreage for sale, commercial zoning.

I headed for the *Cookie Lady* bakery. The men who worked in the bakery said that *no one* should walk those streets. I thought they meant me. Rats roamed freely, they said, the size of cows or maybe ponies.

Anyway, I was not foolhardy. I walked close to the curb, sometimes in the street. I could have called the bakery — it was technically *my* bakery — and asked someone to come and pick me up at the subway station. But I hated to impose. Our midtown offices closed on Fridays in July and August – my idea. Great for morale. I felt bad that I couldn't close the Brooklyn bakery – but the schedule wouldn't permit. The bakery had to stay open on Fridays – winter and summer.

It was only eleven o'clock in the morning. Rudolf and I were giving a party at eight. He might have questioned my going out. But the party was essentially ready. The need for a party was unexpected. Rudolf said that led to the best parties. He said the worst parties were duty events or even holiday celebrations. Rudolf said the best parties were suddenly required – a natural consequence. It wasn't that I didn't want to celebrate – all right, I *didn't* want to celebrate. I was not a good party person. And this was the fourth volume in Rudolf's *Grotesque* series. I didn't feel we had to have a party. But then suddenly Rudolf's editor was coming from Arizona. Or rather, as he said on the telephone – He was going to be in town. So we had this man coming and the book. We had to have a party.

We were celebrating the study called The *Grotesque in Norse Myths*. Rudolf had all his books published by the same university press. The carton had arrived last Wednesday. I unpacked the box and displayed the author's copies – six books standing in a row across the hall table. Rudolf had laughed when he came home, but he had been delighted. So much for humility, he said and kissed me.

I opened a copy that day. Rudolf had dedicated this book to Deborah Farmer. It read *"for her help and inspiration."* None of the previous three studies had a dedication. I closed the book. I was embarrassed. I didn't know who Deborah Farmer was.

My husband had made a request: Please, nothing catered. He hated set platters, loathed anything that arrived covered with yellow cellophane. Simple, he said, no reason why the food can't be simple. Everyone likes cheese, he said. Cheese and wine — and other drinks, of course. I nodded. No one wants to eat heavy in August, my husband said. Cheese will do — and maybe some pate and sausage — yes, Pick's sausage. Perhaps that Pizza Rusticana you do. And a cold seafood platter.

I have made Rudolf's suggestions sound worse than they were. This can happen, words repeated yielding false motives. For instance, Rudolf sometimes called me the family entrepreneur. This, of course, was done kindly in introductions. Rudolf's arm around my shoulders. Theodora, he said, is our money genius. Theodora is the family entrepreneur.

Rudolf has never cooked. He cannot find his

way around a kitchen. It wasn't that he was trying to create work for me. He just didn't realize. Then too, he knew that I was free on Fridays.

So I got up at six for the initial preparations, the dough, the cutting. Prepared the seafood platter for chilling. Then later, I could put everything together. One-two-three. Charlotte would do the cheese, she liked arranging cheese. She would do the table, the flowers. Basically, Charlotte was not too fond of cooking.

Now, I did not go out that morning because of ill winds in my marriage. I went out to bake – no different from the way the man who sells stamps sits in private and looks at stamps or the artist spends his vacations sketching.

The Brooklyn bakery wasn't the original *Cookie Lady*, but it was the main bakery except for the franchises. My plan that morning was to mess around in their test kitchen, largely abandoned. It was a good room, it was old.

The trouble was that the farther I walked the more I became aware that it was August, the frigid flesh was gone, new beads of sweat made the slide from neck to waist. The air was anonymous until you got close to my chimneys.

When I walked, I paid attention. In taxis, sometimes I got carsick, closed my eyes. But I was walking. That's why I saw the car. To tell the truth, I might have thought it was just another abandoned vehicle, but *he* put his foot on the brake pedal for a second. The lights flashed. Someone waiting – and not parked in the *shade* around the corner. Where that car sat, halfway down the block all by itself, the sun took full aim. A man on the driver's side. A man's head.

Anyone else would have gone by. But experience is what we go on. I didn't think of the car as a symbol of my past. What I thought was what the hell was a car doing out there all by itself.

I stopped at the corner where the city wind imitating a sirocco blew at me. Yes, from where he sat, I believed, the man could look up toward the first-floor windows of *The Cookie Lady*. Although what could he see there? A harvest of flour.

I didn't immediately cross the road. No sidewalk on the other side. Two acres of weeds, with a *Lot for Sale* sign. My bakery faced those thigh-high weeds, that sea-wave of refuse besotted with puddles of brown water. The bakery plumb in the middle of its site, an oasis in the boondocks. To the west lived Hassidim, they didn't come anywhere near us, didn't want to inhale the air touched by our burnt-sugar offerings. North and east were brick and concrete buildings with initials for names – but the man in the car was too far away to be interested in them.

I recognized the absurdity of it. A hot August afternoon, a man sitting in a car in the sun – facing a commercial bakery. No quantity of cash on the premises. Still, I thought the man in the car was a potential thief – never mind that it was eleven o'clock in the morning and he was in plain view.

I was seen. In the car, the man's head moved, the neck arched. He had spotted me in his rearview mirror. A figure moving closer and closer. He no longer watched the plant, he watched me. His driver's window was open, his elbow poking out. The tip of one of my sneakers shoved gravel that pinged nicely against his hubcap. The man turned and looked at me. He was so completely at ease, such a manner must be admired. He was clean-shaven, a young man like an advertisement in a dazzling white sport shirt. His fingers pleated the edge of a yellow sheet of paper that dangled from a clipboard at rest against the steering wheel. The man looked less irritated to see me than pleased. Boredom spread like a desert in front of him. I had stopped even with the window. What was I doing? The man smiled sweetly at me. "Sorry, honey," he said, "I'm not buying."

It depends how you look, how you're dressed

– whether or not you want to bash someone for the comment. Sometimes it can be flattering, you know, to be taken for an afternoon hooker. With care I was a reasonable looking woman. But sometimes I was plain, vanity courting truth, my face shiny from heat, the brown cap-cut that was a mistake.

The man was handsome. Someone else might think it unlikely that he be out here. Not me. Looks never told the story.

I caught sight of the strap. Binoculars. My God, the man had binoculars. I didn't say one word, I just started walking again. I crossed back over to the bakery side, where a narrow sidewalk began. I didn't turn in at the main door where he could have watched me. I went around the side of the building. An appointment, he'd think.

I entered through the loading dock. You had to have an identification badge. I didn't. In summer the help was beefed up with high school boys. One of them yelled, "Hey, where do you think you're going!" Someone stopped him. I heard someone else say, "Shut up."

1 thought it was very responsible – a summer employee stopping a stranger. I walked from the loading ramp into the storage level. Didn't that smell good! The ventilating fans pulled out what they could, but it was never enough. What was left was an

intoxication of baking.

Two men wheeling a dolly loaded with sacks of flour nodded at me. One of them gave out a long toneless whistle as they passed. I knew what that was, that was a code, that meant *she* was here. That also meant Henry Arvis would come looking for me, or perhaps today I would find him first. This wasn't a surprise visit, the men were certain that I made surprise visits, but I didn't. If I felt like coming, I came. My reputation rested here in this bakery. No matter who these men thought they were – I was *The Cookie Lady*.

Henry Arvis was sixty years old. A lot of people wouldn't hire a sixty-year-old man. But Henry Arvis was adaptable, that's what I had said uptown. He had tasted one of my cookies. Good, he said. That's what we will make here, I told him.

Henry Arvis had been the manager when this bakery had been owned by *Apple-Cheeks* before they declared bankruptcy. *The Cookie Lady* bought the building and the equipment. It was my idea to hire the same men. Good bakers were hard to find. What would happen when this generation died? I didn't know. So we hired the men who had worked here before – the bakers. And most of those thought this was going to be an *Apple-Cheeks the Second*.

39

Well, it wasn't. The old bakers couldn't figure me. They knew commercial baking. It was not for a woman. Not that I seemed like a boss, I came in from the midtown offices wearing jeans or sometimes a black skirt and a white blouse. I looked like their granddaughters, like their married daughters. The *good* ones, not the smart alecks who went off to college and came back thinking they knew everything. The bakers thought I was a girl who had inherited a business – no sons. Toots, they began to say, commercial is different. It's not, you know, like your own kitchen with one little oven.

That was when I understood about being too friendly.

I held a meeting. *"Apple-Cheeks* made dog biscuits and called them cookies," I said. "Stone-hard lumps that don't even mold." I held up a bag with samples of their *previous* product. The men sneered. I filled my hands with briquettes from the bag and started throwing the lumps at the wall behind the men. The cookies hit the plaster like baseballs, three cracks appeared, the men ducked. The men reported me to the union. But I had aimed over their heads.

Henry Arvis came out of his office, he was hurrying, adjusting his collar. "Theodora," he said.

40

"Henry," I said. "How long has that car been out there?"

He knew which car, he started laughing, "That! The men have a pool on that," he said.

I went past him into his office, from his window I looked down at the car parked on the street. The car had a shine like melted milk chocolate.

"A pool?"

"Yes — how long he'll be here — considering the weather — whether he broils or bakes first. They say he's hiding out from his wife."

"My God," I said. "How *long* has he been here? Why didn't you call me?"

It was then that Henry's face flushed, he's a man with a tic at the corner of his mouth, bad when he's upset. "A week," he said twitching. "He's been there a week. Listen, I went out there. Second day that car showed up and parked, I went out there. Me and Jerry. I asked that man what he was doing."

"What?"

"An actor."

"What?"

"The kid's a movie actor — he's rehearsing a role. He sits out there and says lines or something. That's all he does. A spy movie, I guess. He looks like a young Michael Caine."

"You believed that — an actor?"

The left corner of Henry's mouth flapped.

"Yes, I did. Why not? Clean-looking boy. What do you *think* he wants out here? Going to carry off a carload of our cookies!"

"He's got binoculars — did you know he's got binoculars?"

"Well yes, we saw that."

"You didn't think that was peculiar — a man sitting out here in the middle of nowhere with binoculars and nothing in sight except us!"

Henry cleared his throat. "Maybe he needs them for his role. What could he see with his binoculars? He just sits there. He's like some kind of joke."

I flattened my nose against the window, angled my face. Someone had hired a jerk. A sore thumb. Imagine a cocoa-brown '66 Chevy parked a half-block down from the plant entrance, the tires squat up against those puke weeds, cat-o'-nine-tails, grass stalks coated with sticky hairs. A car with an identifiable dent in the right side, an S-shaped brand.

I had a theory that when you were angry it was best not to say anything right away. Henry's office led into a larger outer room. I went out there, took a Styrofoam cup and filled it with coffee. A paper bucket next to the coffeepot was filled with broken cookies. I took a selection. Three women sat silently in the outer office doing invoices. None of them liked me.

So I sat and sipped coffee and looked out Henry's window. A man sat in his car on a street where people did not sit in their cars. Suppose you wanted to vanish – not be seen. Why, you could vanish just by being there. At noon the man stood up, stretched, took a pee in the weeds, and then trotted to the corner to a Sabrett truck for lunch.

That's how I figured it. I mean when I thought it through, considering the location, how else could the man stake out the bakery – except by being seen. It was another way of becoming invisible. Be seen, be very seen – until he was no more than the scenery. Even the selection of the man who sat in the car was right. He looked like an actor – he could be one. Thieves can be anything. He had a handsome profile, he didn't look suspicious. He had vanished to everyone – except me. Me the man couldn't have counted on, my showing up. Chance was always dangerous.

Henry came back at two o'clock. I was usurping his office. He looked exasperated. I thought he was wondering why he worked for a woman. "Theodora," he said kindly, "what do you want me to do?"

I shook my head. "Nothing," I said. "Nothing we can do right now."

"Maybe you'd tell me what you think that

man plans to do here?"

"A spy."

"Beg pardon – you mean like in a spy movie?"

"Industrial spy – a kind of thief."

"Theodora," Henry said.

"I better go home," I said.

I suppose what I had here was an example of a character flaw. If I were a stronger woman, I could have made Henry Arvis see what I feared. I could have explained. Henry was a sensible man. Unlike the other employees, I didn't think that he saw me as the enemy. Like him I had come up the hard way – I knew baking. I knew baking inside out.

"You want a ride to the subway?"

I shook my head. I didn't think, considering the circumstances, that I could ask for a ride. I went to wash my face. My skin felt like an eggshell.

I left the bakery by the main doors, walked past the man's car again. He smiled at me. Full face – head on – he was very good-looking. I had no idea which actor he resembled. I didn't really know movie stars. How many could I name? Ten. No, at least twenty – but I was uncertain whether I had a face to go with each name. Most of the ones I could name were dead anyway.

The sight of that man in the car upset me. I wished that I could have spent the night at the bakery. Even curled up in a wooden chair. But that was impossible. Anyway, you never knew when someone would make a move. It could be tomorrow or, if he had patience, even next month. I would have been thought totally mad if I slept for a month or longer at the bakery to catch a thief. It's like being able to repair something – no one wants to believe that you can do that, if it's not your business. Baking was *my* business, but I had other skills as well.

At my subway stop, I walked up the stairs to see a crowd gathered on the corner. "What's up?" I asked a man. He smiled. "I think it's Roddy McDowall," he said. I tried standing on tiptoes, then I gave a short leap upward. But all I could see for that second was the top of a head. It could have been *his* head.

The protection of the bakery was as important to me as anything in the world. And often I have returned to this scene in my mind. But a spy story was just that – a story – the movie star playing second fiddle to the acts of daring.

What did we have in common? Rudolf counted fourteen moves before age seventeen. I had eighteen. But during the eleven years of our marriage – two moves. I never thought

45

that twice was too much in eleven years.

One day I walked out of Dr. Samuel Gold-man's office and I felt like a production. A series of round and gloriously golden globes. I was going to have twins. *We* were going to have twins. Rudolf was on the West Coast. I tried reaching him by telephone, but he was between motels. After the last call failed, I went into a coffee shop and had milky-mud coffee and a jelly donut. Also, I began to count. One, two, three, four. We had four rooms. Rudolf, Bonita, John, Sheryl, me. Five of us. We already fit snugly and none too well in four rooms. Bonita and John were away at school but come the Spring Break — where would we all be? Move, Rudolf had said often. We should move. But he was busy. I called the *Cookie Lady* office. I had been on my way back — a franchise meeting at two. I checked the telephone book — made a list of real estate agents. Someone would see me at eleven. I could be back at the office by two.

We needed space. The apartment I eventually selected had ten rooms. Boxy and square-shaped, a large but not a very distinguished apartment, no moldings, no points of architectural interest. Rudolf was sorry that he hadn't been with me when I signed the lease. However, this has always been a good apartment for parties, even Rudolf admitted that. It had *flow*.

That was the apartment where we held the

party for Rudolf's book. He wasn't home when I came back from my trip to Brooklyn, and anyway I was uncertain whether I wanted to tell him about the man outside the bakery. He might be amused or he might make one of his comments to the effect that I saw thievery everywhere and why wasn't I home preparing for the party anyway.

So instead I worked in the kitchen until five, then I went to shower. I left Charlotte written instructions for all the last-minute efforts – she was very good about following instructions – popping trays in and out of the oven.

Rudolf used to tell people that we met when he sold me a car. I was the one who made him stop. People heard that story and their lips set in a certain way. You knew what they thought. They thought money. I wasn't that rich. But I was comfortable. How did we meet? I went into the Buick dealer, one I passed daily on my bus ride to the office. I wanted a station wagon to be used when we went to the country. I intended to rent a house for the children for weekends. I thought my daughter Bonita liked grass, John was too young. When I walked into the Buick showroom, it was almost nine in the evening. Most of the salesmen's desks were already empty. That was dumb of me, because the gold lettering on the window said that they closed at nine. No one likes to bother before they go home.

I stared at a station wagon on the showroom floor. Maroon with metal sides painted like wood. I didn't have a car thing. To me a car was only something to drive. A man walked over to me. He had smooth dark hair, and wore a nice tweed jacket. He seemed exactly like a salesman. Can I help you? he said. Call me Rudolf, he said. Then he began talking to me about the station wagon. Asked me who it was for. And I said that it was just for me and my two children. No one else. Then another man appeared and asked if *he* could help *us*. The man talking to me wasn't a salesman – Rudolf was just waiting for a friend. Rudolf thought it was funny. No one else did. His friend looked annoyed. After all, I was a customer. So I said I would buy the car, and I wrote a check.

Rudolf invited me out for coffee, and I went. Afterwards Dierdre told me that I was mad – to have been picked up that way. He could have been a rapist, she said. Does he know where you live? Does he know your *real* name?

When we were together for the third time, Rudolf took my hand and kissed the palm. What do you want most in the world? he asked. I didn't know him that well, I hardly knew him. I could never confess myself that way to strangers. Later, I said and rubbed his cheek with my other hand. I will tell you later. But he never asked again. I never had the opportunity.

I loved Rudolf very much. Our natures complemented each other. We both had our work, we both had our need for concentration. Before we married, he told me that he understood that people would assume he was marrying me for my money. Well, you're not, I said.

I made a preparty tour of the apartment. Charlotte enjoyed parties. She hinted we should entertain more often. The cushions were all plumped, the vases had a selection of flowers, everything made of glass glittered. What I did was to take a basket shaped like a tray and move from room to room picking up the small things. It was a task that I asked Charlotte to do − but she always forgot. She didn't want to do it. Ruined the setting, she grumbled. I picked up bits of silver, the tiny sculpted acrobats, the Villein vase, the glass paperweights that Rudolf was fond of buying, the statues from Lionel. I made several trips. I had cleared two shelves in the closet in my bedroom. Carefully I put everything from the basket on a shelf. The shelves resembled a display in an expensive store. Rudolf always thought I was very sensible removing, he said, the knickknacks. More room for food and drink. Very considerate of the guests. When I finished, I locked the closet. That way, everything would be there when the party was over.

This was essentially Rudolf's party, I was giving it for him – but it was *his* party. My requirements were simple, someone to talk to. For God's sake, Rudolf said, *my* friends are your friends. It wasn't that I disagreed. Not exactly. But at the very least I wanted Dierdre invited. I don't understand, Rudolf said, she's your basic bitch. I can name a half-dozen people at the party who would be delighted to talk to you. Simone, for instance, is considered to be an extraordinary cook – and a superb baker.

Dierdre in many ways was an old friend. I knew her before I knew Rudolf. At the time I met Rudolf, he was earning his living as an adjunct faculty member – he taught courses at three colleges and traveled around in an old blue Volkswagen like a peddler of culture. He was doing research for an article or maybe a book. Long, he said, and definitive.

Dierdre laughed when I told her. My God, she said, you've got another one. Let him show you something, Theodora – make him show you one concrete piece of paper.

Dierdre was wrong. Rudolf was working on the very first of his series on the Grotesque. He was as he said becoming an authority.

He studied and examined grotesquery both as fact and as principle – in the physical world, in the spiritual world, in literature as symbol. Teratology. He was an expert. When the second study was published, Dierdre admitted that she was mistaken, by that time Rudolf and I were married, and Sheryl and the twins, Rebecca and Robert, had been born.

Just before Rudolf and I married, Dierdre wanted me to go to a psychologist. Hers or someone else's. For the children's sake, she said. Well, I didn't. I didn't ask the children for their opinions either. Bonita was four, John two when I married Rudolf. What opinions could they have had? Rudolf gathered them into his arms. I thought I had it made. They called him Daddy. He treated them exactly the same as he later treated Rebecca and Robert and Sheryl. Undetectable differences.

I only had four *Cookie Lady* stores at the time I married Rudolf, and Dierdre was a merchandising assistant for a sportswear wholesaler. Dierdre lived in an apartment on the next block, it was before Ralph, she was still married to Ben. Dierdre said that when you were ignorant – admit it. She knew nothing about children. She had been an only child, and now she had an only child. Therefore, she read books. Or bought them. Dierdre had an entire shelf of books. Spock, Gesell, Steiner, Bettelheim – other books that I had never seen anywhere else.

She gave me each book as she outgrew it. Her daughter Jane was four when the twins, my fourth and fifth children, were born. I was the godmother for Dierdre's daughter. I made all the cookies Jane ate. I don't believe she ever ate anyone else's cookies until she was eleven or twelve. She had a special cookie – I called it *Jane's Black & White.* I believe that Dierdre during those years mentally saw me as someone in an apron, someone barefoot in an apron.

"You have to have a philosophy," Dierdre said to me one day before we moved further east. "I am not going to give my Jane everything I didn't have. God – there wasn't much I didn't have. A philosophy is what is important." She tapped a book. "Here." She looked at me. "And you, Theodora, what are you going to do?"

"I am going to raise my children to get along without me," I said. "If they have to."

"We'll see," Dierdre said. "We'll see."

Jane turned out to be a very decent girl, polite and good-natured. She lived with Dierdre until she was ten, then Dierdre went to California with Ralph and Jane decided to stay

52

in New York with her father. Afterwards, when Dierdre returned to the city, it seemed unnecessarily disruptive to move Jane again. So she stayed with her father on Eighty-sixth Street. Close to her school too.

In truth, I knew as little about raising children as Dierdre. Rudolf said that I suffered from the orphan's mentality. I can't say that he was wrong. But I stuck to my philosophy. I think it has worked. All of my children have continued to live with me. When they turn eight — soon after that birthday — I send them away to school. I thought it best. Each one cried at the door the first time they prepared to leave. They twisted their hands and shrieked. *Home, home.* I was not hardhearted. I wept after they left. For birthdays, I baked elaborate cookie houses, cookie castles, cookie footballs. These were packed in unsalted popcorn for cushioning, and the inner box tied with streamers of red-and-orange crepe paper before mailing to their respective schools. No one had birthdays like the children of *The Cookie Lady.*

Like all unwilling hostesses, I have never been at ease in party clothes — not when I was younger, not now. The party for Rudolf was no exception. How would I describe myself? Thirty-seven years old, thin, but with big breasts. I wore a minimizing dress for the party, blue silk with vertical silver stripes. Dressed already, clearly too early. I stood in the kitchen doorway and watched Charlotte spreading my special blue cheese and herbs on crackers. She didn't have the knack. Each cracker in a vise — expensive crackers too. One after another the crackers arced, bent, fractured. No, Charlotte, I said. I never got the hang of this, she said. I took the cheese spreader. This way, I said. I slashed cheese across one cracker. Better if I did it. Charlotte tied a white butcher's apron over my dress.

Thirty, forty people filled the rooms, came to meet the man from Arizona. Whom did I know? Rudolf did the inviting. Rudolf made friends more easily than I. There were always people present at our parties I had never seen before.

"Come over here," Rudolf called. I went to him, and he put his arm around my shoulders. "Here she is," he said to the man from Arizona, "the family entrepreneur."

"You know who you look like?" the man from Arizona asked.

I shook my head.

"Jean Seberg."

Rudolf rubbed my hair, cut so short it could not be ruffled. "Her Joan of Arc look," he said.

At this party, standing next to the blue cheese platter, I saw a woman with dark blond hair. How can I explain why I knew that she did not belong or was in the group for another reason. She *knew* people. She wasn't a stranger to the scene. Still, I felt that she was present for another purpose. Not to celebrate the study, not to meet the editor from Arizona. I thought she must be Rudolf's woman. Could she be Deborah Farmer? Rudolf never once looked directly at her.

I pointed her out to Dierdre. "She's an actress," Dierdre said. "Anyway, she gets these tiny parts in movies. She was in the background in *Dune*. You have to look close — last half hour."

The next day I checked the newspaper, found *Dune* was playing in a theater in a mall in Queens. I went to the matinee. The movie started at two-ten, I arrived at four-ten. I saw her, she looked good on the screen, her cheeks painted with a sultry tan. However, she lacked the presence to qualify as a movie star.

When I married the first time, I wore a white satin dress. Not to be mistaken as a virginal symbol. Certainly a most unlikely garment for me to wear and doubly so considering the nature of my first husband. I presumed that Mortimer saw the dress as kind of campy, a definite joke. It was Mortimer's idea — a white satin dress *with* a train. We selected it together from a resale rack — the dress wasn't old enough to have any charm. It looked as if it had originally been part of a cheap package deal. The lace inserts scratched against my throat.

That garment never came up again. Next time I wore a street-length dress — blue. Rudolf and I were married by a judge in his chambers, just the two of us, and witnesses from the judge's staff. Afterwards, Rudolf and I went out and had a fabulous meal. Dierdre offered to take care of my babies for our twenty-four-hour honeymoon. I'll take them, she said. Bonita and John thought of her as an aunt. I had no parents to invite, I had no relatives whom I wanted to know. I took it for granted that was true of Rudolf. Then Rebecca and Robert were born. I bought matching outfits for them, bought all their baby needs in duplicate. The babies went to semisoft cereal at six months. They sat in their high chairs in a new kitchen. One morning I made blueberry pancakes for Rudolf and Sheryl. They ate, while I coaxed tiny mouths open with a silver spoon filled with oatmeal. Then Rudolf said, "My mother and father are living in Phoenix — perhaps we should send them pictures of the babies. Sheryl too." The spoon dropped from my hand, the droplets of cereal drizzled to the floor. Rebecca started to cry, it was her turn to eat.

The parents in Phoenix were Mr. and Mrs. Vestry. They weren't Rudolf's *real* parents, they weren't even his adopted parents — yet in many ways, he said, they were parents. In conversation, he usually referred to them as Mr. and Mrs. Vestry. Rudolf's real parents sold him when he was nine. That was a story that at first sounded worse than it was. His parents were on their way west. But trouble came first, Rudolf said. An automobile repair bill for four hundred and fifty-nine dollars, motel expenses for a minimum of four traveling days, food — gasoline too. Then a few hundred for settling-in money when they reached L.A. In short, his real parents needed fifteen hundred dollars. Rudolf thought they felt that if no profit was involved the transaction couldn't be that bad. At any rate, he never believed they wanted to sell him. His youngest sister, Delores, was too much of a baby, she wasn't even in the running. He thought his parents planned to sell his older sister, Marian. She was eleven. She was smart though, Rudolf said. She could make herself cough whenever she wanted, a convincingly loose, croupy cough. When speaking with Mr. and Mrs. Vestry, she coughed every third word. They took Rudolf, making certain that he had a negative chest X-ray first. His real mother hugged him and said he was going to have a truly wonderful life. Mr. and Mrs. Vestry who were of the age to be grandparents told Rudolf that from now on he was to call them father and mother. They packed up that weekend and left Virginia where everyone knew that he wasn't their son. Rudolf lived with them until he was seventeen.

Rudolf and *Movie Star Cookies*. The more I thought about the imagined connection with adultery, the more certain I became that Dierdre would be the friend to say that. Not to me — not at first. She'll use it as a dinner table story. He was going to leave her, she'll say, and you know Theodora — *she* was never one to waste anything. On the other hand that could be unfair. It was Rudolf whom Dierdre didn't like — not me.

Still, Dierdre pumped me during a certain period. Did he pick fights with you? No, I said. Wait, she said. He will.

I knew he was planning to leave me. Or he was having an affair and not planning to leave me. And when I found out for certain, I would make him leave me. I thought sometimes in the mornings he looked around the rooms as if he were already nostalgic for them. He examined the pictures of our children as if they were Kodak embalmings. How are things? I asked. Fine, he said looking puzzled.

You can't make things too easy. Was that it? Had I given him too orderly a life? Made everything just too easy. Had I?

"Give my best to cookie-land," Rudolf said cheerily and mussed my hair.

"There are signs," Dierdre said. "God, these men leave signs."

I remembered those frantic whispered telephone calls from Dierdre before she left Ben. If my husband calls, she said. Be casual. Remember that we went shopping – the whole day. But he knows I don't do that, I said. Lie, she implored.

A voice on the telephone, a handkerchief over the mouthpiece. Guess where he is? she whispered. Guess?

Did I think that was a joke? Not when you had an unlisted telephone number.

One evening I sent Charlotte away. Go visit someone – take in a play. I set the table with a white embroidered cloth. Embroidered with mysterious symbols. Four roses in a crystal vase. I served Chicken Kiev, tiny noodles with parsley butter, and my sugar-crisp cookies with praline topping.

"I admire you," Rudolf said. "I really do admire you, Theodora. You are a strong woman. You remind me of Ingrid Bergman. You are a woman who has carved her way in the world."

Afterwards, we made love. Rudolf fell asleep early. It was the wine. I had poured too much wine. I got up and went to the window. It was eight-thirty, but the light outside was amber-colored. It should have been dark. We had dinner, made love and here it was still the day.

I received a list of *Signs of Unfaithfulness*. It was anonymous. I knew damn well it came from Dierdre. Who else used that thick beige acid-free paper? It must be one of her second sheets without the engraved name and address. Did she think I wouldn't remember? The list was a game — we had sat down one evening and made that list. Dierdre, Ginger, Margaret, and *I*. It was part of a game, a jest, a pastime. We had laughed as we made up things. Why had Dierdre kept that list? And for such a long time too. I reread the list.

Observe changes in behavior

Rudolf sang bits of lyrics. He recalled a phrase or a line from countless songs, also the correct melody. He shaved and sang. Baby face, baby face. You got the cutest baby face.

I pulled at his shorts. Sweetie pie, I said. Sweetie pie. He turned around, a pirate's patch of lather on his cheek. He didn't look pleased. He didn't look happy. All I had on was my bra, it was morning, and I was late. I was willing to be late.

Rudolf wore flannel pants and a tweed jacket and usually no necktie. That was the way he looked. I was very surprised to see him dressed in a black turtleneck sweater and tailored blue jeans. He looked good, but he certainly looked different. He wore argyle socks, soft cashmere argyle socks. Rudolf wore black socks. He had a drawer full of black socks. They didn't have to be paired, they were all alike. Except for the six pairs of argyle socks.

Observe changes in desire

Rudolf was capable of making love twice a day, widely spaced. I didn't know about other men, but that was Rudolf's performance. I began to count. He hadn't come to me for – Wednesday, Thursday, Friday, Saturday, Sunday, Monday. On Tuesday, he made love to me. Twice. Then again – on the next Tuesday. Why Tuesdays?

I yielded to him. I thought everything about

61

us together was wonderful. I wet my pinkie and rubbed it across his lips. Suddenly he didn't care for that.

"Rudolf," I said, "suppose I made reservations. Suppose we went away for an entire week."

"What?"

"Now," I said. "We could leave on Saturday. Friday. Before you get started on your new study."

"Theodora," his voice was patient, "I am at work now. I began my new study on the very day the previous one was completed – before actually. Well before publication."

"Take a break."

He sighed. "That's the difference, Theodora – I have *only* me to do my work. You are a businesswoman. You have other people – many other people, advisors, other hands. Then too, you are a product-oriented business. When the day is done – discounting special problems that come up – why, you can just drop it all. Turn it off so to speak. I cannot."

"No week?"

"Perhaps later."

Make the ultimate decision

Dierdre thought I should throw him out.

But she had no direct experience, she was the one who always went.

If necessary, have him followed

Rudolf led an academic life. Men who work in offices must have a harder time. They are expected to be in a certain place at a certain time. Rudolf kept his own hours, he came and he went. So not reaching him was negative information. I could not dial a number and when he didn't answer confront him. Where were you?

I decided to follow him. I called *The Cookie Lady*. Do without me, I said. I selected a Wednesday. I wore a dark green wool coat, a print silk scarf on my head, the ends knotted under my chin. He went at ten to the Mercantile Library. I thought I would go mad hanging around doorways. He stayed there until noon. He went into a coffee shop for a hamburger. I selected a similar coffee shop across the street from his. I ordered a cheese sandwich, it was quicker, and I might have to leave abruptly. My neck hurt, I sat at an angle on the stool at the counter in order to watch him through the window. He ate, then he returned to the library. At five, he went home.

I was discouraged, I might have given it up. It was difficult to say why I held on. But I knew that I would try again.

The next time I chose a Thursday. I sat shivering in a tiny park keeping my vigil until he left our building at eleven. I was his shadow, behind him, bus and taxi. He went to Lincoln Center. He walked with a stride I recognized, an eager pace. He met *her* on that wide courtyard littered with pigeons, old people, flanked by other buildings. I was surprised. I never guessed. She wasn't any of the women I suspected. It was Marilyn. She grasped his arm with a possessiveness that *I* never dared.

I could not leave, even though I might have. I went after them. Went with them to a film festival. I stood in line only three people behind them. I listened sharply for his voice — for the tickets he chose. Two tickets. I bought mine. I saw Marilyn reach up to straighten the folds at the neck of his sweater. I thought once he might have spotted me. But I was wrong.

I went into the theater, sat far behind them, saw them side by side, his head, her head, the nodding to each other. Shared remarks. The theater was not crowded. The hour unreasonable.

The movie was *The Cheat*. It was the first and only time I saw Pola Negri on the screen. I never saw such a strong and stunning personality projected. It was truly an experience, never mind the foppish mannerisms, the overstylized movement. Seeing her was an incredible, a savage viewing.

I left the theater as soon as the movie was over. I preceded Rudolf and Marilyn up the aisle. Outside the wind blew a shower of debris, the day had darkened, possibly a cold rain might start. But I had seen enough. I felt lightheaded, like some seed not yet fulfilled.

At the curb a falsely elongated limousine waited. As silver as the moon. Who was in it? People bent over, trying to penetrate the tinted glass. "It's Deborah Kerr!" an old woman shouted. "No," a man said and squatted next to the window. "Not her at all."

I meant to telephone Dierdre. I know, I would say. I know who she is – Rudolf's woman. But instead I went directly to the midtown offices of *The Cookie Lady*. In the test kitchen where everyone looked annoyed to see me, I pulled rank, I washed my hands, scrubbed my nails. With my hands, no electric appliance, I made a batch of one-two-three dough for walnut-studded crisp cookies, and then made a tray of lemon meringue kisses, using up the last of their brown paper. Meringue kisses were firmer when baked on brown paper. Chopped pecans and made a double recipe of date chews.

All of this was a prelude. To whatever would

evolve – a giving out of energy. I was going to do something with what I had seen.

I wrote a memo. I handled my business affairs better through memos. *Some new cookies are in the wind,* I typed. I *presume this requires another staff meeting.*

Vice President Stanley – he represented the *other* investors. "We are doing very well, Theodora," he said, starting off the meeting. "Very, very well."

There were six people present. They nodded.

"I am thinking about a series of cookies," I said. "Just beginning with them – so I haven't firmed the recipes yet. Cookies involving movie stars."

"Endorsements?" a woman asked.

I shook my head. "Why would you think that? But I have the name – I think they should be called *Movie Star Cookies.*"

"You mean shapes – faces of movie stars in profile or full face?"

"My God!" I said. "Like animal crackers? You *think* I mean animal crackers!"

When I thought about a movie star, it wasn't really a person – it was a quality that when seen made you both more and someone else too. That was what I wanted. I made an attempt to dress like Pola Negri. A setting of mood. A woman dressing like another woman with the goal of temporary obliteration of personality. My head wrapped in a black satin turban fastened in the front with a turquoise scarab pin purchased from the gift shop at the Metropolitan, my feet encased in black calfskin thigh-length boots with dagger heels, my dress hung loosely with drapes, scoops, more drapes. I should have closed the bedroom door. Charlotte saw me. She backed away, her pointy ears and her bushy eyebrows rising, then I heard her in the distance, the laughter released. In the mirror my face approached a flashbulb-whitened echo, black mascara-edged, purple lips pouting. I was not Pola Negri. No sultriness, no animal scent projected. I was pure imitation. At least I knew what I didn't want to create. A false Pola Negri cookie. Sometimes knowing what you are not going to do is more important than knowing what you are going to do.

I visualized the *Movie Star Cookies* in boxes not bags — boxes in my standard colors of orange and red imprinted with my logo, each cookie wrapped in tissue paper. The Rolls-Royce of cookies.

The test kitchen at *The Cookie Lady* — I couldn't do a damn thing there. Actually, I could test a recipe in that room after it was developed. But for creating — no. The atmosphere was limiting. I could have worked at home. I had a decent kitchen, but someone was there. I had hired someone to be there.

That was when I got the idea. I rented an apartment in the Bronx. Periodically I left the office, took the subway, and vanished. God knew what they thought. Probably lover. That was the easiest for people to think. Assignations.

I worked in my special apartment, two and a half rooms and a usable kitchen. The kitchen window open, the Grand Concourse below. I could hear voices from the street, three floors down — in English the words would sound worse.

Creation was always a matter of trial and error. But you also needed silence, a chance to think. I tasted cookie *A*, then I tasted cookie *B*. I didn't need any panel of tasters. I thought that *B* had it all over *A*. I must go with the *B* recipe variation. Just work on that one. The cookie crumbs softened in my mouth. Pola Negri. Was this Pola Negri? Close. The cherries I used were a joy. A find from a grove in northern California near Los Gatos. A man named Bolivar. *Midnight Sweets*, he called them.

I nibbled more. I might have it. Batch 64. I kept a notebook. Just because I was *here* didn't mean that I violated the principles of order – I always kept a notebook. Yes, this could be it. The first of the *Movie Star* line. Dark cognac-macerated cherries and a coconut base. Pola.

When did it happen? Consider my theory that people believe the worst events, the most scarifying experiences, occur in the middle of winter, slashes of ice, the sky a shattering grey she-devil. I suggest that nine times out of ten the day is hot, the sun an orange projectile. Later, when we muse upon what has happened, we automatically change the day, the weather, add that discharge of snow, and a whip-cracking wind.

It was hot. Sweat on my forehead. I wore a deep-cut scoop-necked black cotton knit top. A moist furrow between my breasts. My hair pinned up without fashion. A brownout had been announced. Help your city, the man on the radio said. Rudolf turned off our air conditioning. He turned it off early in the morning. Charlotte abandoned the vacuum and went to bed. I tried to explain to her about social conscience.

The apartment was a furnace. I thought the rooms also smelled of rotting fruit, but that was absurd. I sat very still in the kitchen, a glass of lemonade in my hands, rolling the glass between my palms for the comfort of its chill.

The children were at their summer camps – tennis, swimming, sciences, arts and crafts – five camps, two chose swimming.

Rudolf stood in the doorway. "God, I don't know what to say, Theodora. I think I should leave." He spoke slowly, giving bad news to those who cannot understand. "I fell in love with someone, Theodora. You must have *guessed*. Life hasn't been easy, you realize. It's been damn difficult living with your money. I never married you for that money – you didn't even have this much when we married – but try persuading anyone else. Still, I didn't go out planning to fall in love – but there it is – love."

I didn't blow my hand. "With whom?"

"I think I'd rather not say – as yet," Rudolf said. "I need time to absorb this, Theodora – this blur of joy, this dazzle of pain. But my leaving now is better, you know it's better. What's wonderful is that I believe the children will cope magnificently. *Our* children are truly strong."

"The children," I said, "are due home next Wednesday, Thursday, and Saturday. Then expect a two-week gap until the last one leaves for school. I think it would be appropriate for you to wait to leave until then." I didn't mention myself at all.

I thought he was going to tell me to go to hell.

"That sounds reasonable," he said.

I had Pola Negri. Who else did I have? I forced sleeplessness, stayed up late to watch old movies on television, switching from channel to channel. I was waiting to be captured. To see a face and *know*. I required only a few movie stars. I had in mind a series of cookies, but nothing overwhelming.

On a sheet of paper – a list of the movie stars I saw each evening. Maybe I was too fussy. But in the morning rereading my list, if I couldn't remember who they were – if the names conjured up nothing, no glimpse of brilliance – how could I expect the buyers of my cookies to remember them.

My philosophy – don't give up too easily. I kept watching. Also, I had nothing else to do with my nights. Soon after – on television – I saw Sir Laurence Olivier in *The Entertainer*. A show-business heel role. I saw *him* as a nut chunk with a slither of bittersweet chocolate. It was the breakthrough. The others tumbled forth. Perhaps I had begun to pay more attention.

I didn't care what kind of lives these movie stars led or who they were in their other existence. I was not interested in squeaky-clean cookies or family image. Excellence has never been necessarily equated with other virtues.

I was surprised. Suddenly the people at the

midtown office began to like the idea. *Movie Star Cookies*. Why not? There were exclusive candies, they said. Why not cookies? Look, we had investors – it was no longer just me – mainly me – but no longer just me. Public relations or some marketing person saw possibilities. They had additional suggestions – nothing radical, they said. Update the *Cookie Lady* image. Launch at the same time as the *new* cookies a kind of contest. More rightly a search. A search for a new logo.

The Cookie Lady used a distinctive red-and-orange bag. On the side of the bag was the logo. An oval-shaped frame with the photograph of a girl's face. The girl in that oval was *me*. A photograph taken of me when I was age fifteen – taken when I was a thief – not after I had stopped. Not that Public Relations knew about the thievery. Why should they? But that photograph was taken at the time when I sometimes thought my powers as a baker had been at their zenith. What they wanted now was a *new* face. Be the new face on the *Cookie Lady* package – was their idea. It was a trade-off, wasn't it? I was supposed to give them the logo. They'd give me the cookies.

I was sorry that I didn't have a chance to tell Rudolf about *Movie Star Cookies*. After he left, circumstances became the way they are for all separated couples – the level of distrust rose. But I would have enjoyed exploring the idea with him. I suppose I was even scared. These cookies represented a new turning for me. Before, I always started with a sense of what the cookie was to be, a particular taste or texture, a flavor to be evolved. This was different. Here, I had a desire to make cookies that explored a concept. I had to think that through. For me, the translation of what a movie star was into the form of a cookie was an intellectual leap made more difficult because I was not a true movie fan. I hardly ever went to see new movies.

Also, not having Rudolf diminished the number of people whose opinions I valued. Public Relations wanted me to shut up – industry secrets. They did not understand. The exactness of my cookies *was* my cookies. My creation remained my creation even if I spoke about it. I still had friends. I could tell them.

"Who would believe that I don't care about money? Really believe that?" I said.

Dierdre looked up. "Not me."

"I'm thinking about cookies," I said.

Dierdre didn't reply. They had a coatrack near the door in this restaurant. Dierdre always positioned herself so that she could watch her coat.

She was the one who introduced us to this restaurant. She had a friend who came here once with Broderick Crawford. She also saw a woman eating here whom she recognized but could not name. That had been an unpleasant meal – Dierdre with that name on the tip of her tongue but the words not coming out. I saw her in a movie with Joan Crawford, Dierdre kept saying. I know I did. She repeated that over and over the entire evening.

"Yes," I said. "I have been thinking about these cookies for a while – mulling about them. My people like the idea. I call them *Movie Star Cookies*. I have been thinking about them for several months."

Dierdre frowned, nodded, sighed. "Yes," she said, "from a merchandising standpoint I can certainly see the name." She propped her elbows on the table, formed a cradle with her hands to support her chin. "You remember my Aunt Esther? Did you know that she used to go out with Clark Gable? Esther said that when Gable came into New York, he would call her. She was supposed to be quite good-looking when she was young. She wasn't in show business. She worked for a catering hall as a banquet consultant. Anyway, when Gable took her out, they went mostly to a supper club in New Jersey. Aunt Esther said that he was a very nice man, but at that time she had thought he wouldn't amount to anything. I tell you this, Theodora, so you will realize that knowing about movie stars is complex. That's an important world. When did you last see a film?"

I came to.

"What?"

"See a film," Dierdre said. "You know, Theodora — that's when you buy a ticket and stand in line with lots of people to watch a screen. I cannot remember ever hearing from you that you went to a film. I'm right, aren't I? And movie people are everywhere. When I lived in L.A. in that four-family one block off Fairfax, right next door were two character actresses. Their names would mean nothing. But if you saw their faces you would recognize them. Lesbos, though."

"On television — I've seen movies on television," I said. "You wouldn't believe what I've seen. And my cookies won't just be named after a movie star. I have in mind more. I have in mind a different bake."

"Sweetheart, take it from me, I've spent my life in merchandising — all right, women's sportswear — but selling principles are the same. You select certain film stars — image is everything — and capitalize on them. Just anyone won't do. It's not mystical — it's merchandising. You have this apron mentality, Theodora."

What were we doing in the restaurant in which Broderick Crawford had once eaten? We were waiting for Florence. It was an Indian restaurant on Second Avenue where the three of us often ate, where we chatted with the owner, and it was our conceit that between visits he remembered us, and that the Tandoori Chicken served to us was better than what other, less favored patrons received. Unless they were *known*.

"She's late," Dierdre said and pushed at her sleeve to look at her watch. "She's always late, isn't she? I need a drink."

"Dierdre," I said. "when you left Ben, did you think of him? I mean when you first left him."

She shrugged. "No."

Dierdre, Florence, and I were friends in the middle of bad marriages. Dierdre said we were, even when we were uncertain about that. Dierdre said that we were basically similar — marital situations led to similarities among friends, she said, like old dogs and their owners. Except in the matter of children. Dierdre had one girl, Florence had no children, I had five. They tied it in with baking — with the homemaking arts. Did I know, Dierdre said once, that only thirty-five percent of executive women age forty had ever had one child. And there I sat, she said, with five. And I wasn't even forty yet.

"Guess who is getting a divorce?" Dierdre said. "Moira."

"Who?"

"I forget who you know and who you don't. She's from the time I was with Ralph. But you've met her at my place — the redhead with bad posture. Listen to this, Theodora. Moira reads newspapers from front to back — everyone who knows her knows that. She used to work for a clipping service. Well, she's reading a tiny squib. There it was. *Having left my bed and board* — the works. It was her name. Her husband put that in the newspaper."

"He didn't?"

"Absolutely. The little bastard wanted out and *knew* that she would read it."

Dierdre was obsessed with divorce. But she had only one divorce. She left Ben for a younger, a more handsome, a smarter man. She went to California with Ralph, eventually she left him, but she never married him. Now she was married to Len, if she left Len, it would be understandable. She had a collection of divorce stories. The wife who came home and found her husband and a strange woman passed out together on the marriage bed — worse than if she found them screwing — they had come to *his* home and freely passed out together. Dierdre knew a woman whose husband had cut *GO* on her arm with a pastry knife.

Nothing like that ever happened to any of us. Our troubles were simple. We never came home and found a husband screwing on the marriage bed. Anything we found out was by stealth.

I wondered if Dierdre ever told people about Rudolf and me. I didn't think so. All he did was leave me for another woman.

"Where do you think Florence is? Should we eat?"

"Transportation," I said. "Let's wait a bit longer."

I thought it must be transportation. There was the taxi strike, and suddenly the streets were all like Moscow and lumbering buses raced through their routes making light after light. Sometimes the drivers became exhilarated with what was possible — the bus would pass you right by.

Therefore, Florence was late. The restaurant had no liquor license. It was Florence's turn to bring the wine. We needed Florence.

Dierdre drew tracks on the tablecloth with her fork. She did not wait well. "You might tell me," she said. "Who do you have so far — your cookie film stars."

"I have in mind Pola Negri and Sir Laurence Olivier and Maureen O'Hara. And, Clark Gable."

"I expected something like that. I'm no real film buff, but even I could do better. There are genres, Theodora. Different age groups — different levels of the market. You don't just pull movie stars out of a hat. No coordination, no line to your choices. You don't know films, face it. And Pola Negri! Why Pola Negri?"

"I saw *The Cheat*."

"How many times?"

"Once."

"Oh God!"

I cleared my throat. When you start something, you might as well finish it. "Also, I am considering changing that logo on my cookie package — you know the oval with the photograph of the girl."

Dierdre nodded. "That is you, isn't it?"

"Yes. What do you think?"

"Well, I've always thought — with all due respect — that the photograph in that oval was a wee bit too much Pollyanna or Miss Sweet Sixteen."

"Fifteen. I was fifteen when the photograph was taken. And not sweet. No, I wasn't sweet. I was probably bad. By most standards — bad."

I thought Dierdre wasn't paying attention. She looked past me. "Here she is. At last!" Dierdre said.

I turned around. Florence stared at us through the window, her sharp nose blunted, nostrils pushed against glass. She looked as if she had hurried.

"You think she forgot the wine?" Dierdre said.

Florence threw open the door to the restaurant, at the other occupied tables people looked up in annoyance as wind sucked at their plates.

"The streets are empty," Florence announced to us nervously. "Doesn't anyone go out without taxis?" Around her hovered decreasing circles of chill like the rings of a moon.

"What do you expect?" Dierdre said. "It's cold, it's dark, and no taxis. Did you bring the wine?"

Florence lifted her arm to reveal a wine bottle securely gripped by the neck, the torn paper bag peeling damply away in strips.

"Ah," Dierdre said and waved the bottle at the waiter.

Florence sat down. "I think I'll keep my coat on," she said and turned up the collar.

Dierdre shrugged. "Hard to eat, though."

I looked at Florence. She had a flush of arterial color in her cheeks.

"We've ordered," Dierdre said. "The usual for all of us."

The waiter poured the wine. Florence

emptied her glass.

"I'm sick," she whispered.

I looked at her, annoyed, stared at the ruby cheeks, the glazed eyes. "For goodness sakes," I said. "Why did you drink that down so fast?"

"Not the wine."

"Sick? Really sick? You should have stayed home. Have you got a fever?"

Florence was a small woman with blond hair and an inheritance of skin so white that she always looked blanched, so that any color at all was falsely emphasized.

"Listen," Florence said, "let's talk soft — softer. Do you think anyone can hear us?"

I shook my head. "No, not here in the corner. Not unless the next table gets filled. No one else is near enough. What is it?"

Florence put her hands on the table — she had slipped her gloves back on. "Something terrible," she said in hushed tones. "On my way here."

"What?"

"Oh Theodora," Florence said, "I better go to the bathroom. I'm going to throw up."

Dierdre and I looked at each other. We were loathe to follow her. How well did we know Florence? We had met her and her husband at a party about a year ago, later we saw them again at the Reners' buffet. Then Dierdre invited them to a dinner for eight. Then I had them to my place for drinks. That's how adult friendships start. Friendships from childhood were different – they began in school or you didn't remember how they started. Florence's husband was named Jack.

"I feel like a louse sitting here," I said and reluctantly scraped my chair backward.

Dierdre touched my hand, her voice a faint sound. I had to lean forward.

"Do you think she was attacked?"

I hesitated. But I was thinking of the compressed redness in Florence's cheeks. How dark they had been – and that led to an insight into the possible nature of a *Movie Star Cookie*. I should require candied fruit so buried in redness that they appeared black. Considering that took time. I was still sitting when Florence came back to the table, her lipstick retouched, her hair smoothed.

"Feel better?" Dierdre said.

"No, I don't. I have to tell you something," she said.

We nodded.

"A man grabbed me," she said.

"See!" Dierdre said.

"It was after I got off the bus on Second, I was walking here, just past that antiques store, the one with those vases. I was paying no attention. This man – a street person. But he seemed all right – a big man – I didn't feel threatened. No one on the street – but then I thought, well there's lights on here and there, and maybe it's nothing his coming up behind me. But I started to run, I'm wearing these ridiculous boots with high heels. I slipped on some ice. Just a tiny edge of ice. It was very fast, and he caught me under the elbow. He put his other hand over my mouth – dirty woolen glove. Threads were on my tongue, sticking to my lips. And I could smell nothing – just wet wool – but I knew it must be foul."

"You didn't give him money?" Dierdre said. "Why didn't you give him money?"

"I would have – he could have taken my purse. But then he was pulling me between two buildings – a passageway. I didn't even know it was there – yet how many times down that block – a passageway to a courtyard – just a concrete place for garbage cans."

"My God," Dierdre said, *"did* he?"

Florence shook her head violently. "He pulled me back there – I dropped my purse, my shopping bag. I was so scared. I hit him. I raised the bottle – my wine bottle. I hit him. It made such a noise – I don't know how the bottle didn't break. The man had a little beard and a black wool cap. He looked like *anyone*. He fell down. He just collapsed. I picked up my purse – I didn't even realize I was still holding the bottle – I ran straight here. I killed him. I have killed him."

"Oh my God," Dierdre said. "Where did he touch you?"

"On the mouth – just on the mouth. And the arm."

"Did you get close to him after he fell?" I asked cautiously. "Check for a pulse?"

"No," Florence said.

"Then you don't know that he's dead – the bottle is intact. You just hit him hard – a concussion. He is probably gone by now. Got up and walked away."

"Should she call the police?" Dierdre asked.

"I don't know," I said. "Look, if she just hit someone – someone who tried to attack her – and he just walked off. I say no."

"What shall I do?" Florence said. "Nothing but ordinary things have ever happened to me."

"Hush, we should think. We should calm down," I said. "Here comes the food."

We ate everything. We ate just as we were supposed to. We complimented the owner on the Tandoori Chicken, on the *sabzi pulao,* cucumber, *narierl baida* curry, *aloo foogath,* and on the nongummy texture of his plain boiled rice. We went right through to the dessert. We always took dessert. We ate batter sweets in syrup. Florence kept saying she couldn't swallow, but we urged her on. We finished the wine, and the waiter took the empty bottle away. Florence turned her head and watched him carry the bottle away.

We drank our coffee, tiny cups of sweet coffee.

Dierdre sucked at the end of her spoon. "Did you ever do anything like this when you were fifteen, Theodora?"

"What?"

"I was thinking about what you said. Bad — at age fifteen."

"I didn't mean that bad. I never killed a man."

Florence gurgled.

"I'm sorry," I said, "I didn't mean that *you* had killed a man. I was referring to the fact that I had done things that were bad. Kid things. Adolescent."

"I lost the sweater I just bought," Florence said. "In the shopping bag."

"The shopping bag," I said. "You left the shopping bag back there?"

"Yes."

"By now the sweater is definitely gone," Dierdre said. "The man must have taken the bag with him."

"Was the sweater charged?" I asked.

"Yes."

"You have the charge slip?"

Florence shook her head.

I knew what we must do. What friends should do. "I think we have to find the shopping bag – unless the man took it with him."

"You're crazy," Dierdre said. "Walk down that passageway – *us?*"

"Yes," I said. "Look at Florence. She's not up to doing it alone. The charge slip will have her name on it."

Suddenly people were seated at the table next to us. Their chairs rattled, the people laughed. We had no more time to ourselves. We divided the check, paid, and left. The heat in the restaurant had been overpowering. Now the night air heavy with moisture chilled us all the more. We walked three abreast, just women going down the street. I wasn't any less frightened than the others. Florence shivered, turned up her collar. Dierdre had jammed her hands in her pockets.

"Know what?" Florence said. "The man's gloves were weird – like they were made out of bits of wool in red and blue and pink and grey all sewn together."

"Crazy Gloves," Dierdre said. "They're advertised."

Florence stopped. We realized this must be the passageway. A brilliant glare illuminated the sidewalk from a light bolted to the wall and pointed downward. Guaranteed to discourage burglars. We weren't to be stopped.

"Turn," I said, "and walk forward as if we were going somewhere. Have a definite destination."

I went first. I don't know why. The light decreased the farther into the narrow alley we ventured. Florence moaned. I knew what must be ahead. I looked down. None of us must trip. Flattened and dried bits of garbage rustled like unraked leaves. It was a man's leg that I saw stretched across the concrete. Could *it* move? Was he capable of moving it? The light went just that far — beyond a blotch of shadows. Past the leg, at the edge of the light was a crisply new Saks shopping bag, its side tilted against a dented garbage can. I reached for the twisted paper handles, felt my back strain with the effort not to take another step forward. I swung the bag over the leg, and passed it to Florence, she was behind me with a wino's breath and a scent of cumin.

"Let's go," Dierdre hissed.

"Find the sales slip."

"Later."

"Now!"

We marched single file back to the sidewalk. Florence carried the shopping bag. At the corner we caught a bus uptown. We sat side by side on the bus.

"He could be drunk," Dierdre said.

"Just out cold," I whispered.

Suddenly we realized what had happened. We had done it. We had gotten away. We poked each other's shoulders, the camaraderie of the girls' night out. We swayed with the motion of the bus.

"Tell Florence about your new cookies," Dierdre said.

"They're just in the planning stage," I said. "I call them *Movie Star Cookies*. Different cookies named after movie stars."

Florence nodded. She turned her head, and the threads of gold beads hanging from her ears made a defiant cackle. "Consumers are my business," she said. "Do Marilyn Monroe for nostalgia. You want a young market. Do Robert DeNiro, Lauren Hutton, Natassia Kinski, Eddie Murphy. Do people like that. Identification is the key."

"That's what I told her," Dierdre said. "A whole series – do it up big."

Florence worked on greeting cards – consumer surveys. How valuable was her opinion?

"Also," I said, "I am considering changing the photograph of the girl on my package. The one in the oval."

"Change it," Florence advised. "It's like an old yearbook picture. No one wears their hair that way anymore. Did I mention that I saw

Rudolf last Sunday on Canal Street? Nine o'clock in the morning. I think he intended to walk right past me without speaking. I was having none of that. How are *you?* I said. Know who the bum was with?"

"Celia," Dierdre said.

"What?" I said.

"You know Celia Mandel — something. Who recalls that last name. The little brunette with the cleft chin. Divorced. Teaches — God help us — kindergarten. The one he's been taking to what he thinks are out-of-the-way restaurants."

"You're ten guesses off," Florence said. "Helen. Helen the original souser. But let me tell you, she must be on the wagon now. Looked like a young Jane Russell. Tit-tit-hooray!"

"No," I said. "Marilyn."

"Marilyn?"

"Accountant. Ours — no, mine."

"Well, I don't know *her*," Dierdre said. "You never mentioned her. I knew Celia and Annabel Smith and now Helen."

Dierdre called me the next morning. She called so early that I was still in my pantyhose and bra. I sat in front of the closet door mirror and spoke to her, the view wasn't flattering.

"You know what," Dierdre said. "I had a déjà vu about last night."

"What?"

"I suddenly said to myself — what if Florence planned all this."

"Planned what?"

"Don't be so literal. That man she banged over the head. Suppose Florence had a lover — which I am sure she does — and she wanted to get rid of him. You know what her husband is doing these days — big bucks, that's what. Let's assume the lover threatens to tell Jack. So Florence makes plans, lures him to the passageway, where she has already hidden clothing. Maybe he lives nearby. Has to show him something, she says. She hits him over the head, outfits him like a bum, removes identification — dirties him up a bit. His absence won't be noticed — he hasn't as yet established himself anywhere. *Voilà!*"

"You're crazy. What about us? How do we fit in?"

"Florence is smart. You know I have always said that Florence was smart. Suppose she worries in case she might be seen — a lone woman leaving the passageway. She'll muddy the view then — bring us into it — appear to anyone watching to have left the passageway *twice*. Plant the Saks bag. And that, Theodora, is what I think could be the truth."

"That's not the meaning of déjà vu," I said.

Henry Arvis called me.

90

His voice sounded as if he were chewing something. "They caught someone last night, Theodora."

"Caught someone! Why didn't they call me right away?"

"It was three in the morning. Security caught him."

"Was he the Michael Caine look-alike?"

"What?"

"Who was it, Henry? That man in the car? Was it him?"

"No — not him. It was an older guy."

"Doing what? What was he doing — the man they caught?"

"They found him at the file cabinet — the fireproof one near the test kitchen."

"The recipes — the planning cabinet?"

"Yes, that's the one. But he didn't get *in* — not at all. Don't worry your little head about that. The dumb fool dropped a crowbar or something. Made noise. Security heard him."

What could I see? A man making his way between the phantasmal vats of dough, clambering through the mists of flour, and then getting caught.

I didn't make decisions easily. I think that I used to, but now I didn't. How did people make decisions? They slept on them. They drew straws. They tossed phony coins in the air shouting heads to the two-tailed coin. I used to say things like if the flower blooms, I'll go. If the third card is a three, we won't. If the next town has a street named Main, we'll pass it by.

And this decision? This decision concerned a picture on a package. This decision had worked itself into a fugue in my mind. Should I remove the picture? Everyone voting yea, raise your hand. Or should I keep it? The photograph of a fifteen-year old girl framed in an oval on the side of a package. No shot of a naked girl on a rug, no pinup beauty – this was just the face and neck, a head shot. Modern merchandising demanded a new image. Tomorrow, I'll ask my children.

What do you think? I'll say.

She screamed. Charlotte screamed often, raising the sounds of panic, accompanied by an explanation. She swore that a man tried to force his way into the apartment when she opened the door to pick up the newspaper, she said that she saw two mice in the cabinet beneath the sink, she said that she had received an electric shock when turning on the television set. These events always coincided with Spring Recess or Winter Break.

I should have known what was coming, should have foreseen it. Charlotte counted the plates when setting the table as if we were feeding an army. I put it to her simply, if the children got on her nerves, then she must go. We stared belligerently at each other, she did not want to go, I did not want her to go. Anyway, the children behaved splendidly, basically the children were peaches. Witness Stephanie who had been with us for three years, she had *cried* the day she left, and three children had been home when Stephanie worked for me. Before her was Norma.

The scream rose again, a pockmark against the silence. It was not to be a one-time event — no spider sighted on the wall, no fat red cockroach skittering across the vinyl. I slid my feet into my slippers. The scream boomeranged, because the apartment was temporarily bereft of furniture, furniture would have softened the sound, buried it in upholstered shapes, but most of the rooms were empty. This apartment was much larger than the last one, and some pieces hadn't been worth the move.

I imagined the children stirring behind their closed doors, awakened too early on the first day of Spring Recess. I hadn't been asleep, I had been reading a magazine. It was worse if you were asleep — hearing one of Charlotte's screams.

I made it to the kitchen. Charlotte perched on a high stool in the middle of the room, a web of tears on her cheeks, she was an impressive crier. Her stiffened right arm held out like a rod parallel to her lap.

"Look, look," she moaned.

The weal was rising, a dagger-shaped burn. The point near her thumb and the widest part of the blade past her wrist.

The ventilating fan had not been turned on. The air sizzled with the sweet smell of burn. Blue-and-orange flame charged upward beneath a black cast-iron frypan where blackened butter bubbled. A star-burst of yellow melt on the counter. A brown fly buzzing.

"Let's put your hand under the cold-water faucet," I said to Charlotte.

"What?" She pulled her arm back.

"It's the newest treatment. I read that – cold is best."

"Butter," she said offended. "Everyone uses butter."

You can't fight a belief like that so I took a quarter pound of butter and began to smear it across the area of redness. Of course, it hurt.

"What were you doing?" I said.

"Fixing the eggs – for the children."

"Breakfast?"

"Yes."

"But it's only seven o'clock! You know the children won't be ready to eat before nine."

Charlotte nodded, sniffled. "I would have

kept the food warm," she said. "The children are a lot of work."

Maybe it was the move, maybe the move last month and Spring Recess were too much. On the other hand, I remembered the Winter Break. What had Charlotte done? Tripped and twisted her shoulder.

"There was no reason to start cooking this early," I said sharply.

Charlotte began to weep. "Oh," she said and tenderly cradled her hand.

Was I being insensitive? "I'll clean up. Go lie down," I said.

"And the kitchen." Charlotte sobbed. "This kitchen — I can't find anything."

"It's the same as the last kitchen," I said. "We set it up — you and me. We put everything in exactly the same location as before. There can't be one single thing that you reach for that you can't find. See!" I closed my eyes. "Spatulas, by size, left drawer, second down by sink." I opened my eyes, pulled out the drawer. "See!"

But Charlotte, sneezing into a napkin, had already left.

I would make breakfast for the children. That wasn't bad, it would be pleasant to cook. In the kitchen by myself. Omelets. Yes, cheese and ham omelets. They were very fond of my omelets. I'd go into the office late. I didn't really mind. Dierdre said that Charlotte took advantage. But then Dierdre never had to hire and say that *she* had five children. Never mind that they were away at school.

I cleaned the kitchen, best to do that before I showered. The kitchen was new. When I bought the apartment, I had the room gutted, all new appliances installed. I bought the apartment three days after Rudolf left. We needed more space. Charlotte had no rational complaints. I had hired a company to move us. They packed everything, they unpacked everything.

I wiped, scrubbed, polished. When I returned to make breakfast, I would be starting fresh. It was the only way. I moved quietly, stopped occasionally to listen. Mouse-dead silence.

This was the first year that all the children's holidays coincided. Just chance. Sometimes one arrived a day early or one a day late. This time they all arrived on the same day. Bonita went to school in Massachusetts. Rebecca in Vermont. Robert in Connecticut, southern. Sheryl in Connecticut, northern. John went the farthest. He went to school in Colorado. That had been hard. I want to, Mother, he had said. It's what I want.

The children as they arrived had run through the unknown rooms, opening doors, examining closets, bathrooms. I thought my finding the place was a triumph. Now there was a separate bedroom for everybody. Five for the children. One for me. One spare.

"This place must have cost a lot," John said.

"Of course, stupid," Bonita said. "Expensive."

"Was that it?" Sheryl said. "Did *you* spend too much money? Was that why Daddy left?"

"Does Daddy know where we are?" Rebecca asked.

"Of course he does," I said. "He certainly does. And we are only five blocks away from the old building. We are not at the North Pole. This apartment was a very sensible purchase."

"What happened to *his* study?"

I sighed. "He doesn't need a study here, Robert. He has a study elsewhere."

"The whole idea was to get rid of him, wasn't it?" Bonita said.

"You're tired," I said. "Daddy promised me that he would be here on Saturday to see you all. He promised."

Their faces brightened. They were tired, pale, and shut-in looking.

"Daddy never breaks a promise," Robert said.

I spoke to the children before they went to bed. "The picture on the *Cookie Lady* packages — the girl's face. What do you think? Some people say I should change it.

What's your opinion?"

The boys shrugged.

"Change it," Rebecca said.

"Put in Julie Andrews," Sheryl said.

The magazine was on the bed. The one I had been reading before the scream. The best newsstand cum store I have ever known was located on Forty-third. *Around the World – Read.* The store was owned by two brothers from India, turbaned and black-bearded. Just mention the city and one of the brothers immediately said the state. Minnetonka. North Dakota, says the taller of the two. I've seen the strangest people walk in and pick up their newspaper from Little Falls or from Dalhousie. I thought of ordering a newspaper. Thought I might just take out a gazetteer and open it up. Pick a city.

I went to that newsstand. Even when I never wanted anything exotic. I could have bought *that* magazine I was reading anywhere. I wanted to see how the editors handled their interviews for the *Women Entrepreneur* series. I wanted to know what to expect. They were scheduled to send someone to see me next month for an autumn issue.

This month they had published an interview with a Jennifer Oliver. She founded a company that made lenses – government contracts, university contracts, commercial. She used to be a child astronomer. She had her own star or asteroid or something. $\beta 244X7$. An impressive woman with silver-toned hair worn in a French knot that emphasized her well-defined cheekbones. You can just tell, looking at her photograph, that the woman had good bones. She posed with her husband in their living room, a lot of chintz cushions and an antler-shaped chandelier. Ms. Oliver's husband was a lawyer who devoted all his time to Oliver Industries. His last name was Alroyd. They had a Scotty named Frank. They had one son who attended the University of California in Berkeley.

Did she cook? Well, she had this special dessert that she loved to make. She thawed a package of frozen blackberries. That was step one. And then in a crystal bowl she squirted approximately half a can of whipped cream, mushed in most of the thawed berries au naturel and then topped this off with the remainder of the whipped cream dribbled with the leftover berries. It's a great favorite with my guests, said Jennifer Oliver.

I tried to imagine that dessert. Great spoonfuls of purple-colored goop slithering sweetly down the throat. Blackberry stains were really a bitch to remove.

I used to have a purple tablecloth. With certain berry dishes, there was nothing like a purple tablecloth.

I propped the magazine up against the dresser mirror, open to the desirable life of Jennifer Oliver. These lives can be illusory. I needn't come off too badly. I would have my hair done. I would sit on a new couch soon to arrive. A mottled brown. On the table behind the couch, I would have on display the family photographs, framed in a glitter of silver. Children at play, children on horses, children in school uniforms.

Dierdre will find the right dress for me to wear, which I probably will never put on again. I will find it too tight or the drape of the collar will make me feel like a fool. But the dress will photograph beautifully. Unfortunately, no husband cum business manager in my picture. I considered calling up Rudolf. Rudolf, I would say, our divorce is not yet final. Would you come over? Would you sit on the couch to my right and be labeled as husband? Rudolf photographed very well. Rudolf, then, next to me. I rather fancied a bouffant skirt, the edges curling over Rudy's thigh. But no, Dierdre would never pick bouffant. Are you mad? she would say. All right, straight worsted wool, my hands casually placed – where? At my sides. Seated with Theodora Waite is her husband, noted scholar of the grotesque, Dr. Rudolf Tinker, the caption could read. A wonderful choice! Dr. Tinker is the father of Rebecca, Robert, and Sheryl. Bonita and John are the children of the well-known artist Mortimer Dille.

But Rudolf now lived with Marilyn. She stole him from me or otherwise enticed him. I thought of her thick sturdy calves, her love of racquetball, her open nondeodorized pores. I knew her, because she was my accountant. At any rate it must have been her on the end of some of those telephone calls, those breathing and sighing calls. A classic maneuver.

Her Rudolf was a man of integrity. He would never come and pretend that he was still my husband. Hadn't Rudolf said something about having turned a page? No, that must have been Marilyn. Rudolf would never say anything like that.

So husbands must be left out altogether from my interview. Let them go straight to the standard cooking question. When you were a child did you cook at your mother's side? In what? Well, in matching her-and-her aprons. That was the point where I made my correction. It isn't cooking, I'd say. I bake. Always baking. I cook — but my life's work is baking. When allowed to continue, I would say that my interest in baking was scientific. Then I would confess that no one in my family really baked. No one. I was self-taught. They wanted to hear that I was a cottage industry that grew and grew. Did I sell cookies from my kitchen? Never.

I showered, sprinkled myself with talcum. When the children were home I seemed to sweat more. I was going to wear beige. Beige skirt, beige blouse, beige jacket. Except for the jacket, I dressed completely. I wouldn't attempt to prepare a blackberry dessert in that outfit, but I certainly could prepare omelets. A cook with the right attitude is neat. A white butcher's apron was all I required.

I heard stirrings as I walked down the hall. I tapped on each door. If they overslept, they were cranky for hours, especially on the first day of a holiday. Once they got used to the newness, the children should be pleased. We had three bathrooms in the other apartment. Here, we had four. That extra bathroom could make a lot of difference.

No sign of Charlotte anywhere.

The table was set. *She* did set a nice table. I sliced ham, browned onions, slivered a sweet red pepper, grated cheese. Omelets made to order. It was Bonita who came into the kitchen first. She wore her school uniform. A navy blue pleated skirt, a white nylon blouse, and a wide navy blue necktie. I noticed that the children often wore their school uniforms for a day or two when they came home for holidays. Then one by one these clothes were abandoned. Bonita seemed taller. Two inches taller. Did she resemble her father? Mortimer was tall. She looked as if she had dressed hastily. She held up her hand. "This," she said disdainfully. "I found this on the bottom of *my* closet." She dangled something, gripped it with her fingertips.

It was a lone argyle sock. Grey, blue, and white diamonds. I stared at it. Odd how that single argyle sock reminded me of lost love.

Stanley kept his voice even. "You know those mounds — the ones with the thin icing and the silver dragees."

"Yes."

"They're out."

"What do you mean *out?* They aren't scheduled for production yet."

"Not by us. Out as on the market. My secretary bought some this morning. *Bettor's Delights,* she said they were called."

"Idea from the file cabinet in Brooklyn?"

"Henry swore they caught the man before he opened it."

"Then someone else broke in — unlocked the cabinet and then relocked the cabinet. I *knew* that man was a thief."

"Marketing considers it coincidence, Theodora. I think you should know that. A finite number of cookies. Anyway, marketing says we should go ahead — a new name, a different shape — so what. It was *ours.*"

I shook my head.

I decided that the protection of *Movie Star Cookies* would be my responsibility. They would require protection even before they were created.

It might seem easy to draw conclusions and say what led directly to *Movie Star Cookies.* The early meaning of cookies to the child and how those feelings were later translated into a career — the association with warmth and attention. Psychological jargon. It could have been anything. The stringing of beads for a necklace. An attentive teacher complimenting a report. My ability to name unions. I would stand up on a chair. Give me a number, I would say. Any number. Then I would tell them what union that was and its organizational limits. They would applaud.

Icebox Cookies:
1956

I thought my parents' courtship should be viewed as romantic. I thought it was like Romeo and Juliet – both sides of the family feuding. Only this time the lovers made it. I developed a scenario in which my mother's hair was long and thick and hung below her shoulders. My father was wonderful. I had the whole plot worked out. How he sneaked her out of the house. This version of romance held an audience of girls when I was nine or ten. Sometimes, I used special voices, I played all the parts. You're coming with me, my father said. Yes, my mother whispered. Not if I get you first, said *her* father to my father. I would ask for a volunteer and stage a brawl with much shrieking. It was very effective, especially the place where I begged to be allowed to go off with my lover. I could get away with this because my mother was dead and because we moved so much that none of these girls would know the truth. Actually, I didn't know it either. At least I didn't know enough of the truth. I knew they didn't marry because they had to – I had no doubts. They had a *first* anniversary before I was born. This I knew from the photograph – the two of them standing in front of a sheet cake labeled *First Anniversary*. It wasn't until I was almost thirteen that it occurred to me there might have been another baby on the way. But I couldn't prove that. Then when I learned how to twist the lock of a suitcase with a file, I found papers and letters. It turned out that my mother and father weren't even all that young. He was twenty-two when they married, and she was eighteen. As to the feud, his parents gave them ten thousand dollars. That didn't seem like animosity. Her parents gave them nothing. That's when I decided pregnancy – a baby before me.

My mother was beautiful. She fashioned herself into someone beautiful. Certainly, everyone who died became beautiful, but she was young when she died. There wasn't enough time for much to happen to her. The way my father stated it – she kept her looks. Age twenty-eight at the end. I wasn't superstitious. Still, near the last days of my own twenty-eighth year, I became jumpy. Three days to go past the length of my mother's life. What had happened to her, what had she done, what had she seen – couldn't be much. Take me – at age twenty-eight I already had three babies. None of my children were named after my mother. Not for any reason. I just didn't believe in that.

On the last day of my twenty-eighth year I brought my children into the kitchen. A small room, an old-fashioned room with wooden cabinets streaked by layers of white enamel paint. Most of the room was occupied by a rectangular oak table. I need horizontal space. When I baked, I expanded.

"Who's for cookies?" I asked.

My son John clapped his hands. "Me!"

The baby Sheryl cooed.

Bonita frowned. "What kind?"

I had said it wrong. "No, not eat cookies. I mean make them. Want to make cookies?"

"It's hard," Bonita said.

"No," I said, "not hard at all. I have in mind chilled, rolled cookies – icebox cookies. We fix them today and tomorrow we bake them. How does that sound?"

Bonita shook her head. "That's not how you do it. I saw how you do it. You mix the stuff and bake it – one-two-three."

"Not this kind, sweetheart – this kind takes two days. We chill the dough. I made cookies like these when I was little – no bigger than you – and I loved them."

She looked dubious.

"I want to color," John said. "Do a horse."

"Let's try cookies. Who wants to sift? And pick a flavor — vanilla, butterscotch, chocolate, molasses?"

"Vanilla," Bonita said.

I tied aprons around their middles. We sifted and mixed. Was it John or Bonita who discovered once the dough took form that it could be shaped?

"Look," John said. He broke off a bit of dough and rolled it into a ball.

Bonita made a dog.

"Listen," I said, "who's for milk and an already baked cookie?"

Bonita shook her head. "When Grandmother Dille was here in the summer, she said too many sweets were bad. Sugar kills, she said."

The children began rolling the dough into pellets and throwing them at each other. The dough turned grey. The baby watched, sucked her fingers. John gave her a blob of dough. This was a useful play experience. It didn't have to end up as cookies.

Afterwards, I scrubbed the table, swept the floor, washed small hands. My children took crayons and paper, they sprawled bellies down on the floor.

I knelt beside them. "I'll always be here," I said. "Always."

"Or in the bakery," Bonita said. Her fingers held a crayon firmly. Someone was getting silver hair.

In all the memories that I snatched, I was always older and my parents were always older. How well we behaved. So much for memories. But then that could be what everyone did. Thus, I remembered that I was never afraid of strange places when I was a child. But whether this was true, I cannot be certain.

People said that I didn't look anything like my mother. They really meant my stepmother. I didn't respond. I never said that Pauline wasn't my mother so I couldn't be expected to look like her. In many ways I looked more like Pauline than I looked like my mother. We had a collection of snapshots, bunched together in the back of an album of raw black pages. In one picture my mother wore white shorts and a polka-dotted bandanna tied like a halter. She waved and smiled either at the person holding the camera or at someone else. Then in another snapshot she wore the same shorts with the same top but no smile. Hold the pictures side by side, they weren't taken at the same time, the hair was longer in one. Yet I had no idea what occasioned either situation.

My mother wanted to leave her mark on me, especially at the end. When she was already wearing the blue knit cap all the time, she began to get lovey-dovey. It's the pact people made with a deity. I'll do so and so, and you'll back off. She was suddenly trying to tell me things. You have straight hair, she said. You can dip the ends in sugar water and wind them tight with bobby pins. That way the curl holds. You do that, and then every time you make a curl that way – you'll think of where you heard it.

Basically – you cannot regulate other people's memories. I never made curls. So I associated her with different events.

I yelled. I had a hoarse voice, a funny voice for a child. It was because of that husky voice that I could get away with yelling. Tallulah, my mother teased. Tal-lu-lah, my little bird.

"Stop," I yelled. They paid no attention. The ignoring wasn't as bad as it sounded. I was a sneaky child. Weary of bumping roads, carsick and bored, I often shrieked, cried out, begged them to stop. Once I craved a taffy-colored cat that raced across the road. Hal swerved, because of my noise, not because of the animal. He almost ran into a tree. I cried for rusting swings in deserted city parks. You couldn't blame my mother or Hal for not listening.

I yelled again. "Can't you be still?" my mother said. She didn't turn around to look at me. She was sitting sideways and staring at Hal. Always something scary about my mother in profile. Maybe because she didn't look like herself. Only seeing her full-face was I certain that it was her. Hal, I recognized in profile. In fact, I only recognized him in profile.

The car windows were closed because my mother worried about her hair. Hal drove a Buick. He had a black Buick. He said that black was the only color for a car, the only color with class. I would have preferred blue or red.

I squeezed my knees together as tight as I could manage. Then I began to go, a drop or two, but in that shut-up car you could smell it right away. "For Christ sakes," my mother said. "Stop the car, Hal."

I don't know if the Buick had tinted windows or why it was always dark in that car. But once outside I blinked. Sharp light, like coming out of a movie into the world. I had no time to adjust, tumbling from the car, I had to race into the stiff weeds of a vacant lot. I have no idea where all the vacant lots in neighborhoods have gone.

The urine poured through my panties, steaming in the air, and ran like a humiliating faucet down my thighs. Nothing to do but let it happen, balancing myself with legs as wide apart as possible. My scabbed and scraped knees stung, but I couldn't call attention to that. Afterwards, I reached up under my skirt and pulled down my underpants, slipping them over my shoes. That's when my mother called out, "Don't you dare bring those filthy things back into the car!" I abandoned the sodden pink cotton, elastic-edged, in the tangle of weeds. I didn't mind. I had plenty of panties.

My mother then out of the car, her thin heels cutting a path just an inch or two into the wilderness of the lot. "Come and get these," she said and stretched out her arm to me. I was offered a handful of folded tissues to be used and abandoned like the underpants.

I knew they were waiting, Hal and my mother. I ran back to the car and positioned myself carefully on the back seat, the prickly upholstery tingling against my still damp skin.

I suppose Hal and my mother could have been involved in a conversation and not heard me. On the other hand, what happened could have been deliberate. I had been made to wet my pants, I had been made to be a baby, I had been embarrassed. It gave my mother something to hold over me in case I told. But what to tell and to whom — I didn't know. On the other hand, she might have been only careless, indifferent, ignoring. Let me tell you that none of my children could make that complaint. I have always stopped for them.

Hal wished I would go away. I could tell that. However, on the good side, he never asked stupid questions. Never asked me what I wanted to be when I grew up. Never said whose pretty little girl are you. He gave me money to buy comic books, bubble gum, ice cream. Go-away money.

It seemed that Hal might have known mother better than anyone, because he knew her from a period known as Way Back Then. When he was around, he supplied food – Chinese food in cardboard cartons, good greasy hamburgers, reheatable franks and beans. We ate that food sitting around a wooden table. My mother never had to pay attention to me. I had a good appetite.

When my mother wanted to cook she made much better food. She could make roast meats sing. I heard that in a commercial. Use this salt and make your food sing. So I told my mother how her roast meats could sing, and she leaned over and kissed the top of my head. "You're a sweetheart," she said.

Then one day, they were going out. Hal showed up with two hamburgers for me. My mother was nervous. "It will be all right," Hal said. "Christ, where are we going? Only to the corner. The Italian on the corner." So close, she could stop in the middle of *her* meal and see if I was all right. I ate my hamburgers and then, following instructions, I went to bed. It felt good doing this on my own, taking the responsibility. Lying down on sheets that were clean and slithery, I heard the night noises that came through the window screen. I never knew if my mother sneaked back into the apartment and interrupted her meal. I don't remember being frightened. I felt content to be trusted this way. It was comfortable. I wondered if they might do it again.

Hal hated walking around the apartment without any clothes on. His body never meant anything to me. My mother walked around in her panties and bra and also with nothing on. When Hal was naked one day, he complained to my mother. I thought he said that I was looking at him. My mother made a noise like a snort. *"That* sees?" she said. *"That* knows?"

The New York City school system was crowded. There was an age cutoff. I would not be eligible for kindergarten and would not give anyone three hours of relief. My mother altered the copy of my birth certificate. "There," she said, and held it at arm's length, admiring it the same way she admired her nails when the polish was fresh. "A sleek job. How old are you, Theodora?"

"Five."

"Six."

"Six."

"That's right – tall and skinny girls always look older. This experience will be very, very good for you."

My mother took me to registration. We both wore dirndl skirts and white sleeveless blouses with ruffles around the collar and genuine Mexican huaraches bargained down from a peddler on Fourteenth Street. The stiff leather straps hurt my feet and I screamed that I wouldn't wear them, so my mother painted my toenails to make me shut up. I stood the pain, staring down at those tiny pink shells that once were my plain toes. Some of the children in line had on white socks and shoes with laces. It was a hot September day. My mother and I looked just right.

I was not admitted to kindergarten. The women in the school office said that they had seen all the tricks. I wasn't eligible. I was too young. I thought my mother would get terribly mad and perhaps throw something like the vase with yellow flowers that was within range of her hand. But all my mother did was yell, "Stupid bitch!" The woman behind the school desk still had her summer tan, she kept pushing short brown hair behind her ears to show off tiny gold button earrings. No matter what my mother said that woman just smiled, one of those narrow smiles. She was a pretty woman. I thought my mother could see that too.

One library was closed on Mondays, the other on Tuesdays. My mother and Hal dropped me off at eleven o'clock and picked me up at three, sometimes later. I had an apple, quartered so as not to show a recognizable bulge in my sweater pocket, wrapped in aluminum foil with two cookies. "Don't speak to anyone," my mother ordered, "except the librarian. Go into the bathroom to eat and flush all the wrappings down. No food allowed. Understand?"

The libraries had it all over the apartment. Libraries were cool, and the chairs were rump-worn. In the Closed Monday Library, one librarian could have given me trouble. This is no damn baby-sitting service, she said, moving her thick thighs and making a rasping noise. The other librarian shook her head. Leave her alone. She doesn't do anything, she said. She doesn't rip any pages.

I don't know exactly when I learned to read or how. Maybe at school, maybe my mother taught me. But when I was in the library at that time I had a reading vocabulary of four words. I learned those from Hal. I had pointed to words in the newspaper and asked him – not too many. He was an impatient man. He told me four words. I knew *bad, bat, but,* and *hitter.*

To convince the librarians of my continued suitability I always went quietly into the bathroom for my food breaks. In a stall, I ate my apple, the fruit acquired brown edges in my sweater pocket but that didn't change its flavor. I spit the seeds into the toilet followed by bits of core and the uneaten cookies, and flushed the debris away. The aluminum foil I crumpled into a ball and tossed and caught until it finally plopped into the toilet.

I learned which librarians could be asked questions, which not. I would save up words. Point to four per librarian. Possibly that was when I learned to read. When my children started school I knew the limitations of the see-say method and checked out their schools to be certain that phonics were taught.

Ten identical brick buildings formed not so much a circle as a wavy pattern around a courtyard. A beer bottle courtyard, newspapers stabbed on twigs, no grass. Two buildings in from the sidewalk was a playground. "You go in there and both your legs get broken," my mother said. So I stayed clear of that playground. On the other hand, no other children were ever in there to tempt me.

Therefore, it was hard to understand, because suddenly I was enrolled in an after-school group that met in a ground-floor room in one of those very buildings – third in from the street. This was different, my mother said, and if the woman in charge took us to that playground, I could go.

I didn't think we would fool the after-school woman – my mother saying that I was registered in afternoon kindergarten and that because she worked I had to be somewhere until five-thirty. I was wrong. The woman, who said I could call her Anna, fell for it.

So my mother picked me up every afternoon from a library and dropped me off at the after-school building. Anna had fifteen of us. We could do what we wanted, if we were quiet. Once in a while we ran in circles or we sang, repeating one beat late Anna's words. Winter was best, a lot of kids got sick and then the room was emptier.

One day my mother asked me if I thought – if I possibly thought – that I could go from the Tuesday Closed Library to the after-school group. The Monday Closed Library was very far. Tuesday, however, was four blocks away from the after-school building with school crossing guards at the corners. Yes, I said. I'm going to call, my mother said, I'm going to call Anna what's her-name to make sure you get there. Are you positive that you know the way? Swear it? Yes, I said.

It was winter and the six of us in the after-school group who were cold-free were cranky and washed out by the grey cold days. Anna said, "Know what? We're going to go right down the hall to my apartment and do a project."

We marched down the hall, and Anna un-locked a door. "Don't touch anything," Anna said. And no one did. She led us into the kitchen. Six crowded the room, but we were small, we could sit two to a kitchen chair. "Anybody here ever make cookies?" Anna asked. None of us ever had.

The kitchen had a red metal table covered with a clear plastic cloth. We sat on three sides of the table. Anna had one end to herself. "First you get the stuff," she said and opened a cupboard door. I looked — she had boxes and cans similar to what we had at home. Anna put two small round metal canisters on the table. "Flour," she said. "Sugar." She waved a bottle at us. "Vanilla." She unscrewed the cap and held the bottle briefly under our noses. Familiar smell. "Yum," she whispered. "Now we get out the milk and the eggs."

As far as I could tell, the entire procedure was simple.

"Icebox cookies," Anna said. We stared blankly. "Icebox," she said and then pointed. "See, like that — the Frigidaire. That's an icebox."

It was a familiar face, a tooting laugh. I knew that man. That was Daddy! Abner caught me up in his arms. "Baby face," he said. "Pudding," he said. He was not the slightest bit embarrassed to be around me. My mother stood in the doorway and smiled. She had on blue eyeshadow and a matching blue dress.

Abner had one arm around my mother and the other around me. "How are my two bears?" he said. "How are my little bears?"

I could smell him and her — cigarettes, perfume, sweat.

That evening we had roast beef in a chunk, not sliced from the deli, and mashed potatoes and green beans and frosted spice cake from a white cardboard box. I set the table, which was easy because no one cared what side anything was on. I had a friend in the after-school group, and Myrtle said her grandmother hit her because she couldn't remember which side the forks went on.

Just like that Hal vanished and Abner took over. And at no time did my mother take me aside and say don't mention anything. On the other hand, she was prepared. My mother told Abner about my imagination. What tales, she said. Our little girl has a whole make-believe world.

"To tell the truth," Abner said at the dinner table, "I didn't think I would ever find them. I figured they were gone with the wind."

"You think it will do us any good?"

Abner shrugged. "Never hurts to try. I can't believe they lost everything. They were loaded."

"Who?" I asked.

"Guess who's coming?" my mother said.

My mother was going to wear her special green dress from the cellophane bag. One wearing, my mother said, and straight to the cleaners. It holds the smell so.

"Who?" I said, and watched my fingers through the cellophane. I wiggled them, they remained the same but shiny.

"Your grandmother and grandfather."

"Why?"

"Because. And you be a little charmer — and you'll see. You are their very own and *only* grandchild."

I was dressed in my plaid skirt and the white blouse with the ruffle down the front. We sat and waited. I thought we might play Three

Little Bears, I usually ended up getting tickled when we did, but my mother and Abner were not willing. So I sat too.

"How the hell did he get on a blacklist?" my mother said.

Abner sighed. "He signed something or belonged to something. Listen, he was never political — never one bit. But just like that he was out on his ear. Like that."

"Did it have anything to do with you?"

"No," Abner said.

I began looking out the window. My mother kept telling me to go away. Abner kept saying let her stay. A yellow taxi stopped in front. They came by taxi.

The grandmother and grandfather both wore very light-colored clothing. We wore much darker clothes. They examined me. "She looks a lot like my sister," the man said. "Turn your head, honey." I turned my head. "Yes," the man said.

"I don't know what I am going to do," the man said to Abner. "But the truth is I can't help you."

"We have no money," the woman said. "We had heavy legal expenses."

The man cleared his throat. "We are going back to the Coast, Sonny," he said.

"This time further north," she said.

"Up above Frisco."

"Someone will help us," the man said. "There's a possible job — position."

"Otherwise," the woman said, "we don't know. We have no idea."

The man hesitated. "What about *her* people? Can't they give you something?"

Abner shook his head. "I don't think so," he said.

"I'd like to make cookies," I said.

"Don't interrupt, Theodora," my mother said.

"But I want to make cookies, can I?"

"All right, yes. Make cookies."

"We need stuff."

"Christ — what? What?"

"Flour and vanilla. We got the rest. More milk."

"Give her some money, Abner. Give her a few dollars."

The grandfather looked surprised. "She goes to the store by herself?"

"It's around the corner," my mother said. "Just around the corner."

"It's safe?"

"Of course it's safe."

"Does she know about the Lord's birthday? Does she know about Christmas, does she?"

"Of course she knows about Christmas.

Everyone knows about Christmas."

"I don't like you," the woman said. "I absolutely don't like you. You look like her. You look just like her. You look exactly like her. You're half a Hebe. If we hadn't gotten mixed up with Jews, nothing, no nothing would have happened. I'd still have a house, you know. I'd have my house, and a weekly manicure and that woman who did my hair."

I tasted the cookie, slowly bit into it. Better. Better than the ones made in the after-school group. It was better. I could make better than they.

The woman stared at me. She had red lines in her eyes. "I don't like you," the woman repeated.

"I hate you," I said calmly.

"What?" The woman began to cry.

I became aware that I could read. More words than I could count. It was not the right way to read. My own children were taught phonetically. I could print too. My first notebook said *Add more vanilla. Ice box cookies, 1956.*

These people have died – my grandparents. Perhaps one or another baked cookies. Maybe an aunt.

Abner once told me that they died when he

was a young man. People have no idea how much can be remembered. I met them. He was lying. When I was born, Abner said, the money was already slipping away. Abner was probably an accident. Sometimes when people lose everything they try a child. His family moved around. His mother was remote. Life, she said, is a stinking hole.

One day I looked up Abner's father in old newspapers at the Forty-second Street Library. The man was in the business end of life. It was 1954 when his name came up. He wasn't that important. No photograph. Just a name on a list. I retained a historically inaccurate picture of him – I placed him in the Crash of 1929. Grandfather Waite in a pale-colored suit balanced on the ledge of a respectable office building. Behind him, blown by the wind, the papers of his destruction floated from desk to floor. Jump, the crowd yelled.

In turn, I later told Abner's tale to friends. This is my past, I said. My heritage. When they had money – those grandparents of mine – they lived like the kings and queens of L.A. They lived in a house on a hill – a house with a frosting of orange-red tiles. A Spanish roof. Windows, unstained by flyspecks, gave back the reflection of the city at night. The house surrounded by syrup-scented jacinth and myrtle. Two gardeners. I was telling too much.

But I couldn't stop, and the details falsified the tale. I never knew if Rudolf was deceived. He only said that I should pay more attention to my heritage.

I saw my mother naked. I saw her naked before, but one time I tried to see her deliberately. She had come back from the hospital. I was curious as to what had been done to her. I can be excused. I was six years old. She was in the bathroom, naked, leaning over and running water into the tub. What had the fuss been about — the trip to the hospital. Nothing strange about her body except that stripes of red were painted here and there. She sat down in the tub, smoking a cigarette, reading a magazine. She told me to close the door. It was getting cold in the room.

Mortimer — my young artist. He had three brothers and a sister, working-class people, who despised him. My own father, he said, told me that he'd rather I was dead. My own father.

Mortimer lived on Avenue C and roamed the Village in the early seventies. He was on prescription tranquilizers — a wild mixture of chemicals, legitimately obtained. I tried to imagine what he would be like without them, he was always so high, so hyped up. He tried suicide the year before I met him. A real attempt, he said. A bottle of Librium and slit wrists. Did it under the West Side Highway near 125th Street where he could not be easily found. Still, a patrol car had driven by and he was carried to Bellevue. That settled him, he said. That made him know that his art was everything. He had to live for that.

I could tell you all the things that happened during those years — presidents, wars, cultural revolutions. New styles, clothing, music, art. I read about them in newspapers. I never said they didn't affect me. Of course they affected me.

I thought Mortimer was without talent. A painful perception for me, because I already loved him. I thought his canvases were imitative and his use of colors as morose as old laundry. Still, I loved him. We met at a fruit and vegetable stand on First Avenue. He was a vegetarian. He asked me to model for him. My hair was the right color. I told him to shove off. Get lost. He said I didn't understand. A study of my head — I didn't have to remove my clothes.

He introduced me to Ginger. I understood that she was really a friend. Later in the spring when Mortimer and I became lovers, we always went to his room. It was not a choice location for love – cold and damp and smelling of fumigation. But no arguments worked, Mortimer would not go to my place. It represented, he said, all that he had abandoned. He was not prepared to deal with my shibboleths, he said. Not so, I told him – I lived simply. I lived in three small rooms. All other money that I earned was saved for expansion of *The Cookie Lady*.

There was a technical proficiency to Mortimer's lovemaking. Move your leg, now move your arm. No matter how cold his room, no matter how foul the air – Mortimer would not go to my place. I couldn't figure Mortimer out. Didn't fully understand him. He was completely immodest, thinking nothing of slipping his hand under my skirt in the park. Perhaps he enjoyed my embarrassment. My little yelps. He gave me quizzes – asking me to identify strange names. They turned out to be singers or clubs or people whom he said everyone should know. Where are you? he would say to me. Where are you?

We discussed art. His tastes were different from mine. We spoke about Mortimer's plans. He couldn't understand how I felt about my own work. "The truth of the matter," he said, "is that it's not an art form, Theodora. I mean if you created something architectural – equipment – buildings – I could perhaps – and just perhaps – see that. But you bake, darling – someone eats it, it's gone. Art lingers. What you do is fine – but in its place. Business has its place."

I wrote a short piece on the esthetics and limitless possibilities of art. I called it "Art in the Life." I signed it simply Abner. The *Village Voice* published it. "Read this," I said to Mortimer.

"I can't deal with a man right now," Ginger said when I met her on the street. She had a sluggish manner, a tendency to exaggerated sorrow. I could not imagine her happy.

"I am recovering myself," she said. "You do food?"

"I bake," I said.

"Wholesome – decent stuff? *Real?*"

"Yes, I bake cookies. Purest ingredients – sugar, butter, flour, chocolate, vanilla."

"You're kidding? Sugar – you use that?"

"Sugar. That's the kind of baking I do. I sell my cookies in a store."

"Commercial – as in shopkeeper?"

"Yes."

"Then mentally I can't fit you together with Mortimer. Antithetical. Now I can *understand* why he can't make it in your rooms."

I was unhappy. He had told her *that?*

Ginger sent me a secondhand copy of *The Second Sex*.

I sent her a double batch of hazelnut wafers.

Mortimer and I ate together most evenings in a restaurant near the Bowery. The Vegetable Bowl. Not around any more. Styles in food change, the restaurant closed. Someone blew up the building. But once The Vegetable Bowl was a simple restaurant run by three young men, followers of one of the unpopular Indian cults. The vegetables were overcooked.

Mortimer was getting up from his table to leave when I pushed the door open. He regarded being late as an imposition on his time.

"Christ," I said. "Only twenty minutes. Did you eat?"

"No," he said. "Dissension causes me real pain – destroys the pleasure that food gives, and I was low on cash." He sat down again, but his expression was cold and unforgiving.

"I was mugged," I said. "I had a plenty good reason to be late. Coming up from the subway when this bastard shoved me. I lost my balance – nearly fell back down the stairs. He grabbed for my bag – but that swung back when I slipped – he took off with the box I was carrying. Lord & Taylor box."

"For drugs. He'll sell what's in the box," Mortimer said. "Were you hurt?"

"No – not after I regained my balance. He got the box, though. But I yelled – I reached up and caught at his back pants pocket. I wanted to make the bastard fall flat on his face. But instead his pocket ripped loose. Look!"

"Shit," Mortimer said.

I held up a wallet, a slim black leather wallet. "He's got my box – but I got his wallet."

"Everything?"

"The works. Driver's license. Even an identification card with his picture. Sixty dollars."

"What are you going to do?"

"Throw it down the sewer."

"Money?"

"Of course not."

"What was in your box?"

"Cookies."

"You *bought* cookies?"

"No, my own cookies – on display in the box. Leftover box from Christmas. Refrigerator cookies – with chopped pecans. Samples – I was hoping to place them. Get orders from stores, restaurants, groceries."

"You risked getting slashed for cookies?"

"*My* cookies."

"I can't think," Abner said. "My head is stuffed with pain."

I had been buttoned into a white organdy dress that everyone insisted was inappropriate, but a lot of nosy women poking into the closet had found nothing else. A dress printed with Mickey Mouses was less possible. No, the organdy or nothing. Who had time for shopping now. Then they had to find a slip, because otherwise my underpants showed. I could have told them where *she* kept my slip, but I let them find it by themselves.

At my mother's funeral, many of these total strangers leaned over and kissed the woman good-bye. She was my mother. I would have done that, but I wasn't asked. Unfamiliar women had taken over the apartment and could not easily be pushed out. Strangers assumed airs. Their cupboards, their cups, their coffee.

The funeral was the first time I learned my father's complete name. Abner Palmer Waite. The name didn't fit. But people kept saying his name. Then they turned to me. What to do with her? I was the her. What astonished me was that the decision was apparently theirs. And they made it.

"Are you listening, baby," Abner said. "I have to establish myself. I know what I have to do. Then one-two-three Daddy will come for you. Meantime, be a sweetie."

Aunt Arlette was not a true aunt. She was my mother's cousin. She didn't wear black at the funeral — she wore dark grey. Nevertheless, she

132

was the one who won me. Like the other funeral women who hugged me, she had a cushiony bosom. Her bras were strange. I had never seen any before edged with metal. When one hung on a doorknob, it didn't collapse, it kept its shape. This aunt had six rooms all to herself except for Ray who came in three times a week to clean. Aunt Arlette had been married long ago – an experience described by the women in black as terrible. At the funeral they still offered her their sympathies. A saint, they said. Whether the husband had died or what – I never heard.

"We shall get along," Aunt Arlette said, "by observing the Rules."

This turned out to be astonishingly easy. The Rules were not incompatible with what I had learned in libraries. Keep quiet, sit still, and make any messes in private.

At the end of two weeks Aunt Arlette was heard reporting on the telephone, "I am surprised. It's going to work out after all."

I was abandoned into luxury. Carpets on the floor, burnished wooden tables, glasses, and dishes. Where were children? We lived on a third floor. I presumed any children that existed were like me locked away behind the doors in the hallway. Aunt Arlette planned ahead. You'll need clothes when school starts, she said. You'll need well-fitted shoes. Feet are important.

What ended it all? Smoking. I was caught smoking. It never occurred to me that anyone would open the bathroom door without knocking. I had always been curious, but I never had a chance to puff, because my mother always kept her own cigarettes by her side. Aunt Arlette left hers anywhere. On a table, on top of the television, on a counter. So I took one of Aunt Arlette's cigarettes and a sturdy kitchen match. "That's what you do," Aunt Arlette said. "That's what you do. That's what they taught you."

I had been found out. It was expected. I was questioned then. Forget propriety, I heard Aunt Arlette say. Forget that the woman is dead. What had the girl learned?

I thought the big kitchen belonged to no one. Dinners were sent up from what Aunt Arlette called lovely restaurants. The food was reheated to lukewarm and we ate.

Then one day Aunt Arlette took off her dress, removed her rings, tied an apron over her full-length pink rayon slip. She was cooking a meal for the family. Pots, bowls, kettles miraculously appeared. I ventured into the kitchen. "I could make cookies," I said tentatively. "I could make icebox cookies for the family — pinwheels with nuts."

"You know how?"

"Yes," I said.

The pause was long. "All right," she said.

I knew this was a test.

The family came. I was again embraced by women who I suspected were the same ones who wore black but now were in a variety of floribunda prints. Three children appeared. I had nothing in common with them.

"She made the cookies," Aunt Arlette announced. "By herself."

The cookies were pronounced excellent. Aunt Arlette was congratulated. I was coming around, they said.

I got kitchen privileges. I made *mandelchen*, crescents, carrot drops with raisins, leaf wafers, macaroons both plain and chocolate. Aunt Arlette wanted a cake. Reluctantly, I made a banana cake with White Mountain frosting. She thought I ought to prepare an entire meal. I made soup with liver dumplings, a *ragoût fin*, braised celery. Chocolate chip cookies.

One day I had an idea involving almonds and butter and brown sugar. It was a Thursday. Ray came on Wednesday. She came on Friday. Aunt Arlette had gone to the cleaners to return a blouse. There was a spot on the front. An irregular spot, she said, like a figure eight.

Then she was going just two buildings away to visit a woman named Lise whose life was a tragedy from beginning to end. I had at least three, maybe four hours.

The almonds, the butter, the brown sugar. I thought about what was possible and what wasn't. I had my notebook. I dated the entry. *First Try,* I wrote.

I grew hot and sweaty and delirious with joy. What was possible. My notebook had a few spots of grease. I had butter on my fingers. I was already at *Fifteenth Try* when Aunt Arlette came back. What had I learned? I had learned that the varieties of truth were infinite.

I never knew how she found him. Abner came to the apartment. "Good to see you, baby," he said, and picked me up and hugged me. "How's the old witch," he whispered in my ear. I giggled, but softly. Aunt Arlette was in the room.

"I'll pick her up on Saturday," he said to Aunt Arlette, "if that's satisfactory."

I knew from the way he dragged out the word *satisfactory* that somehow he was getting her.

"That will be fine," she said.

Abner took my hand. "Walk me to the door," he said.

We were out of her range.

"You're coming home, baby," he said. "Didn't

I promise? Didn't I promise that I was going to come and rescue you. But first thing on Saturday, you will meet your new mama. I'm marrying this wonderful lady. You'll see."

Where the wedding party was held — Queens, I thought. A fairsized apartment — but already I had a standard of comparison — it wasn't as nice as Aunt Arlette's. One of the guests wore a zebra-striped dress with the stripes running the wrong way. Triangular tuna fish sandwiches with the crusts cut off were served and wine and beer. I would have made cookies for the party, but no one asked me.

Meet Pauline, my father said. Your mama. I knew she was young. I asked her how old and she said twenty-two.

A woman, perhaps a relative of Pauline's, pointed at me and then back to Pauline. "Enough said — that's your bed. You have made your bed."

I was just standing there. Staring. I wasn't behaving badly. Pauline was age twenty-two. She wore shoes with stiletto heels, stockings with embroidered clocks at the ankles, blood-red hair.

I thought she had nothing to fear from me. I had decided to be careful. Abner said he rescued me. Aunt Arlette could have done anything. As a matter of fact, I thought it was great of Abner. No one else in the family wanted me. None of the women who had come to that dinner and eaten my cookies. What would have happened then? A home for bad girls. I — dragged off screaming. No — my father loved me enough. He had rescued me. The least I could do was to be nice to Pauline.

I believed that story for years and years — until one day when Abner said that Arlette had given him two thousand dollars. Two thousand dollars to come and take me off her hands.

I have always thought my interest in baking was prefetal. A cookie is a self-contained creation. I can't sing — possibly tone-deaf. I can't draw. I had a talent for cookie making. I never knew whom I got it from. Everything came from something — genetic disposition. Pauline baked cakes. She made them from mixes. I never interfered with that. My sister used to make cookies, Pauline told me. Oodles of them at Christmas.

That didn't apply to me — that was not usable knowledge. Pauline was not blood. My mother got her baking from white boxes tied with string. Further back on the maternal side I cannot go. We lost all the relatives. I thought that we lost them in a move when my mother's lavender plastic-covered address book vanished.

If they wanted to find us, they could, Abner said. I wasn't sure. Still, somewhere in the past was probably an ancestor with the urge to make cookies.

Bonitas:
1978

"It's your housekeeper," the receptionist announced, although she would have put through anyone. "Important, she said."

I clicked in. I was analyzing a recipe, and it would take me a while to return to the proper mood.

"Yes?"

"It's Bonita," Stephanie said. "I told her to wait — I said call again this evening when your mother is home. She was yelling — sounded very mad. Screaming. Said to reach you, to have you call her back — to get her out of class."

My heart began to beat faster. "Sick? Was she sick?"

"No. She was screeching — I couldn't make out everything. It was about cookies, I think. She was yelling about cookies. On the other hand, she also shouted her name. Yes, I think it was her name."

She had found out. I knew that right away.

How had I thought Bonita wouldn't *know?* I had allowed myself to be talked into the change. All right, I knew from a pure taste viewpoint that the change was right. They were talking costs. I was thinking taste. A *Bonita* was a wreath-shaped, orange-flavored cookie with needles of coconut. One candied cherry half. In the quarterly report – they sold – *Bonitas* have always sold. But they were unprofitable. They cost too much to make.

The cost thing might be true, but that wasn't the point for me – the point was that *Bonitas* were *too* sweet. I kept a plateful on the corner of my desk during the test. I nibbled on them for several days. The sweetness destroyed the basic cookie. Less sugar, better cookie. I must have created them in my sleep – permitting so much sugar. And for ten years too! The *Bonitas* had been on the market for ten years.

I did my own testing – five, six variations. Decreasing the sugar, increasing the orange zest, less coconut. At last I had it right – a better, a tartly sweet cookie.

It astonished me that I believed I could get away with it. Did I think she wouldn't find out? I could have made batches of the *original* recipe and sent them off to her from time to time. But what if she went into a store and bought a bag of *Bonitas* – or even if someone else in her school bought some. One taste and she would know. I carried the responsibility. I had changed the recipe.

I called the school in Massachusetts. Bonita was in Biology, they would excuse her.

I heard the tight voice on the telephone. I felt terrible.

"They are either my cookies," she said, "or they are not. They had the cookies at tea."

I didn't know where.

"That girl's mother said, I understand that these cookies were named for *you*. Well, they weren't! Those weren't my cookies – *you* did something to them, didn't you?" The voice was tearful now. "Then you better take my name off the bag. You just better!"

Oh Lord! "It was just a test batch," I said. "You didn't like them?"

"No!"

"Mistake," I said. "Back to the original recipe, I swear. All right?"

"Yes."

I wrote a memo that afternoon. Return to the original *Bonita* recipe. Some things you had to do. She was age ten, and they were her cookies. I had named the cookies after her. I suppose I was lucky that I had named cookies only after her. I never named the other children's cookies that way. It wasn't that I hadn't given each child his or her *own* cookie – I had. But not the name. John, for instance. I really couldn't see *Johns*. And there was some jealousy. When she lost her temper, Sheryl always said that Bonita was my favorite. That wasn't true. I loved them all. Each child.

On the other hand, I had feelings too. None of the children ever wanted to make cookies. Not even their own cookies. They knew what their cookies tasted like, but they didn't want to make them. They didn't want to talk about them either. They didn't want to hear about my past. Not now mother, they said.

I created *Bonitas* in summer. They were out for three summers before we had weather as warm. Mortimer was having trouble working. "It's so fucking hot," he said. "And the baby squalls all day. Can't that woman take him out?"

"Not all the time," I said. "How can Norma take him out all the time. It's too hot." I took a deep breath. "Look, you want to rent a studio. Rent a studio."

"Remember then – it's your idea. You understand I'd be there most of the time. You know how I am – I work late. I can work all night."

"Yes," I said. "Start looking for a studio –

just hang around until Bonita's interview."

"Sure."

When I was twenty-six I put on a pale blue suit and went for the mother's interview at a nursery school. A foolish and heartbreaking event. You can't prepare. My friend Margaret whose son had been accepted by *three* schools told me this was the school that asked the mother to give a little speech. You couldn't second-guess them, they had a list of subjects. I thought I would die realizing how much of my baby's life hung on my words.

On interview day, two women sat in the room that was furnished like a living room in an English country house. Actually, the school did not look out over Central Park as stated in their bulletin. You would have had to press your forehead to a window and squint to see the park.

We sat on chairs spaced to form a V, and coffee was served. I was faced by the Headmistress and a Chinese lady whose name I did not catch. "What do you think might be a seminal event in your daughter's upbringing?" The Headmistress asked *the* question in the soft voice that denoted power, a deceptive level of sound. If you whispered, that was weak. But if the voice was firmly strong in its very softness, then people must attend carefully. Even though my answer was supposed to be extemporaneous, I gave myself an extra moment by nodding as if absorbing the question. I picked up the white china cup, swallowed one bitter sip of weak coffee. I imagined what this question drew. I myself might have fallen into such a quicklime pit. For if what was seminal had happened to the child, then it must be horrible, because these children were so young. No, the seminal-event question put the parent on the hot seat. I could go that way. I could say that when Bonita was two years old, Mortimer briefly left me. I could even stammer my way through our differences of opinion, his lack of financial success, and then reconciliation and the birth of John. I could even say that Carol Hope, whom I no longer see, had called to say that she had sat two tables behind Mortimer in a restaurant on East Broadway while he ate *dim sum* with a young blond woman. At the same time, I could assure the Headmistress that I doubted if Bonita noticed the family disturbance. She had been two, a self-absorbed age where kindness and nurture can fill any void.

Margaret said that with her interview speech, she was caught so unaware that she almost spluttered that she had a lover and begged them to forgive her. But hers was a different question. On the other hand, I had at my disposal an event that I honestly believed was seminal. The question was how to present it. I made my decision at the moment I put down my cup, I began by speaking about the approach of the crazy woman.

This woman. This *elderly* woman wearing a black woolen coat. Why would anyone wear such a coat in late June? Did that not indicate the sturdiness of her mind, and the level of her character. A black woolen coat with a fur collar. A collar of what could have been speckled rat. She says to me, "If I were you, I would stick her hand in something hot. Hot tea maybe. That would teach her."

Plunge her hand into hot tea! Her hand attached as it was to a three-year-old body. Bonita with hair the color of a cinnamon stick. Hair plaited into a single short braid as wide as an anchor rope. The whole event occurred in a Lamston's on Seventy-third Street. What had Bonita done? She stood humming a tuneless child's song as she fingered doll-size panties, white cotton with pink lace. Admiration and possession. Did a child know what stands between them? She crumpled the panties and stuffed them into the pocket of her jumper. I saw the entire act. Bonita's eyes were neither shrewd nor wary. No subtlety in the taking. It was not a theft. So I gave the child two dollars and led her to a cashier. The old woman following us. The cane. Did I forget the cane?

That old woman leaned upon a cane of rather fine wood with a curved handle that had inserts of bone in a fleur-de-lis pattern. She waved the cane at me. "Stick her hand in something hot!" she repeated.

Bonita, my little princess, will surely remember this incident. And how it was handled. I took Bonita home and gave her back to the care of our Norma. I gave Norma new directions. More time outdoors. Keep her out of buildings and shops. More fresh air. I kissed my baby good-bye. Already she was showing Norma her loot. Together they went to hunt up an appropriate doll to dress. Bonita bounced away from me, down the hall on fat baby legs, her fat baby fingers unscalded by something hot.

This was how things happened. Out of order. As big as a locomotive, that stretch limousine on Forty-fourth. The biggest car I had ever seen. The windows like stylish sunglasses were opalescent grey, but not totally opaque. All the passing people stared, no exceptions, all tried to catch a glimpse of the person in the back seat. Inside the car a movement. Long hair swung. Already then we had a black strand of hair twisted around a button. If you were caught, was it because you wanted to be caught, was that why you were caught. The faintest loss of appetite. I was waiting for him to become tender. Tender was a very bad sign. Are you all right? he says.

See, I told you.

Margaret read a book. We sat in the back of the bus where we shared a seat. We were Mother Supervisors for the picnic. All the Mother Supervisors were working mothers. We volunteered, quickly raising, no, actually waving our hands, in semiannual parents' meetings that we never missed, even though it meant a two-hour ride each way from the city to the school. Margaret sighed as she read. "This book," she said, "is about the Other Woman. It's witty and clever and full of pain. Such traumas and secret passion and humor and the ultimate realization by the character that a decade has passed and she is still with *him*." I nodded. I whistled down the aisle, a thick motherly admonition. Cut it out. All the girls were eleven.

Margaret stayed by me all afternoon. In my basket was adult food. I always brought adult food to a boarding school picnic. We were allowed to share what the children had. I didn't. Margaret took some of the cheese, the crisp wafers of bread, the smoky scraps of garlicky sausage. The cookies in the basket were my sandpipers, rich with vanilla and studded with coarse clumps of sugar crystals.

Other mothers whom I did not know stared at us and wondered whether the school tuna fish salad was still safe.

"In this book," Margaret said, and her finger made a dimple in the cheese, "the man treats the woman horribly, yes basically horribly. And I can see every word of it happening. He swallows ten years from her life."

Margaret turned away. "Don't!" she yelled and jumped up, spreading a galaxy of crumbs. It must be her daughter. She had one daughter. She married late.

I brought the blanket, a blanket gave freedom and allowed you to pick a tree and shade. The book was left on the blanket, its cover design a simple yellow with black letters. I looked down at the book, but I didn't touch it. The Other Woman filled the literature. The Other Woman and her married lover. Margaret was often the Other Woman. She was the Other Woman the way someone might be a tennis pro.

It used to be that was how you met the Other Woman, she was the friend whom you never suspected. That occurred less often. Now the man picked her up, met her at a counter in Bloomingdale's, shared the same dentist, took refuge from the rain in the small store that smelled winey from unground coffee beans. Soon, he kept a change of clothing in the apartment of the Other Woman, taking home what was soiled in his briefcase. He regretted that promises must be broken, he sent flowers, he was sentimental about anniversary dates and certain songs. Weekends, special trips, but no holidays. Holidays were for the children. The Other Woman's married lover had brown hair. He was sometimes belligerent. He began to keep his body in shape. He sat on the shelf of the heart of the Other Woman. But he went home – that was the most painful part – he left the Other Woman in her warm and sweet-smelling bed. He left her and went home. I may have been the person he went home to.

"Now," Bonita said. "The treat." I looked up at my daughter, her eyes were mysterious, like the eyes of ladies from whom knights beg tokens to wear upon their sleeves. She was eleven. The school apples had been distributed. Other mothers were in charge of the Food, they provided the apples. "All right," I said. "The tins are in the back of the bus on the second-to-last seat."

Bonita nodded happily and chose two volunteers. I watched from beneath my tree as the girls brought out the large commercial-size tins in my familiar red-and-orange design.

Eleven-year-olds were partial to my lace baskets made of cookie dough and topped with jam-scented frosting. Still, some preferred chocolate chips and peanut butter jumbles. I had an assortment. That's what Marketing said to do. The lids of the tins were pried up and hands descended. Eleven was not big for queues. No waistlines to consider. "Thank you," said a little girl pausing in front of me. She had five, six cookies clutched to the front of her T-shirt. "My mother said these are probably the broken ones, the seconds," she said. I hesitated, sucked in my breath. "Your mother," I replied firmly, "is mistaken." I leaned back against my tree.

Margaret returned, sank down on the blanket, rubbed sadly at a chocolate stain on her sleeve. "God," she said. "Listen to them! How does anyone manage *more* than a single child?" She stared at me. "Unless, of course, one has help. Like you or Ethel Kennedy. That's a lot different. But for the rest of us mortals — what's next?"

"The show," I said.

The picnic was held on the grounds of a Theater Park. A mime show was scheduled. A man performed a series of tableaus called "Professions." None of the children assembled knew the meaning of the word cobbler. All the girls and the mothers sat on wind-smoothed benches in the amphitheater. It was hot in the sun. The girls liked the entertainment less than moving around. "Nothing happens," says a plaintive

151

voice. "It's not even sexy." The mime in white, his face a cornstarch mask, twirled in that sun and juggled faster and faster the imaginary globes he created with his hands.

The girls grew sulky. Voices raised, exchanged gossip. I went into a rest room and splashed cool water on my face. I touched my lips with lipstick, combed my hair.

The Spring Picnic for this class, held by school vote in New York State, was almost over. The girls would spend the weekend at their homes. The bus was going to the city. Girls who lived elsewhere were relinquished to teacher-driven station wagons.

Almost everyone boarded the bus. "God," Margaret said, and looked at me. "You've smeared your lipstick peculiarly."

The heat and damp fingers. I took a tissue and wiped. On the bus, many of the girls against their will fell asleep. I rested my head against the window. My daughter sat near the front of the bus, she was among those who had fallen asleep.

"You ever see Mortimer?" Margaret asked. I opened my eyes, the lids thickened by the warmth. "No," I said. "He's in California. L.A."

Two of the girls sang softly. They sang the jingle for *The Cookie Lady*. They stopped from time to time and giggled. They were trying to embarrass my daughter. Bonita was asleep.

The bus dropped mothers and girls off on the park side of the street. The driver can't be blamed, that side of the street had shade, and the bus rested like a carriage horse and dripped water onto the concrete. The awakened children tumbled off the bus. Each Mother Supervisor had ten girls in her charge. Nonworking mothers should be waiting, or maids or fathers or the cars sent for suburban girls. Two girls had notes from their mothers – *I give permission for my treasure to walk home by herself* – and were escorted across the street. The luckiest Mother Supervisors had their charges snatched at once. They were free. I was not that lucky. Bonita was cranky and tired. None of the girls remaining cared any more how they behaved or how they looked to each other. "God," Margaret said. "At last! Aren't you grateful that you didn't stay in the suburbs? Now you are a skip and a throw from home."

I bought a house before Mortimer went to California. What did I think a house would do? The house on Henniker Drive had twelve rooms. You could smell water. On foggy days, it seemed as if the water must be there. Half an acre in the front and three-quarters of an acre in the back, all bumpy and poorly graded.

"When *you* were buying a house," Margaret said when she visited, "I don't know why you didn't look a few blocks further east and get a view of the water."

I hired a gardener. His name was Tunroe. He said that the children should have the land on the left side of the house and the rest would be his. He was the one who made a Japanese garden out of that rough and strangely sloped land. He made paths of white pebbles and created a bridge and a pond. Pink and white flowers grew from spring to frost. Sometimes at a party someone would ask, "Can you see the Sound from your windows? In daylight?"

The new apartment looked finished. That's how I described it. The maintenance staff at the building was amenable to bribes. Everything had been hung, nailed, or carried off. Every Friday evening I went to the apartment to see what still had to be done. I would work in the apartment until ten o'clock in the evening. Afterwards, I went to Penn Station and took the train back to the house. Sometimes I had a three-seater to myself and then I would really stretch out. One Friday after the train started the aisle seat was occupied by a thin bird of a woman wearing an old blue suit with a wavy pale hemline like a chalk circle. "My name is Victoria," the woman said. "I have been watching you. We ride this train together every Friday. I would like you to meet my brother."

I was surprised. "I'm sorry," I said. "But that is not possible."

Victoria continued as if I had not spoken. "You seem all right. I'm careful about such things. Introducing is a responsibility. You can have coffee with him to start."

"No," I said firmly. "I will not meet your brother. Not for coffee nor for any other purpose."

The woman began to speak about the weather.

To be honest, I didn't believe that either Bonita or John would recognize Mortimer if he walked down the street past them. Even though he looked exactly like his photograph. The children *knew* Rudolf. They all considered Rudolf their father. They hardly knew Mortimer. He telephoned from California occasionally and yelled in a booming voice. *Hello, my sugars.* They were young but not deaf. Even his choice of words told me how much he had changed living in a warm climate.

When Bonita was angry she sometimes threw clothes into a zippered bag. I'll stow away, she would say. You'll see. I'll go straight to him. But now she was eleven, she was learning

Italian in preparation for Summer Session in Florence.

Once I was asked to appear on the Donahue show. "The Self-Made Woman." But I turned the opportunity down, I knew what they would ask about. The husbands. The children. But then I watched that show, they had on the lady who made silk-screened T-shirts in Duluth and the woman who designed that no-strap kiddie seat. The questions were different from what I had expected. What the audience really wanted to know were the secrets of success. Plenty of women out there with homemaking skills. What was so special about these *two* women? Just look at them — the T-shirt lady and the one with the kiddie seats.

Mortimer had a friend who had gone through three years of medical school and one day just chucked the whole thing. Can you imagine, Mortimer told me, how we used to see him night after night in the library. Then one-two-three he packs up and it's bye-bye. His mother called me before he left. He and I were both from the same town in New Jersey. Do something, she begged. Persuade him. What could I do? We didn't share the same interests any longer. Off he went, we never heard from him again.

Mortimer liked to think of this friend as experiencing events. He thought of him as part of the underground youth movement, saw him on a commune, hitching his way across the country, hiking up mountains. But he never really knew. Sometimes I would say to Mortimer that perhaps his friend had a brain tumor. Maybe he went off to die. Other times I would suggest that he had returned to school and finished up elsewhere. Mortimer said that was one thing about me – I never saw the romance in life, the adventure.

I made for myself a description of the Other Woman. It was intended to be a joke that I planned to share with my friends. In my account, the Other Woman had to be prettier. Prettier, younger, smarter, fatter. When *they* were together she spoke about the coziness of their life. She was filled with the need to tell him everything, to splash her life in front of him. Today, I did so and so, she would say. She would select. All those sharp images that pleased him. He liked exactness. How can you be so precise, he said to his wife, in one way and not in all ways. That need not be said to the Other Woman. She abolished all casual words. Nothing was beautiful or good. Never would she say it was as usual. That was tiring. But didn't she ever want to say – I did nothing. The day was the same.

This was what I wondered. I wondered if the rooms of the Other Woman were strewn with mementos of her married lover. Books, records, photographs, notes. Yes, particularly notes. I believed that the wife hardly recognized the handwriting of her husband. But the Other Woman was the recipient of notes. Letters. Protestations. Every one began, *My dearest.*

The Other Woman cried about the decade to come. How can he do that to her? He parted her legs and she moved, she adjusted, to hold him. They laughed and drank warm white wine. She told him anecdotes from her past. Everything about her was different, he had no idea.

The Other Woman has it all on her side. Everyone said, why won't the wife give him up. If the wife were any good where it counted, he'd still be there, wouldn't he? A good marriage can't be broken. For the Other Woman this was true love. She loved him. First, the Other Woman says that she can wait. But then she can't. How much was asked of her? She never refused him. And she knew so much. The day he gave up smoking. All the brands of everything he liked. The Other Woman kept a ready supply of everything he liked. Then one day she threatens him. I'll go away, she says. I swear I will go away.

After the Other Woman made her telephone call, underwear was checked, handkerchiefs examined. Was that blood on the shirt collar? There, that streak of red. Or was that the shade of raspberry so cherished by blondes? Clothes sniffed. Shirts counted. Should four blue shirts be on the shelf? If so, where was the last one?

The Other Woman wore primary colors. Black as coal, blue as sky, green as grass, yellow as sun. The red of her menstrual blood was pure, carrying with it the salts of her body. She never got pregnant. Not on purpose. Not by accident. She used to. But that was a long time ago.

I was riding a bus to the restaurant when I glimpsed that extraordinarily thick book in the window of Rizzoli. The book resembled in its size the thick one that my friend Ginger carried with her. *The Life of Saint Therese of Avigne.* I was always trying to figure out why Ginger carried this book with her and didn't ever seem to finish it, and whether this represented an affectation. Because at the same time that Ginger was immersed in the life of this Saint Therese of Avigne, she had acquired a new and very young lover who lived on Avenue A. The Rizzoli book of course was not the same book as Ginger's, but thinking about it, I almost missed my stop.

The bus had moved so swiftly, the streets deserted like some Balkan city in winter, because of the taxi strike. I leaped up just in time. I got off at Eighteenth Street, I had four blocks to walk east and then one north. I wore sturdy boots. An Altman shopping bag hanging from my wrist, my purse tucked under my arm, my head bowed to the oncoming wind — a lithograph of winter in the city. I was on my way to have dinner with my friends, Ginger and Margaret. We always went to the same Polish restaurant where we had a favorite table and fancied that because we had spoken to the owners the piroshki we were served were better than those served to other customers unknown to the owners.

I hurried, it was very cold, the last lines of light clinging like icicles to the walls of buildings. My thoughts still on that book, I paid less attention than usual to my surroundings. Not the habits of a street-wise person. I heard footsteps. Was I being followed? No one else on the street. I knew that the lone woman always looked vulnerable; nevertheless, if I was being followed, someone had made a poor choice of location. A window yielded a reflection. A man behind me, catching up. This was a street of converted brownstones, lights on in several windows. The light poles had political and charity rally posters glued to them. Signs of a conscience-ridden neighborhood. If I yelled, certainly someone would have come. The man put his hand on my arm and reached for the purse slowly, confidently. I swung around, the purse's metal clasp banged across the man's Adam's apple, and at the same time, I planted one heel on his instep, first scraping down the skin from kneecap to ankle. He bent over in anguish. Neither of us actually made a sound. I ran all the way to the restaurant.

My friends said I was a fool to have resisted. A purse was only a possession. I insisted that I knew what I was doing. At any rate I was rather proud of myself. I told the story only to women. I didn't tell any men personally, not that I thought the men's responses would be different from the women's, but I thought that unconsciously they would be on the robber's side.

It was Ginger who gave me away. Ginger who asked Mortimer what he thought about his brave wife. She apologized afterwards, she hadn't known it was a secret, and wondered if I had been somewhere before the restaurant that Mortimer wasn't suppose to know about. In many ways that incident marked the end of our friendship – the three of us. Margaret transferred her daughter to another school. After Ginger converted to Catholicism, she moved to L.A.

The children noticed first. Five children sat

at the rectangular table. They had moved their place mats — the silverware, the glasses, the napkins. They were now scattered like buckshot from the womb down the length of the table. Orphans at the refectory. Rebecca mentioned the possibility that *her* Daddy might show up sooner than Saturday.

Then they stared at me. "Look at you," Bonita said. "What did you do to yourself?"

One of the other children put down her fork. "You look weird," she said. "Like a clown." And the boys giggled.

Bonita stood up and walked to the end of the table where I sat. She was my daughter and had been granted the freedom to touch me. I knew that the reverse was not true. With moistened fingers she rubbed at my lips and my left cheek. I thought I must need better light in my room.

The next morning Bonita was angry. "Do you think you are being funny?" she said. "Are you trying to ruin our vacation?" All the children were united. Hostile. I rubbed my own cheek, dyed my fingers a soft pink. Moved the napkin across my lips. I thought perhaps I needed glasses. For close work.

The third morning I appeared with no makeup. Everything was all right. Sheryl straightened my collar. Up in the air, she said.

Rebecca said she was wrong, her Daddy, after all, was not coming until Saturday.

I temporarily stopped wearing makeup. The result was that I looked older. I was asked if I suffered from a migraine. But I did not have that affliction. Still, I appeared pale and wan. I required that artificial color. But I must be in need of some kind of a magnifying mirror. People were staring. Once, I left the apartment before the children saw me, my meeting was early, but from the glances of the passing crowd I realized that something must be wrong. I went into a coffee shop. In their rest room, scented with chemical gardenias, I washed my face. Perhaps the mirror in that room was distorted. I thought I looked all right.

It was not a palsy. I have examined my writing, no tremor displayed. I read perfectly well. Small print.

The new apartment had rooms that stretched from sunny wall to sunny wall. The family that bought the house on Henniker Drive had plans. They were going to bring in a bulldozer and reshape the land. A swimming pool perhaps, the woman said. I nodded. My children don't mind giving up the house. I worry that they will miss the grass. Margaret has come with Ginger and Dierdre to see the new apartment. We walk through empty rooms. Well

Margaret says. You could buy and sell me.

"This is very difficult," Rudolf said. He called me at the offices of *The Cookie Lady*. "I want to take the children away for the weekend."

My heart bobbed. On the corner of my desk was a plate. The cookie of the day. I reached for a gaufrette.

"Look," Rudolf said, "I want to take them up to Ruth's house."

I hesitated. "Ruth? Who's Ruth?"

"The sister of a friend. There's an engagement party – Ruth's son."

"All right," I said.

"The thing is – I want to take Sheryl and Robert and Rebecca."

"I beg your pardon – what have you said? That sucks, Rudolf. I mean that surely sucks. Taking only Sheryl and the twins – that's incredible. Did you say *that?* Who are Bonita and John – The Outcasts of Poker Flat?"

"Look," Rudolf said. "Ordinarily I wouldn't do this – you know I wouldn't do this – but the house we're visiting – small."

"You tell your *friend* and her sister that my children come as a set. We don't break up our sets. You'll take all or none."

The girls have not seen the Other Woman. "I

saw her," John said. "I saw her. She's tall and she's got long hair. Daddy didn't see me. They got into a cab."

That's what it was like in the city, I thought. When we lived in the sticks, that couldn't happen. But here. When *I* saw them I was on Fifty-seventh and Madison. They were on the west side of the street. She was tall, maybe even taller than he. She wore a cape, a classy purple wool cape. Like in a movie.

"All right," I said to John. "How do you know it's her?"

"Come on, he held her elbow. He looked right at her face while they walked. He wouldn't have seen *me* if I stuck myself right under his nose."

"That's enough," I said.

"She does figure eights," Rudolf said carefully. "She doesn't wobble anymore on the corners." He smiled at a daughter.

"Rudolf," John said, "Mommy says that we are going to see the Easter show this afternoon at Radio City, even if the line is seven thousand people long."

Sheryl pushed her chair away from the table. "The hell with you," she said. "The hell with you."

How can I punish her? Shall I forbid her the trip to Connecticut where Ruth waits?

Rudolf looked up. "All right," he said. "Henceforth, no one sitting in this room may call me Rudolf. Everyone must call me Daddy except your mother." He stared at Bonita. She sometimes called him Rudolf. "Except Bonita," he added.

I want you to know, he said, that almost everyone thinks I am crazy and everyone else thinks I am marrying you for your money. They also think I'm crazy. And there is nothing I can do. You think I can say to them hey I love to make love to her. That making love to her is truly the best thing for me. And suddenly I am confused only when I am not with her or planning to be with her.

Remembering that was like remembering when you were young or happier or anything before.

I looked at the tiny clock near the bed. It was early. "Hello."

"It's me," Dierdre said. "Hey, why are you *answering* the telephone? Where's what's-her-face?"

"It's Wednesday," I said. "Charlotte's afternoon off. She does her nails on Wednesday mornings. On Wednesday mornings, I always pick up the telephone."

"Anyway, you sound like you're still in bed. Aren't you going to work today?"

"Yes, I am. But late. I am going to have breakfast with the children first. Everyone's home today."

"Oh," Dierdre said. "Breakfast with the children — well I always say that if I could afford child care like Ethel Kennedy or someone like *you* — then I too would have had lots of children."

"Yes, you do always say that."

"Don't be snippy, Theodora. I'll be late, and I am *going* to work. I meant to tell you this, but it slipped my mind. I got a telephone call last week from someone who wanted to ask questions about you."

"Me?"

"The line she used was absurd. She pretended this was some kind of a survey. She asked me what my favorite *Cookie Lady* cookie was. I said none of your business and just before I hung up, she says, excuse me, but I am doing a book on women and their businesses, and I know that you are a friend of Theodora Waite. Could I ask you some questions? I said no. Of course, I never tell anything to a stranger on the telephone. Write me a letter, I said. Anyway, Theodora, what do you think is up? The last time I was contacted this way was when Arthur tried to get a divorce from Ginger."

"Arthur never tried to get a divorce. That was Arthur's girl friend — she was trying to get a divorce."

"Well, I won't respond of course. Let me know what's up."

Bonita talking to someone on the telephone: "She is really out of it. I tell you it is a step past gross. No, I mean it. Hell, how do I know how it was *before* — I was just a kid. Maybe it was like this before. But she is strange."

It was a midtown group, "Executive Women on the March." An award dinner. I didn't remember when I agreed to go. But I must have. I said that I would present the award to this year's Up-and-Coming Executive Woman. There was no getting out of it. They sent me a capsule biography of the winner. I wore a black linen suit, had my hair done at Lenny's. I was meeting Ginger in the lobby. That was the clue — I had forgotten. How I got suckered into doing this. Ginger and her organizations.

Charlotte would feed the children. They were glad to see me go. They were going to have chili and nacho chips.

Ginger waited for me near the elevator in the lobby. She looked great in grey. Everything about Ginger was silvery. "My God," she said.

"Are you deliberately trying to be humorous? If so, forget it."

"What?" I said.

"And," she added angrily, "if that is some kind of a statement — forget it." She leaned over and sniffed, her nostrils twitching outward. "Are you drunk? Stoned?"

I shook my head. I reached up, tentatively smoothed my hair.

"Not your hair," she said in exasperation. "My God — you don't *know*. Give me your bag. Do you have lipstick in your bag? Any blusher there? If not, we'll use mine. But you are not going like that."

I yielded my purse. Ginger rummaged in it. She pulled out the gold-toned lipstick case. I felt her hands like cool steel. The lipstick pressed on. I had no blusher. Ginger did.

The doorman watched. He was an old man, tired.

"There," Ginger said. "Now don't be funny!"

I opened my compact. Now I did tremble. I looked in that tiny mirror. The lipstick was perfect. Whatever it had been before, it was now perfect. The color on my cheeks a soft shading.

Tomorrow, I would stop procrastinating. I would buy a magnifying mirror. Maybe even a pair of those strange-looking glasses that you hung around the neck — intended for those with poor close vision.

Stanley came into my office. The room messy but not where it looked as if I were making a point.

"I felt that I had to tell you this," he said. "Frankly, Theodora, there has been talk for some time that you were going deaf."

My God. "Deaf?"

"Well, in one ear then. On the left. You see, if someone spoke to you on the left side – on the left side of the conference table, for instance – you didn't respond."

I shook my head. "I hear perfectly well – perhaps I was distracted."

"Then," he said, "it seemed as if everyone was wrong. Maybe you were deaf and partially blind."

I opened my mouth. Stanley held up his hand in the hush sign. "Because, Theodora," he said. "If someone hands you something on the left side – why, you ignore it."

"I assure you – and *everyone* else – I am neither blind nor deaf."

"Then," Stanley said, "the opinions shifted."

"Like sand?"

"I am only trying to *protect* you, Theodora. Opinion said that you had packed it in."

"Packed *what* in?"

"That you had gone nuts, Theodora.

Crazy, straight gaga."

The Other Woman was named Annabel. Actually as in Annabel Lee – her mother named her after a fucking poem. Mortimer called me. I want to give you my telephone number, he said. And my address.

He had been staying at a residential hotel. I knew he couldn't afford that for too long. He would have had to move.

I have a pencil, I said.

He gave me the telephone number, the address.

Okay, I said.

Just a moment. If you have to, in case you might have to, send me anything. A letter. My name isn't on the mailbox. Send it in care of –

Yes?

Annabel Smith.

Smith?

Yes.

The Other Woman was named Annabel. I bet she was full of spirit. Spunky little thing. I bet she happily went to fancy dress parties. Went as Marie Antoinette. She was full of sympathy for him. She thought it was wonderful that his career had taken off. She respected him as an artist. She restored his faith in the romantic gesture. She was too shrewd and cunning to talk about his wife. Let the contrast do the talking.

Ginger was someone special to me. I have known Ginger for many years. Possibly there was no one else with whom I have had such a strong and sustained relationship.

"Ginger, I think that I might be sick."

"What is it, Theodora?"

"Basically, I don't feel sick. It hardly warrants a trip to Lourdes. But *everyone* says that I must be sick. They say that I now behave peculiarly."

"Theodora, I don't want to say this. But you were strange the other evening. Your face —"

"Like a clown."

"Exactly."

"Yesterday, Ginger, when I took off my jacket. My blouse was half-unbuttoned — it buttons on a left-slanted diagonal. I was wearing a sheer black bra."

"I thought maybe cancer, Theodora, when you said you were sick. When did you start acting nutty? When Rudolf moved out?"

"No. Yes. I guess so. Maybe earlier. Anyway, I have been making a list — of what I perceive — that's bad enough. Occasionally, I bump into things. Stumble."

"At least the kids aren't babies, you don't have to carry them around."

"No."

"Do something for me, Theodora?"

"What?"

"Before you get dipsier, weirder — try going out. What do you do these days? Go to *The Cookie Lady* and then straight home?"

"Yes."

"I thought so. I never see you anywhere."

Joseph, the doorman who started his shift at seven, never had much to say in the morning. The doorman whom he relieved had as every resident knew probably slept most of his work shift. There might be on weekend mornings a few tales about drunks or women who were announced and buzzed in, but usually it was midday before much could be noticed.

That's why Joseph spoke and I didn't hear. I almost said excuse me and walked around the three women and one man gathered around him. But then I heard robbery.

"The Mildorfs'," Joseph told his audience. "Sixteen F. The police are still there — see the cop car outside the door." Joseph shook his head. "It must have been a mistake. The thief probably intended to break into the Dodges'. Sixteen G. She has rings that would knock your eyes out. Just last week I heard her husband tell her not to go out on the street looking like a stoplight."

I began to shiver.

The man listening scratched his left ear. "I don't know," he said. "I've been twelve years in this building and it has never been this bad. The Heissmans' last Thursday and now this."

I knew about last Thursday but not the name.

"And," the man continued, "the Brocks' just ten days ago."

"Brockland," Joseph corrected. "Eleven B."

I had to leave then, my appointment was at ten. Three robberies in less than a month. The building was a good one. It was a co-op. Someone should write the co-op board. Heissman, Brockland, and now the Mildorfs. That might definitely be a pattern of some sort.

On the corner I went into a telephone booth and called Charlotte. The telephone rang four times before she answered.

"It's me, Charlotte," I said. Thank God, the children were away at school. "I want you to make certain that the windows are locked. And don't let anyone into the apartment – no cleaners with a delivery, no one. Someone else was robbed in the building – I just heard about it."

"I never let anyone in," Charlotte said. "I would never let anyone in."

"Lock the windows."

"Way up here – lock them way up here?"

"Yes."

Normally I would have taken a bus. But now I was late so I took a taxi. I hated to keep people waiting. I have tried to curb this feeling. When you hire people, you can keep them waiting.

My offices were in a new grey steel and grey-tinted-glass building. I would have preferred offices in a building with gargoyles and a frieze of stone carvings, but such quarters were expensive, and one of my advisors said that those buildings were never in the heart of things.

In the lobby of my building I went to Max who sold newspapers in a glass cubicle. I bought my *Times* and my *Wall Street Journal* from him.

"Missus," he said. "Guess what? They took out the Hassids on five."

"What?"

"Robbed them – diamonds."

"Diamonds? I thought that business was in the forties?"

"No," Max said, "we got one here. Big stuff too, I hear – like the distributors' distributor."

I folded my newspapers and headed for the bank of elevators that went to the odd-numbered floors 1 through 25. I went into the elevator with the *Next Car Up* flashing sign. Two men were already waiting, standing in the back, whispering to each other. Two men in black frock coats.

"I'm sorry," I said. "I heard about what happened."

They looked up but didn't say anything. I thought perhaps they might be two other men or maybe they wouldn't speak to me because I was a woman.

Finally, one of the men spoke. "Thank you," he said. Then the elevator reached 5 and they got out.

The reproduced photograph in the sketched oval on the cookie package showed no background. The picture itself taken on a wet October morning. Pauline held the camera, a small Kodak camera, a cheap camera. The morning air damp, woman and girl alone. Smile, Pauline said. Theodora smiled. The picture was taken. To be immortalized – and neither of them knew it. So the girl wasn't self-conscious. She grinned into the camera.

Mortimers:
1971

"The thing about me," Mortimer said. "The thing that no one believes. Who would believe it? I don't like living off you. I don't care what anybody thinks. It's the middle-class thing, I suppose. Well, anyway — I hate living off you. I thought I could get used to it, but I can't. And I feel — I sincerely feel — that you do not have faith in me. That you do not understand my work."

I held my breath — slowly exhaled. "And she does?"

"Damn right she does. Look, I know what will be said. I know. They'll say I'm substituting one meal ticket for another. They'll say she has more money. *You* know different. What's the attraction? Maybe because she is older — maybe she has the maturity to see my work. With you — I'm not an artist. With you — I might as well be painting *The Last Supper* on velvet. She encourages me, Theodora. She encourages me to explore new forms. I think — I sincerely think I will find my place."

Now was the time to stop sucking in my breath.

"Who's stopping you from doing anything? Who's stopping you? What about the rest — what about *two* children? What the hell are you talking about? We have two babies."

"That may very well be — and I love the children — but I didn't ask for them. I'll try to be a good father. I'll telephone regularly."

"That's it?"

"That's it."

"Fuck you — Mortimer."

"Dierdre, what am I going to do?"

"Do you have any property in both your names?"

"No."

"Thank God. I was afraid you had done that. Don't be upset. I'll fix you up with someone. Lots of men aren't afraid of other men's children. If they don't have to support them, they're not afraid."

"Theodora, tell me. It was the sex, wasn't it?"

"Nothing wrong with the sex, Ginger. Nothing."

"Come on — that was it. Didn't he find you aggressive — just a bit too acrobatic. Didn't he complain?"

"No."

"He told me that he did."

It didn't just happen.

First he bought a book about the Mojave Desert.

I couldn't believe it. A huge technicolor book full of pictures of shadowed particles of disintegrated rock.

Dierdre and Ralph came over, and I served cappuccino and cinnamon stars. Mortimer started talking about our trip last summer. We rented a car, he said, in L.A. Then we drove up to Big Sur. He spoke about what we had seen with great nostalgia.

Later when I was asked when did he decide to go, I replied, I have no idea. They were disappointed. They wanted details of trysts, assignations, despairs. All they knew for certain was that she was older — ten, fifteen years older than he. Older than me.

I never told my friends how much I believed in interconnections of all kinds, in backtracking, in Möbius strips, in the buried coin reappearing. All of this had nothing to do with premonitions or predestination or Tarot cards. One of my tales was about a dinner party. There we were, I would say, a group of people at a dinner party and really strangers to each other and three of us knew this man Joel and we were a thousand miles from where he lives.

One of us had read an article about him and brought it up and another man knew him well and I had spoken to him just six months before. And none of it coincidence.

The summer gone at once and the packing went on and on. We were leaving, we were going in different directions. He seldom spoke. The silence eased his feelings. I went to work every day, and he stayed home and packed. The sweat poured from him. He took three showers a day. I smell like a zoo after a couple of hours, he said.

Once in the morning when I came out of the bathroom wrapped in my towel he leaped suddenly from bed and trapped me, caught me easily when I fell forward. I have to go to work, I kept saying, but I was laughing. He pinned my arms. Gotcha, he whispered.

I didn't know what came over me.

Whoremaster, I yelled.

He wanted me to believe that he was serious about leaving. He had the feeling that I never believed something was going to happen — only that it had happened. He began to tell me all sorts of things, made lists, reminders. He thought about insurance payments, taxes, orders to be given. He remembered how casual I was about opening mail. How, he would say in exasperation, do you know that it is an advertisement?

He was leaving. He felt a migratory urge to go to California. He stared in wonder at California-style commercials, at healthy people cavorting, at life in primary colors. He was going and he wanted to talk about it. He could do that only in a limited way with me.

He believed in reality. For that reason he started packing much too soon. He wanted me to see the concrete signs of departure. Every evening he stopped at the A & P to cajole a few more cardboard boxes. The best ones he got from the liquor store. His inclination would have been to start the packing by removing the contents from the farthest corners of our closets but that had the air of cleaning, of preparing packages for the Goodwill, of discarding. If he wanted me to notice, he must be exceedingly obvious. So he started with the shelves and bookcases. Save all newspapers for wrapping, he ordered. He packed the boxes. Bright-green shipping tags were purchased. He tied a green tag on any box going to California. Then he took down the collection of silver animals we had bought in Mexico. One side of that room became desolate. The white plaster had visible cracks once hidden, a long discolored swath from a rainstorm when the nearest window had been left open blossomed. The boxes packed, taped, and tied began to take over the rooms. They were piled one on top of the other, often three high. The babies didn't mind, they played hide-and-seek in new places.

Tell me, he said, are you different at your office?

Different? I looked up from my book.

Do you behave differently than at home?

I smiled. Do you mean do I take my clothes off and have a good time?

Yes, he said, smiling for a moment. But besides that — do you talk in a different manner? Have another view of everything?

No, I said. I am the same.

We weren't quarreling, at least not exactly quarreling. I thought I knew whom he spoke to on the telephone. Maybe we were quarreling — sniping a bit. I thought about buying a car. I went by myself to the dealer and came back with all those glossy brochures where men and women in evening clothes posed in front of impossibly new cars. We had never owned an automobile. Cars in the city were foolish, and besides I wasn't even a good driver. I didn't show him the literature, didn't leave it out to create a situation. The man in the showroom saw my ring. He spoke to me about the uphol-stery, colors of my choice. Bring in your husband, he had advised.

On the last day use the Styrofoam picnic basket, Mortimer said. Pack the contents of the refrigerator in it. You can carry food over to your new house. There's still a fair amount of eating here. I nodded.

I could find no virtue in emptying the refrigerator. I planned to sweep the contents into a garbage bag and throw it down the chute. Frozen vegetables, meat, poultry, leftover cookies. I could offer the food to a neighbor. But I had never spoken much with my immediate neighbors, we nodded in the elevator, we smiled in the hall. If I rang their bells and held out my food, would they suspect me of something? Who knew what I had put into that food before freezing.

I did not mention to my husband one morning that the seam of his jacket near the left shoulder had begun to open up. A small two-inch tear.

Mortimer's parents came to dinner before they moved to Phoenix. Mortimer's mother was a very small woman with deep red hair. "My boy," she said proudly, "always towered over me. You can expect that *your* children will do the same." I nodded. "Here," Mortimer's mother said, slipping a bracelet from her wrist.

"This is a present for you. Copper bracelet. I always wear them. Best protection against arthritis in the world. What I would like, honey, before we head for our wagon train and disappear into the setting sun – is a couple of your yummy cookie recipes."

"Most of my recipes are standard ones," I said. "It's really a question of ingredients – using the very best ingredients. Being careful."

"Well," said Mortimer's mother, "Daddy warned me. She'll never give you them, he said to me before we came over. Save your breath, Mother, he said. Mortimer has got himself a doozy – and she'll never give you any."

I made the standard Christmas selection. I made Christmas spice cookies, hermits, nut patties, rum rocks, double fudge, springerle. Robert Lee delivered the two trays. I catered the cookies for the Hagen & Hagen Christmas party. It was the Hagen niece who asked me to come by after New Year's. Do you really make it in that tiny cookie shop? she inquired. Barely, I said. She nodded. Look, she said, come and work for us. Get some kid to watch the shop – it can be like a hobby. Or for evenings. I said I'd try it. She sniffed the air – you smell like a bake shop. Nice, but not professional. Go shopping. Get some clothes.

I met Mortimer just before I abandoned the clothing book. I thought I had thrown it out. I almost remembered throwing it out. It was an embarrassing account of my inability to clothe myself. I had no sense of how to clothe myself. Despite what they say, I really believe that women who grew up with natural mothers have a better sense of how to dress, even if they disliked their mothers. My mother had clothes, she had a closet full of clothes, but I can't recall exactly how she dressed or what she put together with what.

How did I begin? I ripped out pictures from magazines of women wearing complete outfits. Then I turned to the back pages where they printed a section called Resources or Shopper's Guide — a listing of stores where these clothes, from shoes to brassieres, could be purchased. With the picture and the list, I would travel from store to store to buy the clothing. If I could, I bought everything in the picture. The final effect when I dressed in those clothes, although usually monochromatic, was synthetic and not exactly as it appeared in the picture. They had pinned back the skirts on the model to create a better line and basting threads concealed puckers across shoulders.

Hagen & Hagen were located in an old building, the air conditioning not trustworthy.

Linen wrinkled badly in summer and perspiration stains bonded to silk. I needed clothes.

I couldn't go on forever with bits of paper torn from magazines. One day I abandoned my reliance on pictures and went foraging on my own. That's when I started the shopping book.

I don't remember the reason, but I began journal entries in the middle of that shopping book. What had I thought? If the writing was in a book not labeled diary, no one would open it.

I made sporadic entries – covering a short period – February through July.

February 2
Robert Lee said that instead of looking twenty-one I alternated between looking either twelve or ninety. Listen, he said, I honestly wonder if you might be color-blind.

I made an appointment with a Dr. Miller to have my eyes checked. I had to leave Hagen & Hagen during working hours for the appointment. The young Joe Hagen winked at me. I hope everything is okey-dokey at the doctor's, he said.

Dr. Miller said I wasn't color-blind, said there was a slight astigmatism, said I might be more comfortable using reading glasses.

March 12
Clothes I remember. I remember that when

I was fifteen I used to wear nothing but blue jeans and expensive sweaters. I slept in blue nylon pajamas that felt good and slithery. Nylon was supposed to be hot, but it always felt cool to me.

In college I wore blue jeans and men's shirts, large oversize men's shirts, sometimes slightly torn. Bought my shirts secondhand from a laundry on Chesapeake Avenue. I slept in nylon baby-doll pajamas, a gift from Pauline. They weren't as comfortable as the ones I wore in high school. Pauline bought me four sets. The panties had elasticized legs with an inch of lace ruffle that I couldn't remove, must have been sewn on with steel thread. The pajamas made me feel like an idiot.

Went shopping, came home with flour sifter manufactured in Denmark.

March 24

Feminine and businesslike. That's what Mrs. Norbein, the Hagen niece, said in her Recruiting Talk. In Food Management, women were to dress not as if they were in a kitchen but as if they could go into a kitchen if they wanted to. The idea is basically absurd. Because if you really cooked, why then you would want to wear something comfortable like blue jeans and an oversize *shirt or a sweater.*

I told Robert Lee to get out. He said he wouldn't go, and I hit him with a cookie sheet — good-quality stainless steel.

April 15
Ginger moved into the spare half-room. I have already gone black. I have black wool skirts, black cotton skirts, black shoes. I have two black jackets and three white permanent-press blouses for contrast. If anyone dies, Ginger said you've got it made.

She fixed me up. She got me a date with someone named Jeffrey, and we went to New Jersey to dance at a club that had a view of the Hudson and New York which we had just left. Ginger lent me a blue dress and a silver belt. The dress had a scoop neckline and three silver buttons. Jeffrey suddenly plunged his hand down that neckline. He had that smug smile that often accompanies true good looks.

Got home at 2 a.m. and made a batch of honey lebkuchen. The smell woke Ginger up. This air is fattening, she said.

April 20
Ginger bought me a crepe nylon blouse with large unidentifiable flowers on a grey back-ground. She said the flowers were the color of

ashes of roses. I paid her for the blouse. Wait, wait, she said. Wipe your mouth. You can't wear that color with that blouse. I scrubbed off my lipstick with Kleenex. Ginger painted on a new mouth from her tube. Almost a perfect match, she said.

Joel Hagen asked me out. I guess ashes of roses is his color. Margaret cornered me behind Filing. He's a womanizer, she whispered.

April 25

Joel Hagen and dinner. We left directly from the office. I made him do that. I didn't want anyone to come up to the door and ring the bell. Is the little lady of the house ready? Perfumed, done up in good clothes, seductive. Anyway, he didn't ask me where I wanted to go. Perhaps he lacked the knowledge to offer me a choice. We went to a French restaurant two blocks from the office. That had the right air, no holding open car doors, no touch on the elbow. We marched down the street, two working comrades. The restaurant was dark. All such restaurants are dark. We sat together in a tiny banquette. We were sitting on top of each other there. Joel had been in that restaurant before. Maybe with everybody. He recommended veal.

I'm getting a divorce, Joel said. I nodded.

What did he expect? He was getting a divorce and wasn't I free too. You've met my wife, he said. I shook my head. At the office, Joel said. She came in one day in winter. No, I said. I must have been out that day.

May 25
I was called into Ralph's office. Joel's uncle — the big man. Ralph must be fifty, skinny, looks wrinkled. I'm an A personality, he says — or B. No sweet tooth. That is his favorite joke. No sweet tooth.

Theo, he says. He comes around the side of his desk and hugs me. Why'd you call in sick? I thought you were sick. Listen, men problems are everywhere. Look at my baby daughter. Look at Bernadette. The guy is a bum. So marriage — shmarriage. Listen, you can use her lawyer.

I shook my head. I don't need a lawyer, I said.

Ralph blinked. Good, he said. Clean the slate then. Best thing. Take some coffee. Have a lemon sponge. They came out brilliant, thanks to you. I'm making them generic for three labels.

I sat down.

Sweetie, Ralph said. We are backed up to here with postings in the ledger. Be a darling and help out.

190

I coughed, a loose croupy sound. Getting sick again, I said.

June 30
I sleep in nothing, but I keep a terry cloth robe on the bed so that I can walk to the bathroom. Bought two pairs of jeans and grey turtleneck sweaters, wool for winter and cotton for summer. Made a find in a second-hand store. A medal and a chain. Cheap gold-plate chain, but the medal was engraved – Third Prize for Acrobatics, Mid-County Gymnastics Meet, South Fork. September 12, 1956.

It's hard to explain how I feel, I feel good in those clothes – jeans and sweaters – I feel dangerous, I feel like I am fifteen. Should I expand The Cookie Lady?

Ginger has taken to wearing dirndl skirts. I'm pregnant, she told me. Then she left about the same time Hagen & Hagen fired me. I think she got married, but that might be just a rumor.

July 10
Bought a khaki-colored lined suit, completely wash-and-wear, and three white tailored blouses of a weave resembling linen. Also, bought four silk scarves to ease the severity. Baked some molasses cookies and

two batches of almond dots. I would have gone on in a blaze of chocolate, but no chocolate.

Before she moved out, Ginger went into my closet and took back the ashes of roses blouse. She is probably the one who slit open the back seam of my favorite black wool skirt.

I did not pack up the books and papers in Rudolf's study. Rudolf packed up his own study. My only request was – do it when I am out. He left an envelope with Charlotte. *Yours,* he wrote. After years of living together, things get mixed up. It was a manila envelope, my name printed in one corner. The flap was scotch-taped shut. The tape yellowed. It didn't look disturbed. Rudolf hadn't opened the envelope, peeked inside. I would have opened his. Now I lifted the flap, noting the resistance of the tape. Inside were notes – my undated notes.

I believe that clothes affect your life. This is more true of a woman than a man. I believe that it has always been more true of a woman. Very little girls seem to crave clothes and ornaments. I suppose that is both cultural and sex-based. I have to say I was late in acquiring this sort of knowledge.

192

Margaret found me a shopper. A woman who actually shops for me personally. She selects and buys my clothes. I thought some sort of a relationship between us would be necessary. A chatty, confiding relationship. The woman's name, the shopper, is Adele. She is quite cool and businesslike. All she wanted to know is my work calendar, what I need clothes for, and how often I go out. And where. I stared right at her. I have a friend, I said. I need clothes to wear for the times I am with him. What you might call nonmarital clothes. Adele never blinked. Didn't ask me if I was joking or what.

She went through my closet. It was an unemotional scene. I thought she might yell, No! No! I certainly know what's there. I have difficulty coordinating colors. I use charts. Quite the contrary, all she did was make notes, then we spoke about money, about limits. She measured me. That was that. Clothes then arrived. Margaret says I have never looked better. The shopper has what is called an eye.

I am accepting. Why not? I don't know what to buy. Occasionally I object. I sent back an outfit labeled by my shopper "Country Wear for Weekend." It was a blue wool cap, a blue wool jacket, and grey-blue slacks. I sent the entire set back. I could have just sent back the cap. I thought Adele might call and ask me why. But instead I received a credit on my next bill.

The blue wool cap was a very thick knit with a flattering brim, and lined in a darker blue silk. The color according to the label was cerulean blue. The color I don't like is a much brighter blue — an electric blue. And I only don't like the color in hats. I could have told Adele why in two minutes. That wool hat looked like my mother's hat.

I have a certain ornamental tendency. I do not have my shopper pick my jewelry. Why do you pick your own jewelry? Adele might ask. I used to steal jewelry, I would say. At age fifteen. Would her cool eyebrows rise? Or would she just write down that client will supply own jewelry.

I have a necklace made of rather nice wooden beads that my daughter Bonita made for me when she was five. That is one of the advantages of sending your child to a good school. When the children make something to take home — the ingredients used are of reasonable quality. The beads are oak and waxed to show the natural luster of the wood.

Of course, Bonita's gift to me is not a bit like the necklace I made. I have one shell left, and the paint still rubs off. My second-grade project. I brought the necklace home. Mother was in the house, perhaps with someone. Either they didn't hear me or they didn't want to open the door. I sat on a step and waited. In Leeward Elementary School I passed a test with a grade that the teacher said was too high.

My friend Margaret wore a uniform when she was a child. I have always noticed that women who once wore uniforms suddenly spring out into peacock colors. She sprang out after she was widowed, although the use of colors I believe is more dependent on a personal past of uniforms than the widowing. Jay died in a motel. He was in his car, had chest pains, made his way to a motel. There, at ten o'clock in the morning, he died. That's what his friends said. By himself in a motel. Margaret wears red, yellow, blue, and green. She blends both colors and fabrics beautifully. She knows all about the cycles of fashion. Very good clothes she saves, storing them in mothproof garment bags on racks in her spare bedroom. One day she told me that shoes with pencil-thin heels were back. If you wear items at the right time, they are stylish. The wrong time tells your social status and caste.

When Pauline wore those stiletto heels, that fashion had already moved down the social ladder. They were not worn by women of *fashion. Women of fashion were wearing low, clunky heels. Pauline should have waited another seven years before wearing her wedding shoes.*

Mortimer was moving in. The light was good. I swore that the light was good and that I had torn down the drapes. He could have the biggest room for himself. I don't need much, he said. I emptied two shelves in the medicine cabinet. The closet would be easy. I didn't have many clothes. Half for him, half for me. Then I found the diary. The diary was a lump of coal in my hands.

I was astonished, because I thought that at age fifteen I was smarter than that. It wasn't the case of a girl putting her secrets on paper. I wasn't just involved in the standard secrets of childhood, I was involved in genuine trouble. I remembered distinctly the extent to which I would be careful that nothing at the scene of a crime could be traced back to me. Then diary entries! Never mind that there were only a few – had I written more elsewhere – left my own trail of crumbs?

The entries that worried me were put down in a pink-and-white leatherette-covered diary, three entries written in ballpoint pink. The book not even hidden. I had unknowingly carted it around for years – caught in the folds of a dirndl skirt. I found the book when I cleared half a closet for Mortimer.

The entries dated from my fifteenth year when we lived in Dover Beach. The handwriting looked slightly familiar — I used to have more of a slant. But still I knew that it was mine.

October 30
The question of how to look enters into my plans. I must look exactly like everyone else. Problems: 1) My belt is too long and the leather hangs down — in fact it flips over into a half-loop. 2) Must discard the blue-dotted bandanna. This is an almost unconscious gesture. I get dressed, I tie the bandanna around my neck. 3) I also wear cheap sneakers. Like the treads of tires, rubber soles have different patterns. Need to survey other girls' sneakers and pick out a very popular brand.
Clothing list: Blue jeans
Rubber band for hair
White top (never, I repeat, never wear a colored sweater when doing it)
Sneakers, white socks (thick)
Navy blue windbreaker jacket (big — for hiding things)

November 6

A thief is a person who fits in with the others, more than blends, isn't there.

February 18

Basically, and if left alone, I would stick to blue jeans. They can be worn all the time. I don't believe that Pauline ever wears jeans. Not that I remember. She could have worn them. They should be part of her generation.

Sometimes I wonder how it must have been for Pauline at age twenty-two becoming my stepmother. I was seven years old. It must have felt weird. Stuck with me that way. It was a standard situation. Abner fooling around with Pauline for two years waiting for mother to die.

Pauline had a first husband. That man was fifty-six when Pauline left him. Pauline said that he threatened to come to her second wedding celebration and blow out someone's brains. When that man did finally come around, I was in school. I only heard about it. He came to the apartment and pounded on the door and yelled, "Whore! Whore!" They said he was crying and that a nephew eventually came and led him away.

There was nothing else from my fifteenth year. I hope there was nothing else. What a chance for blackmail. Child criminal *finally* caught. Suppose I had written more? Pauline could have taken it. Pauline and her memento hunting. At any rate, I was surprised. I never considered myself a journal keeper. I had my recipe collection, but that was different. Pure conversation with myself. Apparently you did these things — these jottings — and either forget or cannot believe that you wrote them.

A *Mortimer* was a thin and elegant crisp topped with bitter black chocolate. "I'm flattered," he said. "God, kid, but I'm flattered. These are dynamite cookies. You're a dynamite lady."

He was sincere. He liked the cookies. Most of his friends did too. Whenever we went to see someone, Mortimer carried along a bag. "Have a *Mortimer*," he would say with a sly smile. "Have one of my cookies."

I was not vengeful. The *Mortimers* could have stayed. They were removed from the *Cookie Lady* list about six months after I married Rudolf. But that was coincidence. In fact, the *Mortimers* were always unprofitable. Stanley wasn't with me at *The Cookie Lady* then. A woman named Louise had the job. Drop them,

Theodora, she urged. *Mortimers* cost too much, and the coating is too mordant. They just aren't worth it. She thought we would argue, but I can be reasonable. No more, I said.

Mortimer told me someone had stopped by with a petition or something. Interrupted him, he said. He told them to come back when I was home. I wish to God, he said, that you could stop this midday doorbell shit. That's what comes from living in a middle-class neighborhood.

When the doorbell rang in the evening, I jumped up to answer it. Two women and a man at the door. It wasn't exactly a petition. They were starting a Neighborhood Organization. Would I join? Come to the meetings? Yes, I said.

Ted Schummer spoke at the first meeting. He had been robbed. Such a bright night, he said afterwards. The stars, the moon. Bright enough to see everything, the face of the young thief. Ted Schummer was a big man. He should have been more aware of his surroundings, but he was wearing a wool suit, and the weather had turned. The winds coming from the west. He was hot and wiping his forehead every few steps, feeling the mist of heat coming from his body as if he were a radiator. He was robbed by a boy with a knife. I should have taken him, Ted Schummer said afterwards. I should have twisted his balls. After his account, they took up Anne Crane's report of prowlers, voyeurs, perverts, simpering old men – all come to view her from beneath the slits of shades. The group added everything up, two purses snatched the previous week, someone's old grandmother and her cans or perhaps it was her fence. So the Neighborhood Organization banded together. They didn't have uniforms or caps or police sanctions. It was a vigilante group, the way they saw it. Taking care of their own. They'd patrol the neighborhood in cars. The men would carry bats and chains. We exchanged first names. Will your husband volunteer? they asked. Maybe, I said.

Well, Frank said, giving his report at the second meeting, a lot of you folks heard what happened. A tragedy – that's what. On Wednesday evening we saw this man running down the street. We never saw more than one. How could there have been more than one? One we saw clearly. We stopped the car and we all headed out. Arthur, our car captain, was running first. That's when someone shot him. The police are taking over. But now we need some women for the condolence group. Volunteers?

The widow's name was Virginia. They told me, she said, that if I went to the Emergency Room and spoke to the heavy nurse with sausage curls, she could tell me what my husband's last words were.

I don't care, Virginia said. He didn't tell me that he joined any stupid organization. Why should he care? Let anything happen to the neighborhood — we're only renters. He made a fool of himself. Know what I have? An insurance policy for fifteen thousand. Nothing, that's what. No other benefits — nothing from the Veterans Admin. He didn't even have a service record. So what was with the American Legion and those parades?

It isn't that money matters to me, she said. He captured me when I was young. I didn't care about money. Hardly anyone came to the funeral. People don't like getting involved with strangers.

The analyst was a woman. She was really very kind. We never got up to my fifteenth birthday. She was interested in women's search for and identification with their mothers. It colors your life, she said. And did you love your stepmother? she asked. No, I said. Was she mean to you? No, I said. Pauline was never mean to anyone. Pauline was a very decent person. But you didn't love her? she asked. No,

I said. Did your mother eat your cookies? she asked. Sure, I said. She never said that she wouldn't – that they were fattening? she asked. No, I said. She ate my cookies. And you felt good when she ate your cookies? she said. Yes, I said. I feel good when anyone eats my cookies. Would you say that they are an affirmation of your existence? she said.

Hank was a pencil-and-paper therapist. He was writing a paper on the sources of success. We went into my earliest baking experiences. When did you start baking seriously? he asked. Age fifteen, I said. He should have lingered there, but he didn't. Listen, Theo, he said. Does anyone call you Teddy? No, I said. I want you to take this paper and write me something pertinent about your husband, he said. Pick a day. Any day. I nodded. I took the paper and pencil.

The man was awkward. Shifting his weight from foot to foot. I'm Vincent, he said. I'm downstairs. I'm on One. Mike said that your husband was missing. Since last Saturday.

Mike was the smirking doorman.

I stared at the man. He rang my doorbell. I had opened the door just a crack.

The man blushed. I thought he looked

unhappy. I'm sorry to disturb you — maybe Mike was wrong. It was just about last Saturday.

What about last Saturday?

I saw your husband — Mrs. Dille.

Waite. Ms. Waite. You saw my husband? You know my husband?

By sight. We spoke — two, three times. We introduced ourselves. It was because we walk to the subway at the same time. Sometimes.

I nodded. Last Saturday?

The man cleared his throat. I saw him in the subway.

If you saw him in the subway before — how do you know it was Saturday — why last Saturday?

I had to go to work. I don't go in on Saturdays — I haven't been in on a Saturday in months. The platform isn't crowded — not up here.

I hesitated, he was being helpful. Mr. Vincent, please come in. Some coffee? A honey bar?

It's just Vincent. Thank you.

I opened the door, led the way into the kitchen.

I was coming home, Vincent continued, pausing to bite into a honey bar. I was getting off at our station. I stood on the platform — refolding my newspaper, stuffing it into my briefcase. Across the way — on the downtown side, I saw Mr. Waite. He was there as a train pulled in — I waved, he waved back.

Him, I said. How can you be certain it was him? Mr. Dille. Couldn't he have been someone else?

Well maybe, well sure. But I think it was him. I noticed because of the way he was dressed.

Dressed?

It was past five — sundown — getting chilly. He — this man was wearing a T-shirt and paint-spattered chinos. No coat. Carrying nothing, as a matter of fact.

How long was he gone? Hank asked. Two weeks, I said. Where was he? With her, I said. That was when I was certain she was the one. What did he say? Hank asked. He said that he was off thinking — said he needed space to think. Did you believe that? Hank asked. No, I said.

"There's one thing I want you to promise," Rudolf said.

I moved my naked body next to his. "What?"

"That you will not give me a totem — that you will not name a goddamn cookie after me."

"If you don't want one, of course, I won't." I was hurt, though.

"Good," he said and rolled on top of me.

When Mortimer came to New York once every few years, we were invited to lunch at his hotel. He always wanted me along. What will I say to them? he implored. So I went.

How long has it been since I've seen you? he would say.

Three years, Bonita said.

The children were well-behaved. I brought all of them to lunch. Mortimer didn't complain. That way they entertain each other, he said. Once he gave each child a pineapple planted in a pot. They were pleased. He was surprised. Afterwards, he sent fresh fruit for the next three Christmases.

The package arrived by UPS on December fifteenth. From the size of it, I knew the package was trouble. I tore off the wrappings, grateful that I had been the one to accept the delivery from the doorman. Inside the box were *two* wrapped gifts. One for Bonita and one for John.

Mortimer was a bastard!

I went to my bedroom, locked the door, and slit the wrapping paper. What had he sent? Samples of what had made him famous.

He was famous now. Famous for his little boxes. Each wooden box contained a surrealistic scene glued in place – composed of bits of felt, tiny plastic toys, sequins, feathers. One for Bonita and one for John – each box signed *Mortimer Dille.*

It wouldn't have cost Mortimer to send three more. Rudolf gave presents to everyone. I knew that the children would be miserable – feelings hurt.

There was nothing else to do. I had to make three more boxes. I would fix them at *The Cookie Lady* where I would not be discovered. It was not difficult once I set my mind to it – it had to be done. I had my people make up three wooden boxes, I gave the measurements. Use oak, I suggested. I bought plastic toys at Woolworth's. Off Orchard Street at a store specializing in ribbons, Velcro, hat fittings, I purchased an assortment. I put together scenes. Still lifes. I practiced Mortimer's signature. With a pen and black India ink I signed Mortimer's name on the lower left corner of each box.

I wrapped all five boxes for Christmas morning. It was tension. I made a mistake. John received a *genuine* box. But I accidentally gave the other one to Rebecca. Bonita got a false one then. I hadn't intended that. The natural children were entitled to receive their father's art work.

What I did was wait until evening. When the

children were out of their rooms — bored with their presents — I switched the boxes.

It was Bonita who later marched out into the hall. "All right," she said, "who took my box?"

Rebecca met her. "Have *you* got mine?"

The Perfect Cookie: 1964

I remember that the year I turned fifteen was not the year I began my search for the perfect cookie, but was the year when I believed that I would create it. I cannot imagine that year different. Or I imagine that year different and know that it wasn't. Yet if I forget the rest – ignore the rest – this period becomes my purest time. The search for the perfect cookie was everything. How I lived was incidental. Yet the way I lived – I can hardly grasp today. I can't imagine *who* I was. I became a thief. Let's face it – I did not consider myself bad in the classical sense. Does that make me sound amoral? Well I wasn't. Nor do I believe that I was opportunistic – glibly selecting thievery.

On the other hand I cannot honestly suggest sorrows or the inner panic of a fifteen-year-old. I became a thief. Yet, I suspect that all I thought about was what I would create – this consuming interest in my perfect cookie. Perhaps that interest insulated me – protected me.

I never intended the creating of cookies to be my life's work. If I had made that perfect cookie — or even come close — I would have gone on to something else.

But I didn't. So I took a photograph of that girl and stuck it on hundreds of thousands of packages. Even more.

"I don't understand," Rudolf said. "I really do not understand. Tell me it's a business problem — I'll understand. Tell that you want to sit in the kitchen on a gorgeous Saturday evening in April and mix up another batch of cookies — no, I do not understand."

"Rudolf, I have this idea. I want to try something."

"Try tomorrow. You have the entire day — don't you?"

"But I'm hot now — sometimes you have to move when you're hot."

"I'm hot too, Theodora. Don't you care?"

"Rudolf, I want to bake."

"So bake then. Who cares — who the fuck cares!"

Abner Palmer Waite came out of the bathroom hitting the rolled-up newspaper against his leg. He was thirty-nine. He looked older. Some very thin men age without the comfort of flesh. "I tell you," he said, "this town is for the birds. You know who I feel like? I feel like what's-his-name – Lee J. Cobb."

"Willy Loman," I said.

"Good movie," he said.

Pauline poured coffee. Her eyes rolled. She bit her fingernails. What was coming? Abner with a migratory urge. He never wanted to move at the beginning or end of seasons – not him – he left abruptly in the middle. Just when she knew where stores were, when streets were explored, patterns established – it was onward.

Not so, he said defending himself. Take geese. The common *Anser anser*. Geese move on in November.

He thought I wasn't paying attention.

"What are you listening to?"

"Sandie Shaw," I said.

"Who?"

"From England."

"No one listens to Sandie Shaw. Why don't you play someone people listen to? Like Marvin Gaye, for instance."

Pauline waited, thought she had an opening. "It's not bad here," she said. "Good stores – close. And think of all they do for Theodora. Just think of that."

"Do?" Abner said. "It's a question of playing the system. They do what they have to do – and they only do that if you know the system.

The same everywhere. Labor has lost its punch. Anyway, what does she learn here that's so wonderful? You think she should go through life as a baker? Do what – stand on some assembly line stuffing cupcakes into cellophane? Is that what you want, Theodora? If that's what you want, then we can sure as hell stay here."

Bethel May High School was big on therapies, their entire educational philosophy based on correction of malfunctions. They wanted to do something for me. Teeth, hearing, posture. We settled on speech.

At the modern clinic they created a map of my speech patterns, the topography of my voice, mechanically reduced to eight by eleven. The city, the town, and the county all paying their share to get rid of my hiss. No distinction, they swore, between those who pay and the freebees.

On my third visit I slid open a file drawer labeled *S to W.* The cabinet wasn't locked. What was I looking for? On the manila folder *Waite, Theodora* – between the comma and the *W* lived a tiny, a discreet pink dot. Pink dots signaled freebees. Sometimes it was a checkmark and sometimes an *x* – depending on the city.

Cheryl the therapist entered smiling. "Hello, Theodora."

"You have lipstick on your teeth."

"Thanks," she said and whipped out a tissue. "Are you ready?"

I was ready.

I positioned my tongue and blew out a word. "Suasive."

It was sibilance that we were working on. Imagine spending your entire life listening to people with weird voices. I'd rather stuff cupcakes into cellophane.

"Smells funny in here," I said.

Cheryl squinted at me. "Yeah? Well kids don't wash anymore. Get twenty kids in here one after another. It's B.O. country."

"It's the curse of poverty."

Cheryl stared at me in case I meant something, sucked in her cheeks. Lipstick scratched her teeth again. "You're kind of a smart aleck, aren't you. Put on the earphones," she said.

As soon as the earphones were on, Cheryl went out. To smoke.

The word list — I should do lost. *Lo-ost*. My first experience with lost as a concept came in elementary school. I didn't even know the boy, a sobbing boy with dry grey nostrils and a puckered mouth. Screaming his lostness in the doorway of the school. Elder, he sobbed, oh Elder. It was *after* school — maybe four o'clock. His family had moved — did he now walk three blocks in that direction or three blocks in this direction? I came up to him. Kid, I said, I know where Elder Avenue is. Follow me. The boy, sniffling and wiping his nose with a crayoned artifact, followed me. Well, his mother said, fighting her doubts, but delighted to get her treasure home. Would you like to come in and have some milk and a cookie? Yes, ma'am, I said. The cookies were Boston biscuits. I tasted. Do you use light brown sugar? I asked. Or dark? Her eyes lit up. Myself, she said, I prefer the dark — even though the standard recipe calls for light. Interesting, I said and vowed from that moment never to get lost myself, to pay close attention to directions, and draw maps in my mind.

The earphones off — I heard a roar. Mama Doll one cubicle over. I suspected freebees were scheduled for the same days as the difficult clients. Mama Doll was a retardee, half blind, half deaf, with a yelping speech defect. Her life a junkyard of pain. Before her appointments she splashed water over her hands in the drinking fountain in the reception area. One afternoon I gave her a cookie, and she squeezed until useless Hansel and Gretel crumbs clogged the drain holes.

My cubicle door opened. The startle reaction got me — I jumped. But the walls were transparent. "You're improving," Cheryl said.

"Thank you," I said.

I buttoned myself into my coat. I left Mama Doll screeching into her microphone. Two clients still waited on the orange plastic chairs. One drooled into her bib. The other must be a freebee.

Outside the winter chill numbed. It had snowed last week. The leftover icy lumps wore a gritty aluminum-colored crust. I walked down the path to the curb. A long maroon car drove past. "Taxi," I screamed. Brakes. The car stopped. Turned out to be my father.

"Smart aleck," he yelled.

Saki wrote this: *The cook was a good cook, as cooks go; and as cooks go she went.* Are you making fun of me? the Home Ec teacher said. The truth was I didn't care how long an egg should ride the boiling waves in a pot. Or whither went the leftover. Why should anyone want to spend their life beating hell out of mashed potatoes?

I was interested only in mastering the art of cookie making. If I didn't sign up for Home Ec – no stoves, equipment, supplies. Institutional jewels. What I planned – and I knew that I was not yet ready – was a new and unique cookie. Tasty. Basically good. Sometimes I thought I had it. Then I did some checking. *Kurabiye,* for instance – sweet butter, sugar, almonds, flour. Simple should be the key. I thought those cookies might be mine. But someone had that idea first. If you wanted to create a cookie, you must work at it.

The beginning of moving started this way. The crocus signal of moving – my father was restless. Ta-ta-ta, he hummed. Drank three cups of coffee. I have always hated driving a cab, he muttered. But it wasn't new to him, this driving of a cab. Once he wrote a poem entitled "Work I Hate." Someone left a copy of the *Village Voice* in his taxi. He sent his poem to the newspaper and it was published. They called him a street poet. He wondered if he could make a living as a poet. But then that was it. He never wrote another poem.

When we came to this town Abner took a job driving one of the town's three taxis. He looked the part, looked tired, irritable, with a two-day-old beard and dry eyes. He carried a bottle of drops. Artificial tears. He hated a man named Hyde. Hyde stiffed him out of the best fares. Hyde recognized people because this was his town. Steered the best tippers to his taxi. Abner didn't express this hatred of driving a taxi directly to Pauline or me. But I looked at him. He had dreams all right.

Every evening Abner was already home when I arrived, he ate between the six-twenty commuter train and the seven-ten. I was usually late, my fingertips Brilloed raw from cleaning up – cleaning up was the Hippocratic Oath of Home Ec.

Pauline dished up meatloaf, mushroom-soup gravy, mashed potatoes, peas. She was not the smartest woman in the world. Any other woman would have raised her voice. The hell with moving. My father wasn't given to violence. So any other woman wouldn't have let him get away with this. Pauline was young when she married my father. I was only seven but I remembered.

"Population is the clue," my father said. "Either it goes up or you stagnate. What you look for then is rising population. The best places to be have rising population. You know what that makes this town? Stinko, that's what."

I considered us to be modern East Coast Oakies. I wrote a report titled "Transient Americans" for a class. The teacher was displeased. You have a bitter, warped, and twisted view of family life, she said. That school was into psychological analysis.

Abner drove up to Dover Beach on Monday morning, slept in the car, and came back the next night. His face was flushed. "There's a town," Abner said.

The truth was that Abner Palmer Waite was good to me up to a certain day. Take money. He drove me to the railroad station so that I could go to the city. Spend, he said. Have a good time. He played the radio. That told you right away what was up. Also he did one-handed jazzy turns. The woman sitting next to me — a paying customer. For God's sake, she said. Turn that thing down. We swerved left, we swerved right. My *kishkas,* she said. What's the matter with you? Don't you realize you have a child in the car?

Buy yourself something to wear, Abner ordered. Bring it back. Can't start a new school looking like yesterday. Pick something smart, honey. So I went to Bonwit's. Each time we prepared to move, Abner gave me money. Like a robin in the snow, as soon as I got this money I always knew what was up. Fifty dollars in my hand. Abner had no business sense. We had no money. We had money. The two situations had no relation to life.

Bonwit's had a sweater sale. Fluffy piles of interlocking yarn, 40 percent off. I picked a grey one, blew at it, umbrellas of grey fuzz sailed forth. Saw three grey geese on the Hudson. This sweater was dedicated to them. Bought a Ravi Shankar record at *Sam Goody's.*

Ten bucks left to blow on white baking

chocolate from Switzerland. And two and three-quarter hours for the restaurant supply stores. The best stores were on Grand Street, north of Canal. I would have liked to buy myself a new stainless steel cookie sheet as a going-away present. Weight 18/10. I had a theory about sheet thickness and crispness of cookies. But I couldn't hide the cookie sheet. Abner was picking me up at the station. The chocolate went into the box under the grey-goose sweater and above the record. But how can you hide something seventeen by twenty-three inches?

Rode the Lexington Avenue Subway to Astor Place with the Saturday morning people – a ramshackle crowd in our woolens looking like modern folklore. I figured that we whizzed beneath low-income buildings each with a discreet pink dot above its portico. I stood near the door connecting subway car to subway car. I had a matchbox-size penknife. On the metal, I scratched *pâté maison*.

I recognized the woman behind the counter in my favorite restaurant supply store. I didn't know if she recognized me. Did all customers look alike? Since I cannot discern one grey goose from another, especially on the wing, why should we look different to her. "Hello," I said. "How are you, dear," she said.

I toured the aisles. The best equipment, the best ingredients can go just so far. Enameled steel, clay, and copper. Rolled steel. Zabaglione pan. Fish poacher. Cookie sheets. Guaranteed not to warp. Tinplate steel. I better not.

No other customer in the store. Just an old man near the window, gumming his lips and probably spitting into the salt shakers. I selected three zodiac cookie cutters. Aries, Libra, and Aquarius. This eliminated my family. The cutters can be fitted into the box, next to the Bonwit's sweater, across from the chocolate, above the record. For supper, I will use the cutters, make cookies filled with raspberry jam, confectioners' sugar frosting, and top it all with colored sequin-style sprinkles. Pauline will say, Abner, aren't these beautiful!

The woman took my money. Next to the cash register was a display of gingerbread cutters, tin people who actually looked sexed. Nipped in waists. Edible escorts.

"Do you know," I said to the woman, "that gingerbread or rather ginger cookies are very old."

"No," she said. "I don't eat that stuff."

"They have been recorded as early as the beginning of the fifteenth century," I said. "King Christian of Denmark used to have great piles of ginger cookies — hard, dry, crisp — crumbled into a bowl then soaked in rum —

before he ate the soggy mess. Ate it with a spoon like porridge. This was reported by Sir John Harington, who later invented the water closet."

Dover Beach loomed on the horizon. "You can ice-skate there," Abner said. He must have passed some kids ice-skating. We were his audience. What we lacked in enthusiasm we made up for in attention. He waved his hand in the direction of our rented yard — as if the harvest had been bad. And so we must move on.

"I tell you," Abner said. "I walked right into this store at the Northvail Mall. Two minutes of smooth talking, and employment. Harry's Suits. Medium priced, customers all day long. J.C. Penney's is the flagship store for the mall."

Pauline listened as she folded paper napkins into triangles. She kept them in a little plastic triangular napkin holder in the very center of the table. She bit her lower lip as she listened. Abner dropped a Dover Beach rent receipt on the table. Ten Rebus Place. Sometimes we arrived somewhere and lived in a motel often named Dream Haven.

This was it. Maybe everything will be better. Who was I to say otherwise. Once we lived above a storefront church. The Church of God's Gift. The elderly Alderbees lived behind the church. He was blind, she crippled. God gives gifts, they said. Wait. Tried to talk me into joining them in worship. One night the old woman hit him with her crutch. We could hear him screaming. Bitch! God will get you, bitch!

"We'll sell everything," Abner said. "Hey — listen up. Why not? I say why ship this stuff. Wear and tear alone isn't worth it. I say sell here and buy new. New is new. We'll start new."

Pauline gasped. Our furniture dated from before my father married her. Except for the marital bed. Abner threw out the old one when he married Pauline. The striped ticking on that mattress was stained and buttons had pulled loose leaving behind metal loops.

"New," Pauline whispered.

I saw the Bethel May counselor. "Transferring," I said. "To North Dover Beach High School."

The counselor looked at my record. "That's unfortunate," she said. "You people don't seem to stay anywhere."

I rubbed the sleeves of my grey sweater. "Yes," I said. "It's a pity, but Daddy is a migrant worker. Picks fruit. We have to follow the crop."

Everything sold. Everything went like hot cakes. Abner said that we would keep the mattresses. Their double. My single. Our clothes. The kitchen things. Abner would have sold the kitchen to the wall. But Pauline drew the line. She wasn't going to go out and scrounge around for a fork.

That last evening I stood up in the kitchen and made three batches of cookies. The stove and refrigerator belonged to the landlord. We still had butter, eggs, and milk in the refrigerator. I shaved white baking chocolate for drop cookies spiced with cardamom. Pauline had a headache, wrapped herself into a blue chenille bathrobe and went to lie down. Abner knew how to manage events all right. Abner had already left on a Trailways bus. Due at Harry's Suits in the morning, he said.

The cookies rose into pale mountains. If the recipe had been mine, I would have called them *Mount Ups*. But the recipe belonged to Câreme. That, I understood. These cookies belonged to the great baker Câreme. I made them, but they were his. I packed the cooled cookies in one of my cookie tins, separating the layers with sheets of waxed paper. You can't just go around handing out cookies. People were torn between greed and fear.

I wrote a postcard to Cheryl. *Good-bye and thanks. My S's will never be the same. Theodora Waite.*

★ ★ ★

Pauline and I packed. What to discard? Take everything, Pauline whispered. Leave nothing. We should have done the final packing sooner, but we were tired. Just before moving, Pauline often got a headache. I thought we moved the same way with my mother. So the moving was male-linked. May be genetic. Or part of an American tradition. My family moved when I was a kid, Abner said. On the other hand, Abner never repeated one actual word that his father had said to him when he was a kid. Surely his father spoke then?

I drove. Pauline was afraid of the trailer, the hitch. I had no license. We skirted cities, went down store-infested strips with interlocking shopping – you can glide from parking lot to parking lot. It didn't rain. Felt like rain, grey sky like rain – but no rain.

Pauline had the map. She folded and unfolded it as if clues were in the creases. By the time we were past the standard fluting of gas stations, I started screaming. Turn left where? But then I calmed down. It was not her fault. I was driving the car. The mattresses stuck up over the boundaries of the trailer that we had huffed and puffed to fill. We started out being neat, but in the end, we tossed, we threw, we piled.

Abner waited. Abner outside our new pink-dotted home when we arrived. Four and one-half rooms. The grass in front turned winter brown, but I recognized the variety. I bet in summer three red geraniums bloomed in that yard. Poor man's horticulture. However, it was my impression that poverty was easier for us in small towns. At least you got more space for the dollar.

"Here's my girls," Abner said. He easily heaved the mattresses that we had struggled to carry. I never thought of Abner as strong.

North Dover Beach High School was into *Make the Most of Your Future.* Already they didn't like me. I stood poker-faced in front of the guidance counselor who had sour breath. Gelusil tablets piled like poker chips on her desk.

"In the *Make the Most of Your Future* plan," I said, "I noticed Honors. I would like to take Honors in Home Ec."

"What?" the counselor said.

"Honors in Home Ec — specifically, cooking," I said.

They sent for someone — a woman named Post. Miss Post. She had a thin face, a beaked nose. Her clothes smelled of smoke. Abner didn't smoke. He had given them up again. Pauline didn't smoke either. My mother smoked.

Attendance was down in Home Ec. North Dover Beach was upward bound. College-going. Typing. No one wanted to cook. Even the subunit in Fast Food Management was almost empty. Administration never had anyone request Honors in Home Ec before. Was I being a smart aleck?

I had them because their gestalt was access. Help the needy. The ambitious.

Miss Post was not quite the fool. She looked at me. "So you are interested in cooking?"

"Yes, ma'am," I said. "I took a placement test."

"I'll be watching you," Miss Post said. "Don't think for a moment that I won't."

I turned fifteen, but my life was not so bad. At Bethel I lost my virginity. Gloria Steinem reported that sixteen out of every twenty-seven college girls had lost theirs. Statistically, probably some of them lost theirs by age fifteen. My birthday wasn't remembered, but that was all right. Moving did that sometimes.

Years later when I spoke of these circumstances to Rudolf, he thought it significant that so few of my birthdays were celebrated. He made a point of seeing that I had flowers or a cake.

We had the family bucket of Kentucky Fried Chicken at 10 Rebus — celebrating this newest of lives. Abner set up a card table â la dining. Three folding chairs purchased that very day at a drugstore in the mall. That was it — mattresses, television. Pauline was excited. Old shopping instincts burst forth, synapses connecting. Abner opened three beer cans. "Here, baby," he said to me. "Try this. A local brand." Pauline shook her head. "It's a celebration," Abner said, "it's all right."

Abner put his arm around Pauline's shoulder. "How's my little sugar," he said. Pauline gave him the it's-been-a-long-time look. I decided to go into my bedroom and read.

On my way home from my first day at North Dover Beach I bought a book in the Salvation Army Thrift Shop entitled *Cooking from America's Past*. Circa 1943. Listed in the index was "Pistachio Army Cookies," supposedly from the kitchens of one Nan Brodwin. I knew the recipe came from the coast of France near La Rochelle. Those cookies were sometimes called Napoleon Bits. I regarded the book as a present.

I have often tried to think of something that really distinguished that evening. Tried to recall if Abner gave us any clues. But what I remember was the cookbook I bought, its slight smell of damp mold. I can recall more clearly an argument with Mortimer. "Get out of my face," he shrieked. "You're always in my face. How the hell can I think? You're like an octopus."

Pauline had her shopping adventure the next day. Pauline exhausted from contemplating so many purchases. She sat still dressed in her kelly green slacks, her shoes off and Ace bandages coiled from ankles to insteps. We were waiting for Abner to come home.

"Theodora," Pauline said, "we have to paint. Can't wash these walls. What do you think? We could get rollers – you and me. We could do this room in a pale green. A spring green. What do you think?"

"Spring green," I said.

"God, but I don't know where to turn first. I made this list, you know, of what we need. Then I went to your Daddy's mall. I went to two other malls, Lord, my feet. Did Sears too." Pauline's eyes filled with longing. "Come with me on Saturday?"

"Sure," I said, opened a tin, took out a double-fudge wafer.

Abner wasn't supposed to be working late. So we waited. Out of money.

"I only have four dollars left," Pauline said.

"The truth is I stocked up on bacon and eggs this morning. I didn't have enough left for supper. How much do you have?"

I checked my pocket. One five, two ones.

"Two dollars," I said.

"We might as well wait," Pauline said. "Anyway I found a Quik-Carry just two blocks away."

It began then — like that. Afterwards, Pauline always said we were into a fiercely cold period, winter storms, soot-grey skies. She never believed me when I said that it was unseasonably warm — almost Indian Summer. Without Abner and money, we watched two game shows. We watched a comedy in which two kids chased a dog. And a mother in a pants suit kept saying, "Now stop that." I started reading.

At eight o'clock Pauline spoke in a thin, tight voice, "We have three pieces left over from Kentucky Fried. Also eggs and bacon." The shape of her mouth puckered, the new life tainted.

I was reading Thoreau

My life is like a stroll upon the beach,
As near the ocean's edge as I can go.

"Kentucky Fried," I said. "Cold is fine."

I ate one piece. Pauline ate two pieces. She was angry. Let Abner find his own Kentucky Fried.

"I know where he is — out with people from Harry's Suits," she said fiercely. "I *know*. Drinking — that's where!"

I thought so too.

Pauline stripped off her pants suit, clutched bathrobe to her early-aging breasts, and walked in stockinged feet into the bathroom.

Abner made Pauline my responsibility. He dropped her at my door. Some responsibilities became yours because of what other people did. Those people can go off — but you still have the responsibility. You can't fight that. The year after Pauline moved to Miami she became sick, forgetful, arthritic. Her bones had doubled up on her. She lived with her third husband, George, in Fort Lauderdale. I didn't know where his sons were anymore. One, George said, joined the Navy — kept reenlisting. The other took off one morning. Cleaned them out of one hundred fifty dollars.

"What do you think I should do?" George said mournfully on the telephone.

"Can she take care of herself? Wash? Dress?"

"No."

"She's young," I said, "she's still young. She isn't fifty."

"You're kidding," George said. "Looks closer to sixty-five."

"What did the doctor advise?"

"Home," George said. "Find her a good Home – long-term care. What do you think?"

"Do it," I said. "Have the bills sent to me. I'll pay."

"You will?"

"Yes."

The night Abner didn't come home from Harry's Suits, Pauline cried herself to sleep. I planned to wait up for the errant father. Never mind what Pauline said in anger, Abner was no real drinker. I suspected he only wanted a fresh audience for his stories.

I awoke with the daylight, my clothes a rumpled mess. I took a twopenny tour of the rooms. Nothing to see but the remnants of our meal, those achingly bare chicken bones. Pauline kept up. But despair and anger took the energy out of you.

I was of two minds – one, he'll be back soon, and, two, to let Pauline sleep and go about my business. But Abner Palmer Waite was a habit-bound creature. He didn't stay out all night.

I wasn't looking for omens. No rending of the heavens. Witches stirring a brew. I thought of a thousand Abner conversations. They began: Are you listening, baby?

Pauline won't go into the station house. We should have comforted each other, but we had so little in common. Our approaches were different. Pauline sat in the car, tears on her cheeks, her eyes lost in fog. "He's dead," she said. "Didn't I tell you about that dream I had last month. Had it twice. A creek. A creek. I didn't know what it meant. I told you I didn't know. But there was rushing water. And *something* I couldn't see. Oh my God, Abner is dead."

No creeks in Dover Beach. None on the Chamber of Commerce map. None flowing past our house. I went into the station house alone, stepped smartly on the grey tile floor with its spiderweb pattern. Institutional cream-colored walls surrounded me. The same color as North Dover Beach School. I figured the mayor called his brother the paint wholesaler. Send over an oil truck full of institutional cream.

The police wanted to know whether I was a deserted minor. Someone looked out the window to see how the Mother, in her black wool coat with a beaver collar, cried in the car. Next, they heard that we had lived in Dover Beach only three days which gave us the status of emigrés. Abner Palmer Waite was described. His body had not turned up – not at North

Dover Beach Memorial Hospital, St. Celia's, or Walk-in Medical Services. The problem was deemed not severe. He'll be back, they suggested. Nine times out of ten. Had a little fight with the missus. Go home, girlie. Take your mother with you.

I told Pauline they thought Abner was sleeping off a toot. We drove back to 10 Rebus. "Make coffee," I suggested, "make yourself some bacon, eggs."

I had my first try at the Garland stove reserved for teachers and those enrolled in Honors Home Ec. Miss Post said coolly that they had acquired a small budget for Honors Home Ec. I had to keep a written record of ingredients used. Responsibility was the keynote. And she wanted a weekly report. Every week.

I planned to make Nestlé chocolate chip cookies. I felt a visceral pounding. I preheated the oven. The bag of chocolate bits had the original recipe on the back. Black letters on canary yellow. I had no interest in the variations. The original Toll House recipe in my experience was the best. I hung an oven thermometer from the baking rack. The thermometer read 350 degrees and the thermostat read 350 degrees. Hooray for truth and justice! The cookies were baked and came out as soft beige circles with a few raised pimples of chocolate. Miss Ruth Wakefield should be proud. Look what she did! The creator of chocolate chip cookies.

It was amazing. Someone was here. Someone was gone. Pauline must have been crying all day, her skin a blotched pink, her eyes ripe cherries.

"Did he call?"

That was absurd. I knew the answer. Still, I asked the question. There was a classic joke, wasn't there? – the husband who went out to buy a newspaper.

Pauline started crying again, she pounded her breasts. Dead was heard, struggling with choking intakes of breath. Oh, dead.

I telephoned Harry's Suits. No Abner Palmer Waite. Not today, not yesterday. Abner worked on Wednesday. A one-day employee. He quit. That meant he was free of Harry's Suits when we sat together feasting on Kentucky Fried. What had recently happened that was different – that was unexpected? I looked at Pauline. "How much did we get for what we sold – the furniture, the junk?"

Pauline looked up, sniffled into a tricorn paper napkin. "What?" She knew what I thought. "Oh no. Never for a moment,

Theodora. Your father. Look here – the boxes, *his* boxes – filled with his clothes."

Suddenly a gemlike flame in my heart. My orphaned heart. "Show me his favorite sweater. Where's his grey cardigan – the cashmere? His belt with the eagle buckle?"

Pauline went to the cartons, dropped to her knees. It was like looking for something you knew you didn't have. Pauline was trembling. "Oh God," she said. "He is dead. And we will die."

No sweater was evidence. The belt gone. We had the car, though. I thought about the car still parked out front. Ten Rebus was next to 12 Rebus to the left and 8 Rebus on the right. No driveways. The mall of Harry's Suits was a short walk from our street. Abner said wasn't that great. He didn't need to take the car. Hard wear and tear on a car with those short hops. The registration was rubberbanded to the sun visor.

With tools from Abner's neat little automobile emergency box, I disconnected the battery. Ours was a family given to doing its own repairs. The battery was an ugly, a dirty thing to be carried into the house.

Before I fell asleep I decided Abner must be in love. Completely taken with a woman. Then only what she wanted mattered. Like that club-footed doctor in that book — the one running after the waitress. After Mildred. So when she said I want to go away, what else could the man do? Naturally he sold all our stuff to finance a pair of tickets. Then twenty years later would come a rap, a tap, a rap at my door. The return of the prodigal father. And he would say, "You have to understand. Are you listening, baby?" And I would shut my ears.

We were eating from a tin of cookies.

"Everyone drops money — a coin here or there," I told Pauline.

In any household, forgotten stashes. Pauline nodded. We hunted and dug through what we had left. Emptied all pockets, rejoiced at each coin.

I can't do his clothes, Pauline said. I can, I said. Never mind wailing in my ears. Once hiding behind a door I saw my father put some money into a sock, pair it with a mate, make a ball. I didn't remember when this happened. But I headed first for the socks. Balls of socks.

People kept their habits. In his grey socks, a hard-edged object. I pulled out a watch. A gold woman's watch, old-fashioned, with a bracelet of metal links. I knew it didn't belong to Pauline. I searched my memory.

Here, my darling, my father says, and gives the watch to my mother. My mother is wearing a white nightgown with an insert of lace. All the necessary medications are on the night table. And thus, the watch remains to this day. Abner's keepsake. My mother's watch.

The face of the watch had the manufacturer's name in gothic script – German, I cannot decipher. I turned it over. The back inscribed. *Love,* it said in less curly script. *September, 1962.* My mother was dead circa 1962.

"What's this?" I dangled the watch in front of Pauline.

She blushed. "I didn't know he still had that."

"Yours?"

She shook her head.

She didn't want to tell me. This was one of those situations. You thought you knew everything. You thought you'd heard everything. The walls of all our houses had always been membrane-thin. Voices carried, whispers shouted. I heard them humph. I heard cries, coughs, curses. Yet what had I missed?

"Okay. Whose?"

"Theodora," Pauline said, "things happen, you know. This watch is a mistake. We should throw it away. Drop it down a drain. It was a mistake. He took it."

"*He* took it? You mean Abner took this watch from someplace?"

"He could have found it. He might have

found two watches."

"You might find *one* watch – nobody finds *two* watches."

Pauline looked away in confusion. In need of a navigator.

"Sometimes – Abner took things. But not often. Hardly at all."

I was flabbergasted. I rocked on my heels. I tried to picture my father – as twice his height, as looming in the darkness, as frowning, pale and nearly bald. The Thief.

"He stole them," I said. I looked at the watch. Abner Palmer Waite supplemented his income. "Did we move because of these things he never meant to take?"

Pauline shook her head violently. "Oh no," she said. "No one ever knew. He would have died of shame if anyone knew."

"What did he do with the stuff?"

"Don't say stuff, please Theodora. It was just a few things. He sold them."

I recalled the name on that watch when I was having trouble with my vision. I couldn't read German but I had made out the letters. Were those the eyes of youth? I went into a store and pretended to be interested in watches. I read the faces. I read the manufacturer's name on the tiniest watch I was shown. I did this before going to the doctor.

Still, perhaps I should have brought someone with me to the ophthalmologist. Dierdre maybe or Charlotte. Possibly I would have difficulty getting home. Eye drops can do that.

I knew the doctor well. I had been to him before. "Shelly," I said. "I seem to be having a problem. Need glasses. I can't do my lipstick right anymore."

"Is that why you have none on?"

"Yes. I think it's all right. When I look in the mirror, the lipstick always looks all right. But then everyone says that it isn't. Messy, they say. Clownlike."

There were no drops.

"We have a problem, Theodora," he said.

"Serious?"

"You need a good physical – might be something."

"I'm in the middle of a project, Shelly. I have something in mind – a variety of cookie. Can this wait?"

"Sometimes, Theodora, we have no options."

The search for the American Father – that Great White Father. He was missing. Think of all the possible horrors that fathers committed – or they just went away. It sank in slowly. Abner Palmer Waite had packed it in. Taken his distilled eye drops, his sweater, his shirt, his belt. I tried to recall some point when he took me aside. Life, he said, life, sweetheart, has reached an impasse with me. Understand, Theodora — and as soon as possible, I'll come back.

I should have cried. Shouldn't I have cried? It must be shock. Instead, I found myself overcome with the spirit of abandon — mine not his. I didn't think for a moment about what was to become of me. A child didn't. Never mind that there was no one to turn to. Pauline moaned. But she had the Protestant ethic to support her moaning. I on the other hand was optimistic and secure. It was temporary.

I worked once after school in a bakery named La Pâtisserie, but what it was really called was Tante's after the old woman behind the cash register, the one with the black shoes from which the toes had been cut out. When they fired me, they said not to worry, it probably wasn't my fault. I got my pay and a large bag of poppyseed hamentaschen. They said I kept staring at Eddie. Eddie was the baker. Eddie said I was giving him the evil eye. He took to wearing a red ribbon. Then a wedding cake — six layers — fell flat as Adventist pancakes. They said outside of that I was a blessing. My change drawer added up. I was strange but not a *goniff*.

The watch gleamed its German golden face at me. The *stolen* watch. I returned the car battery to its cage. I have always accepted full blame for what happened. Wasn't it me who forced Pauline into her good black wool coat with the beaver collar. We're going to Hartford, I said. Picked Hartford because it was close, but not too close. Because I was afraid to do this business in Dover Beach.

How long did it take Abner to *find* this watch? Getting rid of it took most of a day. First, we had to locate a pawnshop.

"You go," Pauline pleaded. "Look at my face, my eyes."

"Perfect," I said. Crying authenticated. I took one of her icy hands. "I can't do it myself. They'll be suspicious. It has to be an adult."

"I never thought I could do it," Pauline said. We were safely back in the car. She was proud of herself. "I want you to know — sometimes your father found these things in the cab. Things dropped."

"Sure," I said.

Pauline was cheerful on the ride back to Dover Beach. Thirty-five dollars richer, we stopped at a roadside supermarket. We bought canned spaghetti, canned beans, franks, and an already roasted chicken. I selected butter, vanilla, and pistachio nuts. At the cash register Pauline whispered to me, "I have never — cross my heart — ever taken anything. And I begged, Theodora, I prayed for Abner to stop."

I thought about Abner Palmer Waite, a man secondhand to the core. He aspired to a '59 Chevy in '64. The cream puffs of secondhand life. He wasn't even a successful thief — still, that must have been the source of those recurring bits of money that I couldn't understand. If you wait long enough everything becomes rational.

Most people like talking about cooking more than cooking. Just read the culinary literature — all those claims to creative cooking. I say they confused creativity with the ability to follow directions. Not to put down the ability to follow directions. Few people can.

I was being watched. I submitted the following list worthy of a three-star *pâtisserie:* gâteau St. Honoré, Robert Southey's tart, ginger drops, Nesselrode cookies, gooseberry tarts, Mexican vanilla cookies. What more did they want? I had no intention of telling the Post woman what I was up to. I did not want to become a great chef, a great baker, a great nutritionist. I wanted to create a new cookie. After that — forget it.

The roots of poverty were extensive. Pull up here, and more appeared there. Well, we were not going to die, but we were not going to live either. For three days I tried to think what to do. The only real property we had was the automobile, the car must be sold.

"No."

"What do you mean no?"

"When Abner comes home – the car has to be here."

"We have to sell that car."

"The registration – in Abner's name."

"I can do a good imitation of his signature – he'll deed it to you."

"No."

Poor people lead less complex lives than people with money. I never knew that. Poor people had no time for complexities. Day-to-day living flattened life down considerably. I listed our options on paper: throw ourselves on the mercy of the Town of Dover Beach, or find work. Neither seemed possible. The rent due in three and one-half weeks.

Pauline was frightened. "I don't want to wait tables," she whispered hoarsely. She had never worked. She married her first husband when she was sixteen. Abner at twenty-two. Now her ankles hurt.

I didn't answer. But the only *Help Wanted* signs seen were those. Only jobs requiring no past. Pauline had no past. I had school records. That was not a past.

I have paid very little attention to the people who lived around me. They annoyed me. Use unbleached flour, they said. Melt a Hershey bar for frosting. Abner never cared much for those people either. Not a one of them, he said, had background. Still, you had to do some talking. I always thought Pauline had an instinct for selecting a pivotal person. In the town of Keene, she picked a woman named Beulah. Beulah knew all the local interesting facts. The man who rented a room at the Stones, he was the one who undressed with his bedroom door just a trifle ajar. See, she would say and point. The Woods, brother and sister, unmarried and always in each other's company. And that's the old man who did it with his fox terrier. All those people are on Welfare, Beulah said.

While I thought Welfare, someone knocked at the front door, rattled the doorknob.

"Hello!" a voice sailed forth.

I moved to the window, the one to the left of the door. Pressed my cheek to the glass, the window shade pocked with tiny holes was half up. I saw a woman in profile, her lips slightly parted as if practicing her greeting. I suppose in an illogical way I thought the knock at the door had something to do with Abner. I imagined he had been caught somewhere.

"Hello!" the woman called out again. "It's me."

I opened the door as Pauline gripped the edge of the wobbly table.

"I'm Fran," our visitor announced. The woman had a secret-holding face. "From Number Eight. I saw you arrive. I said to myself — don't come over until they're settled."

"Come in," I said. What else could I do? "I'm Theodora."

She walked past me eyeballing the bare corners of our rooms. These little houses — every room opened into the next. Take the right path, you can see everything.

"Our furniture is still in storage," Pauline said softly.

"And we don't have the money to get it out," I filled in quickly. No need to create unnecessary mystery.

"Well goodness," Fran said and smiled brightly, "I've done that road. We all go up and down, don't we?"

Pauline nodded. "I'm Mrs. Waite. Pauline."

Hospitality must be among the last graces to go. We served cookies. Coffee. Pauline found

Fran an ashtray. The woman was right at home in this place with its two beds, cardboard boxes, a table and three chairs.

"Good," Fran said. She ate one of my strawberry jam sand bars, licked her fingers.

"Theodora," Pauline said proudly. "Hers."

"Good," Fran repeated and looked me over. "Listen, you could be the right age for my Daniel. Yes, the right age."

I had an instant sense of dread.

"Yes, you are the right age. And he'd like you – he likes skinny girls. If he were here, he'd like you. But Daniel is gone. My two boys – Daniel and Gene – gone." She turned to Pauline. "You divorced?"

I answered. "Widow."

"I'm once divorced," Fran said. "That's why I know how it is with your stuff. I had bad times. Plenty. My first husband – Nathaniel. Nat said I was killing his life. So he wanted to go. We didn't live here then, we lived on Cleremont. Then the boys – they were boys after all. They went with him. Nat wanted to go to California. The boys love swimming. Mind if I try another cookie?"

I found out what we wanted. *The Mayor Helps,* it was called. What we needed, the man said on the telephone, was Aid to Dependent Families. "I'll stay home from school, and we'll go," I told Pauline. "Maybe I can get away with a half day." I could tell that she was nervous and maybe a little sick to her stomach. There was one tin of cookies left.

We took the car. I drove. We parked two blocks away. I didn't know how they felt about cars. Pauline wore her good coat. We took a number at the door and went into the reception area to sit on orange plastic chairs. As soon as she sat down Pauline slumped forward, her back curved. Not a pretty sight.

From a *Help Yourself* bin I picked up a printed list of entitlements: We could be eligible for Emergency Assistance for Families (EAF), Aid to Families with Dependent Children (AFDC), Food Stamps, Home Relief, Medicaid. But, of course, there would be an initial screening. And where did our family's gross income fall? There were need or income limits. Were we economically disadvantaged? The condition of destitution − sudden and unforeseen. What constituted a catastrophe? A catastrophe was us.

They say that the great chef Lorenzo was accused of serving his famous Treacle Pudding falsely. The ingredients cut and diluted. The molasses − the treacle of name − mixed with marmelade. He cheated, he was caught, and he blamed it all on a scullery maid. *She,* he said, having eaten some of the molasses, endeavored to hide her theft by adding common Seville marmelade to what was left. The scullery maid swore he made it that way and furthermore he was always fondling her breasts. He got away with it. It was his appearance. The appearance of honor and truth.

My first trip into crime. If I had been caught that day, I certainly would have stopped. Perhaps an amateur's luck. I did Honors until four o'clock. My mind grew a declivity, a dark drop-off point. I was not going home. I had no blueprint for my actions. Where to go? I followed three girls walking down Beech Street. They parted. One girl walked down her path. I could have chosen any house. I didn't know the girl. What I learned was that your mouth became parched when you were frightened. Your mouth became dry, your bladder filled.

My first house was a modified Cape, winter-toned cottage, two bedrooms on the first floor. All the houses on this street had veils of aluminum siding, side paths to the back door, black wrought-iron fences guarding planters shaped like deer.

I took only one precaution. Pulled my hair into a ponytail with a rubber band. In jeans, jacket, schoolbooks — I could be anyone's friend. The nice part of winter was the early glow of darkness, a blue-black darkness. Lights on only in the kitchen. Boy about thirteen sitting at the table. Girl leaning against the counter talking to a huge-breasted woman who stirred the contents of a pot with a small spoon.

Two inches of window frame to stand on. If the frame cracked under my toes, I would leave. The frame held. Chips of peeling paint clung to me from the splintery wood. Hard to pull my weight up.

Where was I? I smelled disinfectant. Fingers touched a thing soft and slippery. Soap. Then I was calm. A bathroom was safe. The outline of a bathroom – tiles, mirror, toothbrush holder.

I made this entry without proper thought. Could have been a dog. I knew nothing about the occupants. A man might be asleep in the next room.

My maiden voyage – five minutes and then out. I thought I would die from the pounding and throbbing of my body. A television but no voices. Had the group in the kitchen disbanded? Deep and treacherous nausea inside me. I wanted to wail.

I counted on a simple interior plan, on the boredom of the builder. Crossed the narrow hall. Edge of bed to dresser. Dresser had a small mirrored tray. A watch – a man's watch. Put it into the pocket of my jeans. I felt leather. Touched the bills inside. Six or seven. If I took three, would they think theft or just that three were spent and the watch misplaced? On the other hand, suppose I took three singles. What good was that. No, they have been robbed.

Something about the luck of any initial venture. The first time I made Herangues meringues. Cookies with a dough base, a praline layer, and a meringue top. They turned out elegantly crisp. No real understanding of what I had done but splendid results. The next two times: burned the dough layer once, turned the meringue into cement next.

My seven bills — five twenties, one ten, one single. I asked Pauline for a whiskbroom. We had no whiskbroom. She had this wire brush. I eroded the knees and legs of my jeans. The paint chips were institutional green.

I decided to be systematic about this. Rob three times a week. If you perform certain acts in certain ways, you are calmer and less self-indulgent. Therefore, Tuesdays, Wednesdays, and Fridays. I was not looking for profit. I just wanted to break even.

Garrick had it right, though, didn't he. *The Devil sends cooks.*

Anyway, I needed time to keep up with baking. If you haven't tried what exists you are in no position to experiment. Therefore I was determined to make as many varieties of cookies as I could. Extremely difficult to work in the kitchen at home. The entire place was topsy-turvy. I needed drawers. I needed a large level counter or table. I needed a certain amount of balance. Chaos may be all right for personal relations but it stinks for serious work.

The Post woman made me nervous. More understanding than I liked. Her Slavic eyes darkened when she looked at me. Probably shortened her name. She came into my Honors kitchen. Gâteau was being filled. I didn't do it the easy way, with whipped cream. I prepared a crème pâtissière.

I never kept any account of the houses I robbed – just tried to remember the streets. Eventually some idiot will figure out the pattern. The pattern was circular around the North Dover Beach school. Walking distance. That's the pattern. I now examined each house at least once before I attempted to enter. I developed certain requirements: an unlocked reachable window, lights on in no more than two rooms. By planning, I avoided two dogs, one house with a night-employed man who moved about in the afternoon, and houses with small children – who were always unpredictable. I didn't permit the weather to interfere. Rain was rain.

The payoff? Did crime pay? Not for me. I

recognized that this was indeed a low-paying profession. I never again came close to that first amount. But I learned to lift the corners of rugs, to feel under the paper lining drawers, to poke fingers into canisters. One evening ten bills turned out to be ones. But I had five watches – women's. And one pearl necklace.

Bad luck can appear at any time. I carried no identification. Bought a secondhand textbook – *Western Civilization*. Text for a course I didn't take. That was the book I carried.

Sometimes I thought about Abner Palmer Waite. I was uncertain how life challenged Abner. He wasn't nearly as pushy as he said. If someone crowded him in a line, didn't he step back? Little bastard, he might say. But could the little bastard hear that?

Pauline crying. The sight of her sitting and weeping. I only stared. "If I could find a job," she sobbed. "Something good – we would be all right."

"Sure," I said.

Fran waved at me.

"Hey," she called. "Wait up."

I paused.

"I swear I never see you," Fran said. "But also I never hear you – you don't play that loud rah-rah music?"

"No," I said. "Possibly I may be tone-deaf."

"No kidding? Anyway, you're a mighty quiet girl. Too bad my son Daniel isn't here. My new husband – you've seen him, haven't you – short guy, balding. Would you believe that he was in the Air Force? He was wounded too. A hero's wound. Appearances prove nothing."

I dozed. Sitting at the table reading Gorky, I fell asleep. What woke me was my elbow gave way and my chin dropped. It was a startle reaction. I was alone. As soon as I opened my eyes I remembered. The man's name was Hal.

She called him Hal. It was Hal this and Hal that. He had sandy-colored hair. He was a young man – probably her age. A man of limited conversation and somehow a weighty step. It can't have been all that romantic a scene. Was it romantic to be trailed by your progeny? But perhaps they truly didn't notice. They would sing to each other in thin, quavering voices. He must have been her lover. Most of those days were yellow afternoons. And I don't see any of the red hospital streaks on her body.

I didn't believe my mother was an exhibitionist. No. At one point he protested. She laughed. *That* sees, she said. For goodness sakes she's a baby. Go into the other room, Theodora. Go play, sweetheart. They were naked. They were walking around the room. They were drinking something. I have no recollection of Abner. So he wasn't in this scene.

It shows you – there's no way of estimating how young is young. I remembered.

I avoided the moral issue. I couldn't afford not to avoid the moral issue. I was afloat in lies, and my behavior ignoble. I did not think about the people I stole from. My criteria for picking them were incomprehensible to me. Still, I maintained some rules: Never go back to the same house, leave the houses as they were, and never take too much.

At the same time I cannot equate what I did with the theft of a loaf of bread. I robbed to live. Pauline does what she can. That cannot be enough. She became a baby-sitter.

Rudolf never asked for the details of this year – not the real details. Perhaps he believed they were painful or too lurid to tell. I would have told him it was mostly fear that I felt. I might have added that watches were worth very little secondhand. That first watch must have been *something*. The rest never brought more than a few dollars. And the pearls broke under a hammer. I would however have told him about my sense of fear – both its attraction and its despair. When Rudolf was working, he didn't like to be interrupted. Go and do something, he would say.

I was in a house when the man and woman began to fight. I had seen them talking in the kitchen before I entered. The trusty television as background. Then when my fingers were actually inside the purse on a chair, he yelled.

"Don't tell me!"

"I'll tell you — if I want. It's a free country.

"No you won't! Now I don't know where she is — that's final. I don't know."

"You've seen her."

"No!"

"Don't tell me!"

My breath banged against my rib cage. Either one of them might stalk down that tiny hall to the bedroom. She, I thought, She would come. She would slam the door. She would throw herself sobbing on the bed.

My fingers touched one of those old-fashioned coin purses attached for safety's sake to the internal workings of the larger purse by a chain. I clicked the pronged clasp open with one hand. Bills, neatly folded. On top of the shouts, the accusations, wouldn't this be too much? But then, of course, the shared loss could reunite. I might be responsible for mutual comfortings.

Pauline thought I wanted to bake cookies someday for a husband and two kids. Abner said I was crazy. Sometimes I thought he was jealous. Still, my baking was something separate. I told Abner that baking cookies could be the creation of a work of art. It was a question of intention.

Had anyone done a literary work about a cook – about a great baker? I didn't mean one of those marriage and family situations where people wander in and out of a kitchen. But where a baker was followed around. His craft, his art detailed. His mind explored. A genuine three-star invented Michelin baker.

Then, for instance, someone came in and attempted to bribe the baker. Get from him secrets – the very ones that were the property of the restaurant – *gloires de la cuisine.* The baker did not take the bribe – de *piston pas de pot de vin.* The sins of rum raisin.

Pauline wasn't crying, but she looked pale. Not trembling, but pale. Wearing her coat she sat at the table, but the house wasn't cold.

"What is it?" I asked.

She shook her head. "I'm numb," she said. "Have to catch my breath."

"Are you sick? Pauline, are you sick?"

"No. But, something happened."

I thought she'd lost a baby-sitting assignment.

"A man," she said.

"What?"

"I got mugged."

"My God, did he do something to you?"

"My purse," she said. "He grabbed for it."

"Are you all right?"

"He didn't get it. We stood on the corner near the A & P. It was near dark – him pulling, me pulling. Not a word said. If he'd been a bigger man, I might have lost. But suddenly, Theodora, I pulled it away from him. Then I hit him over the head with it. He didn't yell, but he ran away."

"You should have given it up."

"Never."

I entered a house without lights. Hadn't tried that before. Oddly enough I equated the presence of people in any house with safety. The occupants were then *somewhere*. A side window gave access to an enclosed porch that led directly to the house. A sweet-smelling house. A cook's house. I detected vanilla – followed the scent to the kitchen. I lifted the glass cover of a cake plate – revealing a jumble of cocoa drops. Rough-textured cookies, oatmeal base. Not bad – although the baker hesitated too much with the sugar. A false caution, equating sugar with illness — too sweet can kill you. The kitchen had that simplicity — that neatness I admired. What caught my eye? The gleam of a metal tube. A cookie press. A cookie press with heft to it. Made by a craftsman, this press from the kitchen of someone's Old World grandmother. It must shoot dough through its smooth cylinder like a rocket gone to space. I moved the exiting pin. I wanted that press. I stuffed it into the pocket of my jacket where it protruded with a flashlight belligerency. Then I took a deep breath. Christ, I might as well have written my name and left it on the table. I put the press back on the counter where it rolled to nestle against a shining avocado-colored side of the refrigerator.

I was wrong. My method. My pride in *my* method. I exposed myself too often. Three times a week, just to exist. I needed to minimize my risks — more money per house. One house entered, one theft. All these trips took time. I estimated two and one-half hours per theft. That's seven and one-half hours a week. One day of prime work time. Then too, sometimes when I came home, I was unaccountably jumpy. Particularly noticeable on those evenings when Pauline had a baby-sitting assignment. Not that we discussed what I had done. Or where I have been.

I had to think through my actions. The problem could be geographic. My choice of theft locations – I might be picking up ten dollars at some house that looked right and bypass the very place where two hundred waited. I had to find out where the real money might be. Last week I went into a house and found nothing. No watch. No money – or what there was must be in the pocket of the man in the kitchen. Or the woman hid hers. The purse in the bedroom held an empty wallet and a handful of coins. I didn't have enough time to try another house. A Tuesday wasted.

I decided to become popular.

A rat appeared in the Home Ec room. Screaming that could accompany the arrival of a rock star. I often went into Home Ec in the morning. I did not interrupt the class. I came to check the refrigerator or the cupboard. I had detailed lists of ingredients needed and ingredients used. When I opened the door, a draft entered. Perhaps the air ruffled fur. The rat crossed the floor, a click of nails on cream-colored tile. Screams. It wasn't that I didn't scream. Only that I was too surprised. And the tops of all the chairs were taken.

The rat was a large and painfully ugly animal. I wondered if he had been in that room a long time. Was he present late in the afternoons when I worked alone?

"Get him! Get him!" someone shrieked.

I grabbed a broom from the rack near the door. An absurd gesture. I had no intention of getting the rat. But what I did was mark a circumscribed circle. One of those magical unseen circles.

In a house near Poughkeepsie there were mice, tiny grey-colored mice. Pauline opened the cupboard door beneath the kitchen sink one day and two mice ran out. She screamed. I screamed. We leaped on top of chairs in the kitchen. Later we went to neighbors next door. I had a glass of milk and Pauline had a cup of coffee. Her heart, she said, was going to burst forth any moment. When Abner came home he set traps. Two big girls like you, he said.

The maintenance man arrived in the classroom.

"What do you think you're doing?" he said.

But the voice was more amused than disdainful. We were a bunch of girls in the right place. Home Ec.

"All right," the maintenance man said, "all you *big* girls climb down and file out of here."

Later, the maintenance man swore he caught the rat.

Everyone believed him.

"Hey, Miss Prissy-Prig! I know your type."

"For God's sake, Ed."

"Shut up, Fran. Look at her — a little pussy-prig. See her march up and down the goddamn street. Head up. I know her type. Thinks she's hot shit. Hey, Miss Pussy!"

"Ed — shut your mouth. You're drunk. Ignore him, Theodora."

"Hey Miss Prig-Prig! You don't speak to a goddamn soul, do you?"

The first approach on the road to popularity came fortuitously. In the school hallway a girl said, "I was scared to death, weren't you?"

This was one of the bodies on a chair.

"Yes," I said. I examined the girl. She wore a cashmere sweater and jeans. On the other hand, I too owned cashmere. But — she had that air — people took care of this girl.

"I'm Theo," I said sweetly.

"We know who you are," the girl said. "You leave those fantastic gooey things in the fridg."

"That's me, all right."

"I'm Patsy," she said.

At lunchtime I timed my arrival carefully. A quick-handed wave. Suddenly I was at lunch with Cindy, Mindy, Patsy, and Susie.

For a while, until popularity took over, I used an ancient method. Itisket, Itasket. I pick

261

you. Brick house. Ranch-style with bedrooms of necessity on the first floor. Not a converted Cape in sight. Lights on in one room. It was my very favorite situation. The kitchen with the eating area. Woman in the kitchen. Five-thirty. Ah — best yet. The man at home. I heard voices. But no argument. Periodically the woman said, "No, Winifred."

An unlocked bedroom window. I lifted upward and even the storm window moved easily. I raised myself up to the ledge with my new-found skill in push-ups. The growl was low, poignant, full-throated. I didn't know the breed, but the growls were distinct over the rushing fall of blood tumbling down the banks of my ears. It didn't matter which course of action the dog took — barking or leaping from the window and attacking me. I would be caught.

What I did was this. "Winifred," I said softly, "Hi there, girl. Hi, Winifred." After all, it could be the dog's name.

The growls slowly wound down. One must assume that the dog had not met an adversary in the window before. It was for both of us a new experience. "Winifred," I said, "good girl."

I thought in the gloom that the tail wagged.

The extent of my idiocy was that I did not drop to the ground and bid Winifred adieu. No, I pulled myself forward, one leg over the sill, cooing away at the dog. I reached out, patted its head, trying for a firm touch. Winifred's damp muzzle in turn rubbed against my denim thigh. We waltzed together across the room. Wallet on the dresser. A thick wallet. I slid the bills from the wallet to my pocket. I saw a purse dropped on the cushion of a two-seater couch. The room bloomed with lilac-laden chintz. The purse yielded more bills. I had never put so much in my pockets. Of course, they could all be ones. Not impossible.

Good-bye Winifred. God bless you. Good dog.

"You know," Pauline said, "It would be nice to have a dog someday. I don't believe I ever wanted one before. But now I can see a dog — not a big one, but a smallish dog. What do you think, Theodora?"

"What?"

"A dog. Doesn't have to be a puppy, could be one already housebroken. A sweet little dog would be like extra company."

I was very careful. "Why do you mention a dog?"

"I was sitting for this little girl today. Little girl and her baby brother. They had the sweetest dog. The mother is a nice woman, but the baby, you know, could be cleaner. She had this awful rash on her behind."

"What kind?"

"Little white poodle. Named Lace. She begs, Theodora. Sits up on the tiniest feet."

"Maybe someday," I said. "We'll see."

In the bathroom I pulled down my jeans and sat on the john. Both pockets bulging, absolutely bulging. I pulled out the bills, both sides simultaneously, from the pants around my ankles. I never expected this. I had four hundred dollars in twenties, six tens, three fives. I hadn't any one dollar bills. None.

On Saturday I suggested shopping. We could not buy everything we needed at once. People noticed if a truck pulled up and unloaded a houseful, not a street for windfalls. But a few things. That would seem all right.

I left the choice to Pauline. I only insisted on the size. I measured to see what was possible. I can't work on the tiny counter space. I needed a table to operate properly. Pauline selected a white formica-topped table with a pink-and-white spiderweb pattern and embossed metal edging. The chairs covered in matching vinyl. We can afford this. Pauline talked the man out of a delivery fee. "Right around the corner," she said. "You can spit to our house." I was proud of her.

A girl brought a slip into Calculus that summoned me to the Vice Principal's office. I had to stop first in the john. I had the runs. Then I drank from the fountain. If I was sent to jail — what then? Or even to some juvenile facility. Who would come for me? I knew the answer. Pauline, even if she were my mother, wouldn't know what to do. Pauline would in time wander off somewhere.

The Vice Principal had an office with a half-glass door frosted with a snowflake design that belied the theory that all snowflakes were different.

"Come in," the Vice Principal said heartily. "Theodora, Theo."

I entered and was waved to a chair.

"Now Theo," said the Vice Principal. "North Dover Beach is observant. We *know* our students. And the reports on you" — Vice Principal checks a paper. "Tired. Yes, a good student — but recently presenting as tired."

I only stared.

The Vice Principal wrote on a pad of pink sheets. "This is a referral. Take this, Theo, to the nurse's office. We'll take care of you."

"Yes," I said. "Thank you."

I kept the old wire bottle brush and some rags in a wooden box in the yard. I regularly brushed my jeans and my jacket. That's what I was doing, so I wasn't eavesdropping. The lights on in the kitchen. We left the window open a crack for ventilation. Two coffee mugs on the table and a plate of my florentines. The woman was Fran.

"It was bad at the time," Pauline said. "It was terrible. But although I remember — like it's not me. Know what I mean?"

Fran nodded. "Like when I got my divorce. Like it wasn't me saying those things. And like he wasn't there with Madeleine."

"I wasn't wild," Pauline said. "I know I looked wild. But I wasn't. He buys me a Coke. They had a machine right outside. So I stand there drinking it. Hey, he says, I admire you, kid. Then he invites me out. Can you? he says. I arrange to meet him near the movie theater. Now, no one ever, you know, took me out for dinner. Leonine's was a regular restaurant. We had tablecloths, veal, spaghetti. Red wine. I felt stuck-up. No one asked how old I was. I knew I looked more than sixteen, but this was proof positive.

"I became silly from the wine and feeling good. No — great. He was telling me how sweet I was, how pretty I was, how nice I was. I don't know. Maybe I would have done it with him. I might have.

"But he drives us back to this garage. He

266

unlocks the parking lot fence and we drive in. I am wearing a cotton blouse and a skirt. And he rips the blouse. Now he didn't have to — you understand. It buttoned right down the front. But he rips it. I start to scream, and he grabs my mouth, he puts these dry cracked fingers across my mouth. I'm scared. Then it happened.

"He drives me home. I'm living with my married sister and her husband. But he doesn't go off. He comes in and he tells them he wants to marry me. It made no sense to me. He said he knocked me up. He said I might be pregnant. For a week they yelled at me. My brother-in-law said I had to. My sister too. But maybe I wasn't pregnant. He wanted to marry me. He wanted to have a girl. He was forty-something. I was only sixteen.

"I thought three times of dying. Once I held the knife right at my wrist. I was married to that man for eight and one-half years before I met my second husband."

"Your second husband?"

"Dead," Pauline said.

Pauline took out a photograph of Abner. Abner standing in front of his car. A '57 Ford Fairlane. One hand fondling the fender. A debonair, relaxed Abner. He was wearing a hat. How many men today could be photographed wearing a hat? I stared at the picture balanced on top of the television.

Pauline blushed. "I tell you," she said, "I put it out for a reason."

"Like what?"

"It was a dream, Theodora. A terrible dream. In this dream I am chasing Abner. But when he turns around, he doesn't have any face. I woke up in a sweat. So I thought I would put out the picture for a while."

Once when I was enrolled in Rideway Middle School, I took LSD. It wasn't better than I thought or worse. I took it with three friends. A girl named Helene said we should go shopping. We went to the mall, but all the stores were closed. So a boy said we should go to *his* neighborhood where life is always on. Meanwhile, I thought I had an idea for a cookie, but no one had paper. So this boy took us to a street with stores. We rode in a Ford. There were more people now in our group. Suddenly many stores were open, a lot of selling going on right on the sidewalk. I wanted to buy some cologne. Cologne was being sold in the largest bottles I had ever seen. And phony Vuitton purses and phony Gucci shoes. The prices were very reasonable. But everyone spoke a rasta lingo, I thought. I kept saying I didn't understand. So I left the others and went home. By

268

the time I located paper, it was too late.

Dierdre hummed a song. I didn't know the song – tried to think of the words. Rudolf would have known. One night of love, shall we dance, begin the. No, I didn't know the song. Perhaps Dierdre made it up. No, she didn't do that. She hummed quite well.

The Wellingtons, she said. Had me over for dinner. I can't believe they have that much money. They did the room over again. That seems somehow wrong, you know, not tasteful – changing all the time. Blue suede on one chair. Luxuriant, somatic. I sunk in. That Neber man was there. He's getting a divorce. Can you imagine? The old goat came home and found her. It was the same situation, so tacky. Found her with Miller.

I listened. Miller and Neber's wife. Neber's wife had short black hair. Did he grab it, close to the scalp, push her down, she resisted the token amount. Miller pulled her skirt up, pulled down the pantyhose. Neber's wife gone moist.

I suspect it will blow over, Dierdre said. He won't let her go. I mean what did he expect, those twenty years between them. He was forty-something when they married, but now he's past sixty. What did he expect?

After Mortimer left, I felt bad. But I didn't feel as bad as I thought I would. Ginger said I had to look for a different type of man. Part of the problem, she said, was that I kept the same life patterns. I kept picking and finding the same paths. She wasn't thinking about cults, she said, or formalized internal instruction. But still, if anyone needed a group — I did.

Margaret said no, that the problem was one of looks. Rudolf was handsome. And she didn't necessarily trust good-looking men. It wasn't vanity she was thinking about — but wasn't there something — well, slimey about men who were truly handsome.

The handling of chocolate was a skill — like weaving. Sometimes, I believed that *understanding* chocolate was a vocation. Think of the varieties, and each idiosyncratically different: semisweet, bittersweet, bitter, dark, milk. Chocolate liquor like a mother lode. Anyway, chocolate must be handled properly or not at all. You can't just melt chocolate. I preferred the *bain-marie* method. No risk then of separation, no scorch. Otherwise, how can you make glazes or *ganache*. Then too, I tempered chocolate to retain that shine.

If you were careful how you did it, handing out chocolate products eased the way into popularity.

When we lived outside Poughkeepsie I knew a girl named Monica – I met her in Home Ec. Monica always said that she had a lousy home life. Try getting a dime out of my mother, Monica said.

She came up to me one day with a proposition. We would go into the city together and spend an afternoon – just one afternoon – picking up guys and making money. It was the weirdest idea. Bet it's easy, she said. So we went into the city together one Saturday. We wore jeans and tight T-shirts. We rode the subway to Union Square and then walked over to Broadway. Monica said we had to stand near the curb. We stood near the curb. Two cars pulled up just like that, one after the other. Monica grabbed the first one, a beefy red Camaro. We'll meet back here, she said. I had a black Chevy. The man was overweight, and definitely older than Abner. Cutie, he said. How much? Ten dollars, I said. Where do we go? he said. Your car, I said. He didn't look pleased at that. But it was his car or nothing. We drove further west. It was Saturday, plenty of empty factory-lined streets. He parked and we did it in the back seat. My legs parted and one, two, three. He sort of slapped softly against my thighs. It's funny but there were no details to this encounter. Drive me back? I asked. The place was deserted. Sure, the man said. He took me right back to the same block. Be careful crossing, he said. It was like being with an uncle. I waited a while, but Monica didn't show up so I took the train back. I didn't see her until Monday. She had on a new suede skirt. Our kinship based on need ended. We never had much to do with each other after that.

Did I belong? The Patsy entourage was not too sure of me. I can't be glib about my favorite movie star, my favorite singer, my favorite boy. I had to pick up on what they said. I would rather not spend time with them — and a few guessed. Anyway, who among them can do more than singe a steak or mix an oil-and-vinegar dressing. Easy on the vinegar.

Still, I needed those girls. So I worked a friendship. Patsy offered the first invitation. We should go over to her house. We rode in Cindy's car. We crowded together, sitting on each other's laps, laughing healthily.

Patsy's house was a shopper's paradise. I could easily clear enough money from Patsy's house to live for a month. It had that look you saw in women's magazines — for instance, everything matched in the living room, two chairs, two lamps, two tables. I resisted examining anything, turning over a candlestick to check its heritage.

Cokes poured, splashed with rum. A large ripped bag of potato chips went around. I noticed chips dropping from fingers, slipping behind cushions, sizzling greasily into the carpet. No one cared.

"The john?" I asked.

"Sure — next to that hall closet door."

I wanted to go upstairs. That could be fixed. I walked into a tiny silver and grey-striped bathroom. I made certain that the doors to the miniature vanity were painted on. Carefully I removed the roll of toilet tissue from the spool, opened the hall closet door, and dropped the roll into a corner, kicked a winter boot over it.

"No paper!" I yelled.

"Shit! Go upstairs, Theo. End of hall. Door in front of you."

I walked up thickly carpeted stairs. What a delightful experience. The walls were painted a creamy white, no visible smudges, no dried dribbles from a careless paintbrush. Close your eyes, open your eyes, see where you are. Remember! Fix the location, make an internal map. I headed toward the bathroom. Was anyone up here? All the doors were open. Four bedrooms. Almost gliding, I stepped into one bedroom. The room smelled of beeswax. I cannot imagine anyone sleeping in this room, anyone being sick here. I checked the tops of furniture. A ring on a dresser. A diamond ring. I didn't for a moment doubt its reality. What could it be worth in Hartford? In a second I had the ring, wadded in tissue, stuffed in my pocket. I raced to the bathroom. Flushed. I didn't know if pipes could be heard in this house. Did I keep the ring? I never got as far as the stairs before reality returned – Who had I thought they would say took it?

During the period when I collected cookbooks, I'd mark up the margins, underline, make emphatic fat *no's*. Abner was annoyed. Every time we moved, we hauled cartons filled with my cookbooks. Then a roof leaked – the books grew a moldy life. I saw the truth. Dragging around great piles of cookbooks after I explored their cookie recipes was pointless. Now I still bought books but I sold them before each move. I believed that true originality required a long and careful search. But it was worth it.

Pauline suffered from insomnia. I heard her wandering around at night. Yesterday she knelt by my bed. "I was asked to join a group," she whispered and poked my arm.

"What?" I was pulled upward from a dream.

"Some ladies had a card table set up outside the laundromat. They were signing up people.

It's called *Women Against Poverty*. It's free."

"What do they do?" I asked.

"It's to promote laws, they said, and to offer support. They meet all together – sit in a circle – in the basement of the Y. Talk – exchange thoughts – just women."

"We can't do that," I said.

Popularity was very hard. Most of the time it gave me a headache. First, the matter of clothes. Abner didn't sell my clothes. But popularity required more than I had. And I must buy expensive – because these were friends who respected expensive.

Popularity meant visiting. Which was the point of the whole effort. I resented the time. So far, six different houses. But I was careful, being friendly, and thus one friend led to another. Sometimes the urge to keep a notebook or at least write a list of addresses or floor plans overwhelmed me. If such a notebook were found – no, I had to keep all this in my head. What stairway led to where. The likely drawers to open. What to avoid. Some houses no matter their size will not be worth a trip. Some people were borderline bankrupts.

Nell was giving a party. Who was Nell? Patsy stopped me. I was on my way upstairs to Honors Home Ec. The girls knew when I was not available. I was annoyed.

"Come," Patsy said.

"Hell, I wasn't invited."

"That doesn't mean anything. All Nell doesn't want is crashers who don't *know* anybody. Here's the address. Come around nine. You want to be picked up?"

"No," I said and took the piece of paper torn from a notebook.

"Nell gives great stuff."

For the past three weeks I have been concentrating on chocolate. Chocolate drops, chocolate kisses, chocolate macaroons. Cassell's recipe for chocolate biscuits (1877) — an endless heaping of chocolate. Then — to make the Posts of the world content — I did poached eggs in *matelote,* pumpkin and rice soup, and an elegant Easter bread.

Should I stop chocolate? I have a great basic fondness for vanilla. Vanilla as spice, as scent, as the conduit for flavor. Maybe I'll experiment with different types of vanilla in vanilla cookies vanilla sand dollars, vanilla macaroons, vanilla Washington favors.

My school acquaintances were the Home Ec girls — but when we went to their houses no one ventured into the kitchen unless she wanted a drink. Clean and sterile kitchens. No one cooked in those rooms. The girls in question had no real interest in food preparation. I would look like a damn fool if I took a general tour of their kitchens − checking out cupboards, ingredients, appliances.

My curiosity was the main quality of my behavior that I kept in check. Fade. Do not stand out − neither smile too much nor be too sullen. Fade.

A boy insulted me as we entered Calculus one day. We were taking an examination. "Are you here to serve milk and cookies?" he said. I allowed myself to take the bait − use the insult − I came in first in the class. I defended myself brilliantly at the blackboard. I forgot my rules.

Bought a toaster in St. Celia's Thrift Shop − an old-fashioned model, circa '56. It was a Sunbeam. I liked the shape. Four bucks well spent.

"I think it's really nice," Pauline said. "You should go to parties more often."

"Pauline," I said exasperated. "Not that kind of a party. This is a *business* party. That *kind* of party. Understand?"

Pauline looked away.

"Now, you have to pick me up," I said. "A map − I have it all sketched out for you. Watch for the light. We have to time this. Remember the Southside Mall – you'll see a Walgreen's when you drive in by Kiplard Street. Left hand. Park up close. Be there about midnight."

I made it to Clinton Avenue by nine-thirty. I'm cold, though. Party noises penetrating that thin chilled air. Such loud music. Two acres of insulation protecting the neighbors. I'm not good at judging land. Could be more, could be less.

The house impressed. I felt a tingle of anticipation. Bigger than any place I have yet entered. Who the hell was Nell? I gained admittance so easily. It should always have been like that. I didn't know anyone. I employ a smile – casual, weary – and I "Hi there" to death. And they "Hi there" back. I didn't know where to go first. Movement from hall into the next room was blocked by bodies. A tall blonde pushed next to me. A girl – almost a woman – with what I identified as contemporary hair. The kind that swung out and then swung back.

"I don't know you," she said accusingly. "Do I know you?"

"No," I said. "But Patsy does – and Susie."

"I'm Nonnie," said the blonde.

"I'm Nell," I said.

I sometimes thought I was tone-deaf, all this music sounded similar. I detected differing

278

rhythms – but I suspected that nuances were lost to me. Someday when I had time, I planned to explore this. Tonight I wanted something to eat. I was starved. I didn't have a chance to eat anything earlier, not even Pauline's leftover meatloaf.

It had been my experience, although limited, that garbage circulated first at parties. Any good food remained inexplicably on trays in the kitchen waiting to be served. Did it ever get served? Not usually.

I asked a passing girl where the kitchen was but the direction she sent me led to the john. So I moved down the hall. The dining room had couples clinging to each other. Astonishing what people did in public, as if there were no public.

Past the dining room was a walk-through pantry. The kitchen was a miniature skating rink rented by careless people for the evening. What did they care, tomorrow they'd rent someplace else. Napkins floated across the floor like crumpled swans, amber puddles on counters, fingerprints on the walls. The room itself was an appliance-filled void. A black-and-white room. A six-burner stove. Le Corbusier. Two ovens in the wall, one huge one beneath the burners. A wall barbecue pit.

I was right, food waited in the kitchen. Plastic platters imitating glass held pyramids of meat-filled triangles of flaky dough. Good-looking ham, rye bread, mustard. I made a sandwich for myself. Opened the refrigerator. Poured milk. I stood there and ate, watching the occasional soul wander in and out – a drunken girl, one noisy couple, a fat boy who grabbed a handful of miniature hot dogs.

When Nicholas came into the kitchen, I greeted him. I had seen him before – at Patsy's. He hung around Patsy or Susie. I remembered seeing him at their houses. And occasionally I had turned around and found him staring at me. It was unpleasant those times – that I should be the one to turn. Me, not him. I say "Hi there." He was exactly what I liked, dark and dashing. That's what I liked. But I had very little time to bother with either boys or men. I was in every sense the sole support of my family.

Come on, Rudolf said. This Nicholas was the adult – he took advantage of you. He could have turned you into a *real* criminal – instead of those juvenile antics you two did. You should have considered yourself lucky to have escaped with so little damage. But you have a streak of common sense. I can't see you, Theodora, enthralled by some junior hood. But then, you weren't really, were you?

No.

* * *

Nicholas poured himself a glass of ginger ale and left the kitchen. I thought no more about him. I should have gone and looked for Patsy, Cindy, Susie, and what's-her-name. Instead I opened a few drawers, kitchen utensils were well-arranged. A paid cook in this house — you can sense a certain impersonal feeling about the kitchen. It worked. But the person who used it — probably didn't own it. An employed environment.

Flour. I found flour, tasted a snip caught between my thumb and forefinger. Everything else I needed were the staples of life. The kitchen had a large bottle of Guiana vanilla. The bowls logically placed. A mixing spoon. What was I going to do? I was going to make cookies. I hummed but not to that music. You can't hum to that music. Cookies don't deserve a raucous beat. But cookies can survive that.

I decided to make simple and pure vanilla-flavored sugar cookies. People entered the kitchen, but no one said anything. No one questioned my right to make cookies. I should learn from this. The value of decisive action. No triple batches. Just a reasonable amount of cookies. There were cooling racks. More than I owned.

Rows of thin and crisp cookies. The room

smelled good. The fat boy reentered. Grabbed cookies.

Time for me to explore the second floor of Nell's house.

"Hi!"

It was Patsy.

"Hi!"

I waved a frantic hand and went up the stairs. Ahead of me was a wonderful hall. A Queen Anne table with a vase filled with never-born pink to ruby-red silk flowers. The bloody palace had six bedrooms. I placed the setting in my memory. Best bedroom second from right.

I doubted if I could ever get into this house on my own. This place must use a burglar alarm system. I would if this were my house. Maybe essentially a wasted evening. No. There were the cookies. I hunted for a john. Might as well use the best one. The Mommy/Daddy bathroom.

The biggest bedroom had a mountain of coats burying the bedspread. A quilted lilies-of-the-valley flower garden. My coat? I was still wearing it. A lined jacket. I must look weird. The burglar habit. Don't relax or remove anything. I baked the fucking cookies wearing my coat. On the other hand maybe they thought I was on something. Shivers and shakes.

I slowly closed the door. Some girls had

dropped their purses on the bed. What could you get from these girls' purses? A five, a ten. But take twenty to thirty purses — I often got less in an evening. I reached for a purse. Probably purses with real loot were hanging from shoulders. The first purse had the expected five. Five was five. I moved faster. Two fives, one ten, then a lousy single, then a five, then two tens. God, this one had fifty dollars! I tried a few pockets of masculine coats. Nothing. No money. I returned to purses. Burrowed beneath the coats. I might come away with more than two hundred. My hands slipped in and out of purses as if this were some kind of dexterity test. How many in ten minutes?

Never heard the door.

"Hello," Nicholas said. The open door set off a blast of aggravating noise from downstairs. He closed the door. He turned on a wide smile. And his eyes resembled that Home Ec rat except he was not trapped.

Nicholas was not someone who improved after you knew him. Rudolf always said that Nicholas clearly had the advantage. You were fifteen and he used that — fifteen to twenty-three was an experience gap, Rudolf said. Just listen to your description.

I described him as he was. Twenty-three years and good-looking — under any circumstances, a girl was flattered by his attentions. At that time he drove a black '56 Thunderbird with an engine you could eat off. He had been thrown out of a school somewhere – maybe two schools.

"Didn't occur to you that someone might come in?" Nicholas said. "Wasn't smart. Shall I watch the door for you?"

"I am looking for my purse," I said and kept digging among the coats. The search itself was a frantic heaving of purses and coats.

"Hey," Nicholas said. "I *saw.*"

"Here it is," I said. I grabbed a purse, hung the skinny strap from my shoulder. "Good-night."

Nicholas blocked the doorway. I had no idea what brewed behind his eyes. I had a desire to yell either rape or fire. But I didn't.

"You're a thief," he said. "Don't worry – I won't tell. You take things. I wouldn't have guessed that. Something else maybe. What is it – party kleptomania?"

"Mind your business."

"My business? Dumb, you were very dumb – the rug is thick, the hinges don't squeak – I opened the door. And there you were – hard at work. What do you do, feed a habit?"

"I take money," I said sweetly, "for my poor sick mother – poor dear can't work."

"Yes," Nicholas said.

"I do it because I like it," I said. "It's a hobby."

"Do you shoplift?"

I stared at him grimly. "No, I do not shoplift."

"Just stuff at parties?"

"Yes," I said. "It's fun."

Nicholas nodded. "On the other hand you don't look as though you are having a good time."

"Well," I said and abruptly tossed the purse back on the bed. That's all I needed – to be seen walking out with someone's purse. "I have to go now."

"You need a ride?"

"No."

"You have one?"

I could say yes, but if I couldn't find someone who was leaving – I'd have to walk. And I believed that he would certainly drive past me – pacing me slowly. How was I going to handle any of this? Someone knowing.

"All right," I said, "I could use a ride as far as the Southside Mall."

"No problem," he said. "Just wait until I find my coat in this heap you created – nothing in *my* pockets."

We walked down the stairs together. Cindy saw us leave and nodded encouragement. It's called fitting in.

The seats in Nicholas's car smelled of neat's-foot oil. I slid carefully into a corner. Should I go home and pack? Should Pauline and I race through our possessions, dump them into the car, and leave? I really fixed it this time. Allowed it to happen.

"I never did this before," I said. "It was an impulse."

"No," he said. "You were basically cool. Not the first time then. What do you do with the money?"

He wanted some. A bribe. I reached into my pocket. "I spend it," I said. "You want a share?"

He shook his head.

"For what?" he asked.

"Things."

We were at the mall. Pauline waited in the car, parked according to directions near the entrance to Walgreen's.

"Here," I said. "I can get out here."

"Sure."

I opened the car door. He didn't do anything, didn't grab me, didn't touch me.

Once in a while I had dangerous ideas. The ideas I had were the ones I acted upon. Trips. I got an urge to move – find water, find the source of cool and damp air. Without saying a word to Pauline, I took the car and drove too fast down a highway. Sometimes, I took an exit and pulled off the road and stopped at one of those soft ice cream drive-ins where relatively undesirable young men congregated. They whistled and made suggestions. I said nothing. It was as close as I came to mystery and eventually I went home.

"I think I saw Abner. Honestly, I think I did."

"Where, Pauline?" Something pulled inside me.

"In the A&P."

"What did you do?"

"I called out to him. Abner, I yelled. Abner. He was through the check-out line first — but he didn't turn around."

"Because it wasn't him, Pauline. Do you honestly think he was shopping in the A&P nearest us?"

"No."

I thought a compartment in my mind was labeled desperation, in this abattoir anything can happen, no matter how chaotic. I was about to hit one of the Home Ec houses. Belonging to the girl nicknamed Bats. A location with problems. On some streets any car can be parked, each vehicle looking like another. The Bats street was not such a street. No cars lined the road, no cars of any type. It would have been folly to pull *my* car into that driveway. How could Abner's car belong there?

From the Bats house, perhaps a ten-minute ride to a shopping center. And a car could be parked at the shopping center attracting no attention. That was it then. I must be driven to the Bats house and later picked up. I was sorry, but no other way was possible.

I felt terrible. Worse than if we had the argument I anticipated. "All right," Pauline said, her face white and abnormally dry-looking. "When?"

"Wednesday."

She brightened. "I have a sitting engagement."

"Cancel."

Pauline wore her good black coat with the fur collar and her gold-tone hoop earrings. Her brown eyes stared intently at me. Her hands must have trembled and in anxiety she put on and rubbed off lipstick, finally abandoning it. But all that frenzied activity left a bruised red circle around her lips like clown's paint. Well, if we were seen, if they wanted to identify anyone, we were it. Pauline had also slipped on her highest heels, black sandals. I could smell her sweat, a sweet caked-talcum odor.

"Pauline," I said, "all you have to do is

drive me. That's all."

The house I wanted was the second from the corner — not exactly a corner, more like a curve in the road. I had Pauline stop in the shelter of that curve. We compared Timexes. I prepared for the unexpected. "If for any reason you will be late — car won't start, you forgot the hour. Don't come! If you aren't here, I'll leave. Walk, something."

Pauline nodded. Her eyes now turned into slits, as if she were squinting into the black night. I left the car, didn't slam the door. Pauline drove off. I heard the screech of tires, the whistle of a crazy turn.

I trudged around the corner. I was not an ogre, but still I didn't think about Bats. The evening light made the lawn look charred. I can't imagine Bats thinking about me. On my visiting day I never even made it upstairs in her house. There were twelve of us crowding the rooms. Bats had a mother who was home unexpectedly that afternoon. She wore a dress with puffed sleeves, and she had ridiculously young legs.

I moved around to the side path. The rhododendron branches scraped against the house, and I pushed my way among them. Three of the windows were locked. I visualized myself huddled outside for an hour — locked out. But then the fourth window slid up. The ledge was too far off the ground for me to pull myself up, but I placed my foot in the fork of two branches. I tried not to injure the plant.

The window led to where? A closet? A pantry? My luck – *that* door will be locked. I smelled a sour mop. The doorknob turned. I was in a back hallway. I turned on the pen flashlight I carried. But there was also some low-level light – to guard against burglars, I suspected.

I moved quietly down the hall that led directly into the kitchen. The light was on beneath the ventilation hood. What a filthy kitchen! It even smelled. A shocking sight. Dry curds, onion peel, decaying garlic, a putrid end of a ham. How people lived. No one emptied the *clean* dishes from the dishwasher so no room for the dirty ones. At least three days' supply of dirty dishes, acid-based foods etching the glaze of a dish, a can opener consumed by what it had opened, a Dead Sea of coffee. Between the burners, the enamel green or green-hued. The place spore-heaven. My foot touched something fleshy on the floor. I recoiled. When was the sink last scrubbed?

Suppose Bats's mother had a lover. Suppose the poor man wanted a drink of water. Would the mother bar the door – throw her body across it. I'll fetch the water, she would have to yell. Don't go in!

What happened to me at that point — I cannot say. I opened the doors beneath the sink. A package of sponges. Comet cleanser. I sprinkled the sink with cleanser, taking swift hard swipes at the sides. Thwacking the sponge. I polished the faucets. If the lover touched the faucets, at least now he wouldn't vomit.

Sometimes you start something and you can't stop. When I finished, the kitchen looked good — except for the curtains. Of course that was all I could do. The hour was up, I had worked at breakneck speed.

Pauline waited for me in the curve of the road.

She didn't ask me anything. I didn't say anything. I rubbed my hands — chapped.

Pauline used to dance before her ankles gave way under her. She and Abner went out dancing, mostly on holidays. My mother danced, but it was a costume-party type of dancing. She would grab a scarf and hold it taut as if the ends were the hands of a partner and then she would whirl around the room. A lot of chanting. Ah one, ah two. Once after spinning around the room she collapsed in Hal's arms. I thought she was crying. But no, she was laughing. My little flower, Hal said. Hey Pearl of the South Seas.

I bought a mortar and pestle. Fran saw them on the table.

"What the hell is that for?" she said. "Starting a drugstore?"

"Spices," I said. "Pulverizing spices."

"You are a weird kid," Fran said. "I'd swear you must grind up funny stuff in that thing."

I made a batch of cookies in Honors. That was risky. I hadn't submitted the recipe on my weekly list. Now, I could have stuffed the cookies in a bag and lost them. But no – I put them with the other spoils. What I did was combine flour, sugar, eggs, a touch of milk, and dried currants macerated in a rum-and-sugar syrup. This tasted extraordinary. So I left the cookies. And Post found them.

"What are these called?" she asked me.

I didn't hesitate. *"Gone,"* I said.

"What?"

"I just named them – *Gone*. You know – so good that they're gone."

"I see. Not on the list?"

"No."

The Celts had a cookie – a biscuit based on oatmeal and raisins soaked in rum. I tried them, put them first on the weekly list. They lay on the stomach like welts. I suppose it had something to do with the climate, the heavy moist air dropping on everyone – heavily. Also I made pastry coffins from the original *Martha Washington Cookbook* and filled them with chocolate mousse.

Everyone yelled at us to hurry, the seats in the blue convertible were filling rapidly. I slid into a corner, pressed upon by too many thin girls. We rode to Melanie's house.

It was an ordinary house. I might enter that house all on my own. This Melanie turned out to be nineteen. She used to go to North Dover Beach. She didn't graduate, she left. Some said to have a baby. Others said that Melanie was not that dumb.

I liked Melanie. We had cream soda and vodka – a strange union – with slices of reheated pizza. We ate in the kitchen, and when soda splashed and strings of melted cheese were crushed by shoes, I didn't feel so bad. The debris can be cleaned, the floor was tiled.

"I'm staying," Patsy whispered to me. "You stay too."

Why not? Too late to case another house anyway. We remained in the kitchen when the blue convertible reloaded.

Melanie sighed and got out a broom and a dustpan. I took a damp sponge and washed down the table. Patsy went to the bathroom. The silence of people working was in my mind a very companionable silence.

"I like things clean," Melanie said. "I was this way even when I was a kid. My boyfriend Chuck said that was abnormal. We went together long enough to tell each other a lot, and afterwards he said I was bossy because of what happened to me when I was fourteen.

"When I was fourteen my mother got cataracts. The doctor who examined her had an office on the first floor of that apartment house on Klempnew. My mother was crazy scared. Don't worry, that doctor said, we'll operate and take care of the whole thing. I guess he didn't know how to talk to someone like my mother. The world, my mother told me, turned creamy. Like skin on heated milk. If I go to sleep by artificial means, my mother said, I will die. We cried in each other's arms. My father could have talked her out of her fears, but he got pink-slipped that summer. He was sixty-three and in charge of floor repairs at Whipperwill, Inc.

"So my mother sat down and my father took up braiding rope. I shopped, I cleaned, I made the decisions. It was chance that my father got another job. Just like that the trouble was over. I slipped back into my role as daughter – but by then I was sixteen."

"I never had any parents," I said. "They died in an automobile accident when I was three. I was raised by my married sister."

Mortimer kissed me. We bounced together on the bed. His mattress flat on the floor. Everyone he knew had a mattress on the floor, he said. I heard an insect sizzling above us. The sheet was grey, the sheet had turned ash-grey. Mortimer patted my belly. Love you, love you, he sighed. His teeth poked at my earlobes. Then his head buried between my breasts, he turned and bit me. The torn skin let loose a road of blood. Hell, Mortimer said. I never — do something. Do something to me. Do something back.

As much as I understood that we needed a telephone, I hated it. All that ringing whenever it wished, last week someone wanted to sell me a freezer plan for meat. I hate frozen meat, I would sooner become vegetarian.

The telephone jangled. Just like that, tyranny began. These were largely Pauline-generated calls, baby-sitters were in demand. I personally did not give out my number. Pauline turned down the television sound, reached for her Week-at-a-Glance, and answered the summons. "It's for you, Theodora," she said.

I had been preoccupied, preparing the next

week's list for Honors Home Ec. I would make a *dacquoise*, the meringue base for a multilayered dessert. I used to call it a *janosia* — but now I prefer *dacquoise*.

"Hello."

"Hello," a man said. "It's Nicholas."

I couldn't answer.

"You still there?"

"Yes."

"You want to go to the movies?"

"What's playing?"

"Who the hell knows."

He wasn't going to pick me up. He knew where I lived. But no, he said, meet me at the Lakeville. I knew the place, an old dead-style movie house. On a bus route. Where did Pauline think I was going? She didn't ask. She looked frightened, nervously biting her lower lip.

I can't remember when I last went to a movie — before we moved. Who spent money that way? We had trouble making the lousy rent.

Fran came over yesterday. Hey folks, she said, can you lend me ten bucks until Friday? Sure, Pauline said. I would have done the same.

Lakeville was going down the drain, the marquee had a *the* minus the *e*. What's up? A movie about World War II starring Tab Hunter.

I waited in the lobby in front of the velvet rope beyond which you must be a ticket-holder. Some old theaters have decaying class, clouds painted on the ceiling or rococo carved pillars covered with peeling gold leaf. The Lakeville was just old. Popcorn and commercial oil – a pseudo-butter smell.

Eight-thirty – one minute to movie time. I thought I had been stood up. Maybe that was what he liked to do, maybe that made him feel big. He didn't come up behind me, he appeared right in front of me. I didn't recognize him for a moment, wearing a tweed overcoat, he looked like someone's father.

"Here I am," he said. "Two tickets. You want popcorn?"

"Love some."

He didn't ask me anything, did I want to sit in the back, did I want to sit up front. He picked two seats. Ten people around us – the nicest thing about going to the movies was the sense of shared adventure. The movie itself wasn't important, if there had been two features, I would have suggested walking out on this one. We sat side by side. I thought at some point that he would take my hand or do something. But the only contact came in the popcorn box. Maybe he was saving up for something labeled the Big Moment.

From time to time I looked over at him, he

had a surprisingly short chin, considering that full-face he was good-looking. I didn't know anything about him. I didn't know if he's smart or dumb. Smart, he's smart, didn't have rabbit eyes. He's smart, he could be mean, he could be crazy. He was old enough to be married. I can hear his father. Why the hell aren't you married? A man your age should be married, working, respectable. Yet there he was chasing after high school girls. Had he nothing better to do with his time?

The movie ended with one of those flourishes of music, as if the musicians were deeply grateful to have finished. I shoved my arms back into my denim jacket.

"Aren't you cold," he said, "wearing that thin coat?"

"Yes."

"Buy yourself a coat — your mother has a coat."

He *did* follow us.

"That's her coat. It's all right."

"We have to get you a coat."

"Yeah."

I didn't know whether I was expected to return home by bus, but I followed him to his car anyway.

I guessed I had a ride. Okay, whatever happened can happen, and then I will forget it. He turned on the car radio, pushed buttons until he found something soft and dark.

"What do you do?" he said. "Just steal at parties?"

I thought about how much I could get away with saying. The level of the lie. Still, he could have followed me more than once.

"I break into houses," I said finally. "I live off that — we live off that."

He knew. I thought he knew.

He slapped the steering wheel. "You know what? We'll get you a coat. Coat money."

"I don't need a coat."

"Coat," he said.

I thought at that moment he was on something. Or maybe it was just the kick of the idea.

"Listen," I said, "I don't do this for fun."

"Sure," he said.

I know what I can do, I can do nothing.

"Where are we going?"

I recognized the neighborhood. We pulled into a driveway. Nicholas cut the motor, turned off the lights. "This," he said, "is the house. The people are gone. Out of town, be back tomorrow."

"How do you know?"

I looked at his eyes. He *knew.*

"What do we do?" he asked. "Break a window?"

"Crazy," I said. "Don't be crazy."

Outside in the bright moonlight, I pulled at his arm, moved him into the shadows of a tree. He was excited, interested, sweaty. He put an arm around my shoulders, he squeezed, but that was fellowship.

Not since the early days have I gone into a house so blind. Dogs, maids, alarms. I didn't know what might be here. Idiots left a window unlocked. I could have lifted myself, but he hoisted me up to the sill, his hands supporting my buttocks. It was pathetically simple then, window up, I put one leg over the sill. "I'll go to the front door," I said. "Let you in."

In this house selected by Nicholas, this house of rich people, I was disturbed. I looked around. A piano in the far corner of the living room, a German piano. Sheet music open to *Schelomo*. Family pictures, framed in leather, framed in silver. Old people, young ones. No idea if any money was around. Could I pretend that I was alone? I headed for the stairs. Nicholas humming "Stouthearted Men" went his own way. I selected a bedroom. An enameled box on the dresser. I lifted the lid — jumped back. The box played "Some Enchanted Evening" — but the box also held money. One, no, two hundred and ten dollars. I could have left then. Nicholas came into the bedroom with silk scarves like banners dripping from his fingers. "Hey," he said. "Want a scarf? Want *two* scarves? Here, the colors of your choice."

"No clothes," I whispered. "Never take anything that can be identified — like a scarf — especially a scarf with a pattern."

For the first time, I noticed that he had taken off his overcoat. Somewhere in this house he discarded a garment. Who knew what could have fallen out of the pockets?

"No scarves?" he said. "Well, suit yourself. Me — I just acquired a nice half-dozen shirts — white on white. My size too."

"They'll miss them — know that someone *his* size was here."

"The hell they will. All nicely folded from the laundry — cardboarded and fixed into place. You think *he* knows how many white shirts he has?"

"Enough," I said. "Let's go."

"Why?"

I hesitated. "I have school tomorrow."

What happened? Why didn't we just leave? No, Nicholas said. They have to *know*. Our mark, he said. That's important. So he drowned those silk scarves — Scheherazade's dowry — in bath oil. The pictures — photographs snatched from frames. Rip them up, them up, he ordered. Like confetti — first

301

this way, then that.

Nicholas drove me home to 10 Rebus. His finger traced my lips. "You were really great," he said. "Great." He reached over and I felt his hand in the pocket of my denim jacket, the pocket over my breast.

"I found money," he said. "Buy a coat."

I didn't answer, he didn't push it.

I got sick later that evening.

Pauline made me a cup of American Rose tea. "Careful, it's hot," she said. "I put honey in it for you."

I couldn't thank her — sometimes you cannot speak.

Someone stole the *Mona Lisa*. Truly happened. In 1911 — think about it. What an act of bravery, the world's *most* famous picture, snatched off the wall. Even the thief had glamour — the Marqués de Vafierno. I was always certain that if I turned to someone and said I was the person who stole the *Mona Lisa* — their eyes would light up. They would most assuredly want to know how it happened, the details. The entire act would have romance. Never mind that it was a theft and as tawdry as any theft can be. Think of any of the great train robbers – renegades and brigands. The James brothers, Younger brothers, C. C. Haswell, John Renom, Jack Davis. Maybe at age fifteen we were all kin.

"Suppose we go into the city," Nicholas said, "hear some music, grab something to eat."

"I don't want to," I replied.

I was waiting, waiting to hear the menace in his voice. Instead, he changed. He became anyone.

"Listen," he said. "I bet you're annoyed that I didn't call before. Had to run some errands for my father. I really want to see you, Theodora. You buy a coat?"

"No."

"We'll eat, I know a place on Eighth Street, near Avenue A. I know several places. I know good ribs on St. Mark's. Eat, music. Tomorrow?"

"No."

"Friday?"

"Friday."

Pauline was impatient for me to get off the telephone. When I put down the receiver she grabbed it. The baby-sitting business was fraught with crises. On Tuesday Pauline sat for a couple who came home drunk and then wouldn't pay. They could hardly stand, Pauline said. The woman claimed to have spent all her money. Fuck off, she said to Pauline. On Thursday, the woman called to make future arrangements. I got to the telephone first. Fuck off!

Pauline was talking to a Mrs. Appleby or Applebuy. On Saturday, she was saying, we need you for Saturday. She gave an address. Not ours. Be there at seven-thirty.

"You subcontracting now?" I asked.

Pauline looked as if her memories were being disturbed. Her eyes were Bette Davis wide, an effect achieved when her hair was up in curlers, pulling the skin taut across her cheekbones.

"I need to get someone for Mr. Letwin for Saturday night," she said. "Reliable people are hard to find. They don't come, or you can't trust them. He's got two boys. A lot of women won't take boys."

"Yeah," I said. "Isn't he your regular?"

"What?"

"The place you sit every Saturday."

"Yes, except this Saturday — I'm going out, sort of."

I liked the city when it was dark. Nicholas held my hand. A cold but good night. I was wearing a navy blue coat, nipped waist, gold buttons with anchors embossed. Nicholas cut off the tickets with his penknife in the car. In the pocket of the coat, a receipt from the store in case the coat didn't fit, in case I didn't like it. The coat was paid for with cash. Two hundred fifty dollars. The coat fit like a charm.

He picked the restaurant. We had ribs, thick and glossy with molasses. The smells made me ravenous. There was a drag-queen floor show. Judy Garland belts them out. Bloody Marys. Nicholas ordered a pitcher. I could have that restaurant's liquor license lifted.

"Patsy says you take a special cooking class?"

"Yes," I said. "A class just for me."

"You want to be a cook?"

"No."

I wiped my fingers on a thick paper napkin. "What do you do," I said, "all day long?"

Nicholas didn't hesitate. "I keep busy. My father owns buildings – I look after things, run errands. That takes a lot of time. Perhaps one day I should try the Army – you think I should try the Army? It's my father's favorite suggestion."

He had a place to go in the city, an apartment in a building his father owned. The rooms furnished, clean, warm. This was no back seat of a car, nobody's borrowed bed.

"My father uses this place," he told me, "my father's fucking pied-à-terre. I almost puked the first time he said that — he's got this woman — this *educated* woman. So this, Theodora, is the pied-à-terre."

"Yeah," I say. "Well, *merci.*"

"Here's the bedroom."

I thought he liked that I knew what lovemaking was supposed to be. Well, I did. What didn't he know? That I didn't know how I was supposed to feel. The truth was that when I felt something, it was like feeling nothing at the same time.

"You must tell me," he said in an even voice, "what you want me to do to you."

We undressed and threw our clothes on the floor. I hope he noticed that I threw the coat on the floor near the jeans and the cashmere sweater.

We did five houses in the next three weeks. He broke china, cut upholstery, poured bleach over a table. Do something, he ordered me. I threw a lamp on the floor, it bounced. The brass dented.

There can be nothing crazier than breaking into a house in the city. All those windows with security decals, all those *Beware of Dog,* all those wired alarms, all those secret devices.

We were walking down a street, attached brownstones, most renovated. Nicholas smiled, left me, and walked up the stairs to a house with mostly darkened windows, just a dim light coming from the interior. He rang the doorbell. I knew what he was doing, if anyone answered, we were looking for someone.

No one answered.

At the corner we climbed a fence, went past a passageway with garbage cans. Tiny yard to yard, we climbed fence to fence. It was the third house. All the windows in the back were barred.

Post had frosty eyes. "I want you to enter a Bake-Off contest – college tuition and expenses."

"What?"

"A Bake-Off."

"I don't have an original recipe ready," I said. "Maybe by spring I will, but I make no promises."

"Submit your *Gone* cookie recipe."

"Its not good enough."

"It will do."

"It's him," Pauline said and held out the receiver.

She didn't like him. She never directly mentioned it, but now I can see that she didn't like him. I hardly ever thought of Pauline as having such opinions.

"Yes," I said.

"I want to see you," he said.

"No, I'm copying recipes. *Pâte feuilletée*. Cornets. I am going to make cornets tomorrow."

"I don't give a damn about cornets, Theodora. My father has an apartment here, *here* as well as in the city. I'll pick you up in a half hour."

"Hour."

This time we made love in a wicked way. He banged at me as hard as he could. But I did not yell. Instead I wrapped my arms tight around his shoulders. He licked my ear, my nose, my forehead.

Afterwards he found a beer in the refrigerator. We drank out of the bottle, passing it back and forth.

"You know Clements?" he asked.

"What?"

"That little lane — off Belmont?"

"No."

"Six houses on that street. Big cutesy-pie houses in Ye Village setting. You'll like the houses, Theodora. Fucking architectural wonders. What I have in mind — is a particular house."

"I don't need any money."

Nicholas laughed.

"I *want* to do this house, Theodora baby. I

want to do this house tonight — then you can go back and build your crumpets."

"Cornets."

It's interesting how things change. The man says hello, and you fall in love with him. The man says hello, and you stop loving him forever. All things change. Someone closes a door. And so I became a criminal. Never mind that it seemed as if I was already one. Not true. That night I became a criminal. And it seemed as if nothing — not even my search for the perfect cookie — could save me.

That's it, I told Rudolf, I believe I became a true criminal that night. Everything vicious and contemptible was me. Rudolf didn't agree. You were a victim, he insisted. Consider Bonita. Do you think that in a few years when she is fifteen — she would be able to resist the blandishments of a man like that — if she were poor?

"When I bake I am happy. What do you think?"

"About what?" Nicholas said.

"Does that make me crazy — I mean it's a deep interest. I don't see how that's different from anything — from liking cars, for instance. When I bake — it's real love, excitement, adventure."

"I don't care."

"About what?"

"Whether you bake or not — if you want to bake — bake."

Evil has nothing to do with creation. It's terrible, but it's true.

Two nights ago Pauline crept to the side of my bed in the middle of the night. Her finger-nails dug deeply into my arm. I woke up, and my leg muscles twitched violently. "What is it?" I said, whispering the way people do in the dark.

"This man," she said. "Nick."

"Nicholas."

"Don't do anything — don't let yourself be caught."

"Caught?"

"Don't get pregnant. And if you do, don't marry him. He may try to make you — but you don't have to."

"I'm not pregnant," I said.

"Remember," Pauline said, "what goes around, comes around."

I tried to think what kind of cookie was appropriate for this morning. A morning in which if there was a cliff I would jump off it or if there was water I would walk and walk until the salty spray covered me completely. Were there special cookies for a funeral? As a matter of fact, for some cultures there were. But for ours – should I just make any kind and burn them?

I went to the store yesterday – went to three stores – when I had enough money I bought a lot. I made molasses hermits. Then, I searched my spice cabinet. Did I have carbonate of potassium? I made honey lebkuchen. Afterwards, I did peanut butter cookies. I followed this up with nut patties and Shrewsbury wafers. Hickory nut kisses, date bars, cinnamon cookies, oatmeal crisps, spice cookies, cornflake macaroons.

The kitchen was as hot as the hold of a ship in which William Bendix shovels coal into a furnace. I packed my cookie tins with cookies. I had ten tins. I packed ten tins. What was left? A Great Wall of China, a pyramid of bound crumbs, a dike without a hole.

I took some Dover Beach newspaper, and careful not to read a word, squinting my eyes into slits, I tumbled cookies into a paper cornucopia. I carried my horn of plenty into the damp outside air under a sky faintly red from the twenty-four-hour neon top hat signature sign of our nearest mall, original home of our table and chairs. I put the newspaper on the short path that led to our front door. Ten minutes later, I heard cats fighting among themselves the way uninvited guests always did.

A policeman on the telephone.

Pauline began to cry as she handed me the receiver.

My mouth overflowed with saliva. Would it come this way? On the telephone? Would they still consider me a minor in making the charges?

"Hello," I said.

I listened, could hardly hear. Pauline squeezed my elbow. "What? What? What?" she hissed.

"My mother is distraught, sir," I said carefully. "That was her speaking before. No, he hasn't come back. No, we haven't heard from him."

Pauline grabbed my free hand. "Who? Who? Who?"

I hung up. Pauline and I wrapped our arms around each other and she cried. Abner Palmer Waite hits below the belt every time.

Pauline had two qualities that amazed me. She could pinch pennies with ease. Nothing in her background gave her this training. Sometimes, she said, they think potatoes are pearls. Chinks eat rice — rice can be good.

Pauline's other quality was a peculiar ability to be steel when it was unexpected. I said no

Nicholas. And he called maybe ten, twelve times an evening. No, Pauline said smoothly, not available. She never said – Drop dead! Shut up! Fuck you! She just spoke her words and then returned the receiver to its cradle.

It was inevitable considering the growth in Pauline's baby-sitting business that I should from time to time answer the telephone myself.

"I want you to come to dinner," Nicholas said.

"No."

"Listen, I mean I want you to come over here, to *my* house. I want you to come here on Sunday."

"Are you high?"

"I don't need to get high. You think an invitation has to come from being high?"

"To your house – yes."

"My mother will like you. You look sweet. She hates girls in high heels. She hates girls with eye shadow. She wants an old-fashioned daughter-in-law, she says."

"Drop dead!"

Patsy took a deep breath. "I'm going to tell you something," she said. "Only promise not to tell."

"I promise."

"I don't want the girls to know, you understand. When I graduate – well, I'm not going

313

on to college. I'm going to get married."

"Congratulations," I said carefully.

"The man is named Franklin. He's like a friend of the family. He's older − I get sick sometimes of little kids. That's why I like you, you always seem older." Patsy smoothed her hair, cheeks grew pinker.

"This Franklin is older?"

"He's maybe ten years older than me − maybe thirteen. But he's relaxed, he's easy."

Patsy put her fingers to her lips in the universal shut-up sign, although no one else was around. Home Ec girls can be secretive at times. She reached down the front of her sweater and hauled up a chain, a ring dangled from it.

"See," she said.

I reached over and examined it. The ring was warm from her body. "What goes around," I warned, "comes around."

I never noticed. I was busy. Pauline lost weight. Pauline looked at least five pounds down. "I don't sit on Saturdays," she said to me.

"Yeah?"

"I *get* a sitter instead."

This time there was no mistaking the tone.

"Mr. Letwin and I go out," she said. "We go to the movies, twice we went dancing."

Robert Lee was stealing from the cash register. It wasn't a register – it was a drawer. Should have been at least fourteen dollars. Ten dollars before I had to go back and bake some more fig bars. Then when I returned to the store – the tray of chocolate chips was almost empty. Robert Lee wasn't a sweets eater. He sold those cookies. I calculated fourteen dollars in total. Where were they? Three dollars left. Where's the money? I said. What the hell do you mean? he said. The money, I said. We could have gone around like that for hours but suddenly he left. I don't need to take crap, he said. I couldn't believe he would do this to me. I felt terrible. But then I calmed down. Suppose I was wrong. Suppose I had taken the ten – and forgot. Suppose he had eaten the cookies. Or given them away.

Post said fill out the application for that contest. For the *Gone* cookies. She told me that after I complained that the cold water faucet at Cooking Station One dripped and squealed. Water sputtered from it. My concentration decreased accordingly. Such sputterings were rarely rhythmical.

Sometimes I thought Post was an idiot. The sort who cannot differentiate between a true pastry and a cookie. *Gipfelteig* was not a cookie. That was a bloody pastry. Also, the woman told me I strained the Honors budget. I was able to account for every dime expended. Good ingredients cost. My shopping lists were accurate to the farthing.

Post's husband came for her one day last week. I was just shutting down Honors. He looked like a flattened loaf of bread, his voice bleated, and he smelled like a *rumtorte*. Post introduced us.

I asked to have Honors hours increased. Request denied. Except for Wellness Clinic, my afternoons were suddenly mine. My Home Ec friends say that I have begun to act like I was better than them. The short life of my popularity was being sucked up.

"It can't matter now," Dierdre said. "Can it? I always wanted to tell you – cleanse my soul in a fashion. *He* made a pass at me. A grope. He groped me. There's no sin in telling you – the sin would be in my response. No response, Theodora. He actually slid his hand under my skirt way up. We were sitting at a table. You were sitting right across. He did it then. Another time I walked past him and he pinched my breast. I said cut it out. So you see – from me – no response. I never did – never with a friend's husband. The only thing – he wasn't drunk. Neither time was Mortimer drunk."

Fran pacing the sidewalk in front of her house. I suspected she was waiting for me.

"Hi, Theodora," she said. "I knocked, but your mom isn't home."

"No."

"Had something to talk over with her."

"Come in?" As I said, hospitality lingered on.

"Sure."

I unlocked our door. Pauline kept a neat house. No need to worry about the unexpected guest.

"Wheew," Fran said and sat down. "Good to take a load off the feet."

"Coffee?"

"Sure — you don't have some of those cookies of yours, do you? Any kind will do."

I pulled a tin down from a shelf. Poured coffee.

"The thing is," Fran said and looked at her watch, "will your mom be home soon?"

"Can't say. Sometimes she goes from one baby-sitting job straight to the next."

"Well then you'll have to tell her good-bye. It's only temporary, but I'm going to the Windy City to stay with my sister. Chi is a good place for cooling off. I'm cooling off."

"You're leaving *him?*"

"Yes, I suppose you could say that. Only I say it's temporary."

"I thought the house was your place? — your lease, your furniture."

"It is."

"Then why the hell doesn't *he* leave?"

"He won't, Theodora. He says if I don't like what's going on, then I can get out. What do you think I should do?"

"I think you should hire a van, wait until he goes to work or wherever the hell he goes, and then pack the place up, strip it to the walls."

"You think I should do that? Don't it seem too cruel?"

"No. Your stuff. If you don't, ten minutes after you're out the door, he will."

"You think so?"

"He'll sell you to the bed boards and go off with the money."

"You think so?"

"It's a transient world, Fran."

"What?"

When you look for trouble, you never pick the right site. It appeared. I had been disguising my voice when I answered the telephone. I watched the front of the house, locked the door. But I took precautions only at home.

Honors ended at five-thirty or six if the janitor wasn't anxious to get home. I turned the lights out in the room, double-checked the burners, twisted the faucet tight. Shortening was on my mind, qualities and temperature sensitivity. No one was around. Suppertime or close.

The car was parked at the curb like a drain at the foot of the path. You think I noticed? Then he got out, he was at my side in less than a second. He was lucky that I didn't scream in surprise before, in the twilight, I saw who had my arm, fingers holding tight.

Analogies in life – think about Picarin. At the feast of 1873, his great chestnut soufflé was a failure. Quite suddenly – perhaps the result of a draft from a window opened by a rival – the soufflé fell. The notable chef Picarin bowed before the king of Austria and left the room. In his kitchen the chef shot himself, bending neatly over a trough.

Pauline sat on the couch. We had to pay for that delivery. What was she wearing? A black dress with a lace ruffle. I didn't even know that Pauline owned a black dress. Her legs looked thin, her body smaller and narrowed. She was either worried or frightened.

Could it have happened? I half expected *him* to walk out of the kitchen, beer can in hand. Theodora, he would say, Daddy is back. I was gone but now I'm back.

"You got a sec?" Pauline said.

"Yes." I pulled a kitchen chair opposite the couch and sat down.

Pauline fingered her neck where a strand of pearls might have hung, if she had one.

"Theo, you know I have been seeing this Mr. Letwin."

I nodded.

"He's nice," Pauline said. "Two boys, ages eight and ten – quiet boys – kind of scared. Mr. Letwin – George – he thinks we could be a family."

"Right."

"You too," Pauline says quickly. "You, me, and them."

"He doesn't even know me."

"He says it doesn't make any difference. He says what comes with me, comes with me."

"What?"

"His first marriage wasn't apple pie. Lots of problems, he says. Mr. Letwin wants everything to be all right between us. Between him and me. So he thinks that we should go away for a week to Atlantic City. And if it works out, we'll get married."

I hooted. The woman was a walking idiot. "Come on? You're kidding? A bedtime story like that, Pauline!"

"I said yes, Theodora. I said I would go."

"Pauline, what about Abner? You're married to Abner."

She shook her head. "I think he's dead."

"Suppose he turns up?"

"He'll never turn up, Theodora."

"Letwin is bull shitting you."

"Saturday," Pauline said. "We're going to Atlantic City."

"Right," I said. "I can give you fifty dollars to take along. We can spare fifty dollars."

"Thank you, Theodora."

"Susie's uncle. You remember Susie? The man keeps cash. The man has to keep cash — our local chemical dealer. He can't put it anywhere. His wife has rings. They can't be declared, could be sold, uninsured pieces. Unkie can protest just so much. Can claim to be robbed of just so much. It is as sweet as heaven, Theodora."

As soon as I unlocked the door I saw that the boxes had been moved, setting up an earthy cardboard smell reminiscent of abandoned stores and homeless people. Pauline wearing her kelly green slacks suit knelt in the middle of the living room floor with two open suitcases that I had never seen before. She looked tired, lunar shadows under her eyes. Atlantic City loomed like a Babylonian paradise.

Pauline put on her good coat, hugged me, kissed me. She took one suitcase, I took the other, and we carried them out to the curb.

I went back to the house. I wasn't wearing a coat. The car when it came was a black Ford. Probably a '64.

Pauline left no clothes in the house. On the other hand Pauline didn't have a lot of clothes. Two suitcases could have easily held them – clothes for all seasons.

I thought it was absolute coincidence that in the book I was reading by Céline – in *Journey to the End of the Night* – Bardamu hates everyone. Or at the very least, who was left?

If Pauline didn't come back, I could manage reasonably well. I could forge her name where necessary. I could do the sick mom forever, if I had to.

I baked a batch of *Gone* cookies.

I called Nicholas.

We did a big house on Sommerset. Nicholas smeared mayonnaise on the upholstery. All the dining room seats. They were pink silk with an embroidered design of roses. The food thing was fun, he said. Why hadn't I told him the food thing was fun? Chocolate syrup, melted butter, wet flour.

We drove up and down the streets. We worked seven, eight hours. I forgot some of what we did. Money piled into a brown paper bag. In the evening I counted. Eleven thousand dollars. Nicholas didn't want any. He cut tassels off drapes. He made a skeleton of a chandelier.

I never once said stop.

"This is what we are going to do," Ginger said in the ladies' room of Hagen & Hagen. "We — you and I — are going to throw a party."

"You're kidding? In that dump we rent?"

"Don't be nuts — lots of parties are in places far worse. It's *who* we are that counts. Anyway, a lot of nice men have been taking us out. We should return the favors."

"What do we do?"

"You — nothing. I don't think you know about throwing a party, Theodora. I've always felt that. Never mind, though, leave it up to old Auntie Ginger. When do we ship — on Wednesdays?"

"Who ships?"

"Hagen & Hagen, stupid. They ship on Wednesdays, so this is what you do. Just list a couple — no, make it three — trays of their mixed hors d'oeuvres. Be sure and pick some of those yummy pigs in blankets. Also, a cracker assortment. Miniature pizzas. And three loaves of Italian."

"What?"

"List them, sugar, and have them loaded.

Then I'll bring someone's car around and remove."

"Christ, Ginger, you are out of your mind! Why do that – discount. We can get a discount. Hagen will give *me* a discount."

"Discount is not the same as free. On top of everything – are you afraid?"

"Yes."

Nicholas picked all the houses. This house, he would say. The house where I found a small suitcase filled with money. I thought he found something else in that house. I didn't ask what.

Nicholas called me up. "Go buy the newspaper," he said. "We're in it."

"Read it to me."

"Burglary rampage," he read. "That's us."

I knew what I had to do. I had to move quickly. I would give it until Sunday, then grab my clothes, my shoe boxes of recipes, and a selection of other things, and get out.

All day Saturday I stayed in, drinking coffee, eating from one of my tins of cookies. Nervous, jumpy, kept looking out the window. Saw the black Ford pull up. Pauline got out with one suitcase. The other was where?

I waited until the car pulled away before I went out and helped her.

"It was wonderful," she said. "It all worked

out, Theodora. I won twelve dollars."

The wedding cake was composed of layers of cookies. It was rather an extravaganza. The main course was chicken with a *beurre blanc* sauce dotted with slivers of carrots. A salad of *mâche* and walnut oil. Ravioli stuffed with sweetbreads on a bed of endive. A veal mousse. You've done too much, George said.

We broke into a house guarded like an armory. Nicholas had a key. He carved hearts into pecan paneling.

Now I bought the local newspaper. A skinny newspaper born for advertisements. The police had clues, I read, to the local rash of robberies. Arrests were expected soon.

Nicholas said the report was a lie. What they always said. But for me — I was in a closet. Can you travel from a closet? They would have to catch us. We took no care.

I began pacing my floors. Walking magical circles. I would never, I vowed, never go out again. I baked mighty windfalls of cookies. George was frightened. But I bought all the ingredients.

What did Nicholas do when he wasn't with me? Ran errands for his father. Perhaps he was on an errand when his car hit a concrete pillar, a support for an overpass. The contents of the car were reported to be suspicious. Before he died, Nicholas confessed. I did it, his deathbed words, said the newspaper. I am that burglar. He knew the right details, the police said. The mayonnaise, the syrups, the flour. He did it all alone, he said. The newspapers called him "The Kitchen Burglar."

Pauline and I read the account. We read it when George wasn't around. "He knew he was dying," Pauline said. "He wanted to be noticed. That's why he said what he said. Big famous burglar – that one!"

Now, on the face of it, she could be right. But Pauline never liked Nicholas. He must have reminded her of someone from her own past. I have always believed that Nicholas accepted me as I was. Life with him would not have been placid – it wouldn't have lasted. But I could have baked while he did whatever he did. There was a caring relationship between us. In extreme situations such relationships can turn into love. So when he knew he was dying, he confessed for me. He did it because he loved me. Nothing to do with fame.

Movie Star Cookies: 1987

I was proof of the fact that it was possible to function when you were sick. Especially if you didn't believe that you were sick. What was wrong with me? It had to do with my body image. With my sense of me — as in this is *me*. "What you have," one doctor said, "is a disorientation of your body orientation. You cannot recognize the left side of your body."

Charlotte was with me. She gasped and reached for my hand. Right hand? Left hand? I took a deep breath. "Stress?" I asked. "Psychological origin?"

"Could be a lesion, Theodora. Autotopragnosia — is rare."

"Progressive? I mean will I be unable to recognize *other* things?"

"Usually not. Not if it's true autotopragnosia. What can you do? You can look. Some people, when they *look* very hard — concentrate, that is — the missing side appears."

"I'll take you home," Charlotte said crying.

"I'll give up lipstick, take up concentration, reduce stress. By the way – how come I can still walk – move the left leg?"

"Movement memory."

Rudolf called on the telephone.
"How are you, Theodora?"
"Fine." If he thought I was going to ask how he was, he was crazy.
"Do you want to have dinner?"
"The children aren't home. The children are in school."
"I wasn't inviting the children. Can we have dinner together?"

I practiced looking. Those were my hands. Hands. Was I seeing two hands? I thought I was. How could I be certain? When I baked I used two hands – didn't I? I took a test. I put on lipstick. Went into the kitchen. How do I look? I asked Charlotte. She stared at me. All right. I would have danced around the living room, but Charlotte would have been certain I was crazy. Still, I had to practice. Looking at me. That was hard.

"I never should have left you," he said.
"Hah!"
"I know what that sounds like – I was mad – into my own period of madness – my own

grotesquery. You know I never married you for your money."

"I know that."

"I don't give a shit for your money. But who believes that — no one. So I went off with — well, several people. Nice women, intelligent women — but different. They annoy me — you never did. When I want to work, so often they want to do something. You understood. I miss you — I wake up missing you. I miss those damn cookies. God, Theodora, can I return?"

"I don't know."

"Listen, Theodora," Rudolf said. "Ever since the Winter Break, I've been unhappy. I had this terrible vision of growing old alone. Totally alone. I have lost the children. Don't tell me no. They blame me. That wedding, for instance, in Ruth's house. The girls were all dressed up, you sent them all dressed up. Ruth looked at them. Your ribbons, she said kindly, are tied at a slant. I'll fix them. They drew back. Such fierce faces. No thank you, Bonita said. Our mother likes them this way. You bet, Rebecca said. Their angry faces turned from her to me. They were unrelenting. They hated me, Theodora. And it will get worse."

"The only thing I can offer you at the moment is the spare room," I said. "You can move into the spare room, if you want."

"I'll send my suitcases and my trunk over tomorrow."

We sat in our favorite restaurant. The rain had been falling for hours, and the air was disagreeably damp. Dierdre looked at me, but I was calm. Charlotte had inspected me already. The lipstick was all right.

"I truly, truly cannot believe this," Dierdre said. "You are going to permit that man in your house."

"Spare room."

"Spare room nothing — he'll wheedle his way back into your bed in two seconds."

"No."

"Where is your sense of pride — all those hot ovens have addled your brain. He left you — for another woman — for other women."

"I wasn't always easy to live with."

"Who told you that? You're a pushover, that's all."

"Well," Florence said. "I would never have let him back in, Theodora. Out the door in my book means out the door. I could find someone for you. A woman with means can always find someone."

Put the *Movie Star Cookies* on the back burner, I told Stanley, until I am completely well. There they stayed. I heard the people in

330

the company kitchen wanted to take a whack at them — but they were mine. Let them find their own cookies. But, God, suppose I was never well enough to make the *Movie Star Cookies.* They represented such a leap forward for me. I looked for my left hand. Made it hold a glass and drank a whiskey and soda. Spring Break was coming up. Charlotte yelled. Must have hit herself on something. I didn't get up. Let her find me.

The children tumbled into the house. I was wearing slacks and a sweater, sitting in the living room. The children were taller and thinner, they smelled of schools and dried leaves. They crowded behind Bonita, peering at me. "You're up?" she said. "You were sick."
"Yes."
"What was wrong?"
"I was sick."
"Har, har."
"Something with my eyes."
"You're all right now?"
"Getting better."

We had dinner in the dining room. I heard Rudolf's door close. Maybe it was wrong, but I didn't invite him. The children wore their uniforms. I thought they looked fine — all of them. They exchanged news with each other.

331

What had happened, what they had done.

It snapped that night, clicked in me. I got up, put on my bathrobe, and quietly made my way to the kitchen. My kitchen at night, nobody else's. I thought about what I had in mind. The mood I wanted to convey. Nothing transparent or thin or sweet. Something strong and glittering. That wouldn't fade with time.

I made my cookies. Left hand, right hand. I didn't know which. The first batch were dazzling in the moon's glow. In the room – only the light over the stove. The smell from my oven was bewildering, foreign, and vital.

I had made no noise. But the odors spoke. The children woke up. They moved sleepily into the kitchen in their white pajamas, white nightgowns, bare feet. We all looked pale and blurred.

"I'm sorry," I said. "You woke up."

"We might as well eat some," Robert said.

I nodded. They grouped themselves around the kitchen table. I poured glasses of milk. Rudolf came out of his room and perched on Charlotte's stool. I poured milk for him.

"Here," I said and passed around a tray of cookies.

They tasted them. They had all been taught how to eat a cookie, slowly, carefully. I took one too.

I watched them eat, watched them stare at each other.

"They make me think of movie stars," Bonita said, licked the crumbs from her lips. The others nodded in agreement.

I closed my eyes.

Movie Star Cookies.

But they weren't perfect.

THORNDIKE-MAGNA hopes you have enjoyed this Large Print book. All our Large Print titles are designed for easy reading, and all our books are made to last. Other Thorndike Press or Magna Print books are available at your library, through selected bookstores, or directly from the publishers. For more information about current and upcoming titles, please call or mail your name and address to:

THORNDIKE PRESS
P.O. Box 159
Thorndike, Maine 04986
(800) 223-6121
(207) 948-2962 (in Maine and Canada call collect)

or in the United Kingdom:

MAGNA PRINT BOOKS
Long Preston, Near Skipton
North Yorkshire,
England BD23 4ND
(07294) 225

There is no obligation, of course.